Dear Reader,

There's nothing like curling up with a good book on a crisp fall evening, and this month we present four new Bouquet romances that are sure to warm your heart.

With Thanksgiving only weeks away, Adrienne Basso's **Sweet Sensations** is a perfect first course in a month full of captivating stories. Adrienne's heroine is a pastry chef who finds that only one man will complete her recipe for love. Next, Zebra and Avon author Jane Kidder serves up a second chance at love in **Heart Song,** when a pianist with a precious secret must face the man she once loved . . . and lost.

Of course, once Thanksgiving draws to a close, Christmas is just around the corner—and this month our authors are inspired by the spirit of the season. Longtime Zebra and Harlequin author Patricia Werner offers the charming tale of a woman in charge of a retirement home who rediscovers her Christmas cheer—with the help of a resident's handsome son—in **Jenny's Star.** And in **A Christmas Bouquet,** three of our favorite authors spread holiday joy. In **"Amy's Gift"** by Suzanne Barrett, a young widow whose child is looking for Santa meets a bachelor who just may fit the bill. Then a Christmas decorating enthusiast and her bah-humbug neighbor clash—passionately—in Kate Holmes's **"Merry and Her Gentleman."** Last, in Vella Munn's **"Silver Christmas,"** a small-town shopkeeper with contemporary flair meets the handsome, if old-fashioned, man of her dreams.

So build a fire, make a pot of tea, and get ready for the kind of smart, sexy love stories we know you adore.

The Editors

KISSING THE COOK

Lauren flashed Jonathan a comfortable smile and rolled a thick zucchini onto the cutting board. He felt the urgency within him rise to a higher level. He wanted to kiss her.

He noticed her catch her bottom lip between her teeth, and he realized his intentions must have shown on his face. Lauren's hands shook slightly as she lifted the cutting board and pushed the sliced vegetables into a copper bowl. Moving closer, Jonathan grazed his knuckles gently across her cheek and stared down at her with a sexy, intimate look.

She cleared her throat. "Now I'll show you how to stir-fry all these vegetables."

"Mmmm, sounds fascinating." The fingers caressing her cheek slid down to the nape of her neck. "But first I'd like to show you something."

Without giving her any more warning, Jonathan pulled her close. He extended his head and met her lips. He kissed her slowly and gently, deepening the kiss only after he felt Lauren's acceptance. . . .

SWEET
SENSATIONS

ADRIENNE BASSO

Zebra Books
Kensington Publishing Corp.
http://www.zebrabooks.com

ZEBRA BOOKS are published by

Kensington Publishing Corp.
850 Third Avenue
New York, NY 10022

First Printing: November, 1999
10 9 8 7 6 5 4 3 2 1

Printed in the United States of America

To Pam Hopkins,
without question the best agent in the business.

I will always be grateful for your kindness,
professionalism and optimistic attitude.

You were right, Pam. Persistence pays off!

JONATHAN'S DESSERT RECIPE
CHOCOLATE-AMARETTO CHEESECAKE

CRUST

8	ounces	chocolate icebox wafers, crushed
3	ounces	(3/4 stick) sweet butter, melted

FILLING

6	ounces	semisweet chocolate, melted
6	ounces	almond paste, cut into small pieces
1/3	cup	Amaretto di Saronno liqueur
24	ounces	(3 8-ounce packages) cream cheese, softened
4	large	eggs
1/2	cup	heavy cream

Butter sides only of a 9-inch springform pan. Mix crushed wafers and melted butter and press firmly into the bottom of the prepared pan. Refrigerate while making the filling.

Place cut almond paste in small bowl and beat on low speed with an electric mixer. Gradually add the amaretto liqueur and beat until thoroughly mixed. Set aside.

In a large electric mixer bowl, beat the cream cheese until smooth. Add almond paste and Amaretto mixture, beat until thoroughly mixed. Next add melted chocolate, beating again until smooth. Set mixer on low speed and add the eggs one at a time, beating only until they are incorporated. Add heavy cream, beat until incorporated.

Turn into prepared pan. Bake 50-55 minutes at 350 degrees in a preheated oven. Cake will seem soft, but will become firm when chilled. Let stand at room temperature until completely cool, then refrigerate 6-8 hours or overnight.

To serve, carefully remove sides of springform pan. Top with whipped heavy cream and chocolate shavings.

ONE

"Jonathan's recipe! That's *my* recipe!"

Lauren Stuart set down the large box she was precariously balancing in her arms and reached across her sister's pristine white kitchen counter to retrieve the magazine. Angrily clutching the offending material in her hands, she quickly scanned the recipe and accompanying article.

A PROFILE OF MARYLAND'S MOST SUCCESSFUL
MOVERS AND SHAKERS

Snorting loudly at the condescending tone of the title, Lauren flipped rapidly through the pages, finally finding the section about the pilfering Jonathan.

Eligible bachelor Jonathan Windsor, thirty-five-year-old president and CEO of one of the state's largest seafood companies not only earns his living from the sea, but spends much of his leisure time on the water. A staunch environmentalist, he supports a variety of causes aimed at the preservation of the Chesapeake Bay. He graciously shares with our readers an original dessert recipe he enjoys making on special occasions.

Adrienne Basso

"This guy can't be real." Lauren lifted the magazine closer to her face, carefully studying the photograph of Jonathan Windsor. He stood comfortably behind the wheel of a huge sailboat, the crystal blue waters of the bay glistening behind him. Shards of sunlight highlighted the blond streaks in his windblown hair and heightened the sparkle in his deep-set green eyes. Over broad shoulders he wore a white crewneck cotton sweater that showcased his tan and emphasized the brilliance of his perfect smile. He even had dimples.

"You are a rotten, no-good, rich preppy thief!" Lauren rolled the magazine into a tight wad and smacked it over the counter. Twice. Then she marched out of the kitchen, shouting loudly for her sister. "Eileen? Eileen? Where are you?"

"Upstairs. I'm giving the kids a bath."

Lauren heard her sister's muffled voice and doggedly followed the sound, stomping her feet as she climbed up the winding oak staircase. She burst into the center hall bathroom and discovered her younger sister kneeling over the edge of the spacious porcelain tub.

"Warren!" Three-year-old Michael shouted his delight at seeing his aunt, stood on his feet and attempted to climb out of the tub.

"Hi, big fella. Are you and your little sister having fun in the bathtub?" Lauren greeted her nephew with a grin, and watched Eileen gently, but firmly, push Michael back into the tub.

"Hello, Lauren." Eileen smiled faintly and pryed away the washcloth eight-month-old Ashley was furiously sucking on. "We're almost finished. I just have to wash their hair."

Lauren sat on the edge of the tub and unrolled the magazine.

"Have you seen this?" she asked, shoving the journal beneath Eileen's chin.

Eileen sat back on her heels, but kept a firm grip on the baby in the tub. "Hmmm, Jonathan Windsor. Not your usual type, but he's very cute."

"Oh, please." Lauren rolled her eyes disdainfully. "Did you see his *original* dessert recipe? That's *my* recipe for chocolate Amaretto cheesecake. It was published in *Cuisine* magazine several years ago when they ran that feature on promising graduates of the Culinary Institute. I slaved over every detail, spending weeks perfecting the technique and adjusting the ingredients."

"Are you certain it's exactly the same?"

"Of course. I know my own recipes, Eileen."

Lauren huffed with indignity as she watched Eileen carefully rinse away the clouds of white suds from Ashley's head. Even though she was two years older than Eileen, Lauren occasionally suffered pangs of inadequacy around her sister.

Eileen was a successful attorney, married to one of the town's leading physicians and the mother of two adorable, young children. She was beautiful in the classic mold; fair-haired and blue-eyed with delicate features, a flawless complexion and a willowy figure that could still turn male heads even after having two children.

In contrast, Lauren had a face that everyone automatically referred to as cute; brown eyes and hair that wasn't quite light enough to be considered blond, a complexion prone to freckles when exposed to sunlight and a body that demanded constant exercise to avoid a steady increase of clothing sizes.

After taking five years to graduate from college, Lauren had worked at several uninspiring office jobs before deciding her true talents and interest lay in the culinary arts. She studied at the Culinary Institute of

America and completed her education by apprenticing in some of the finest restaurant establishments on the East Coast.

She had returned two years ago to Salisburg, the small town on Maryland's Eastern Shore where she'd grown up, with the idea of writing a cookbook. But not just any cookbook. This was to be the definitive, ultimate book on desserts that would appeal to both the novice and experienced cook.

Thus far the creation of mouthwatering recipes and writing pages of valuable advice on techniques, ingredients and equipment had been a challenge Lauren met and conquered admirably. Unfortunately, finding a publisher for this future best-seller was an entirely different matter. The pile of rejection letters on Lauren's desk seemed to grow weekly, yet she refused to give up.

She supported herself by catering part-time and baking an irresistible assortment of pastries and sweets for a trendy coffee shop in town called Just Desserts. Her parents tried to be supportive of her career choice, but they were honestly confused. Although they managed to refrain from constantly saying it, Lauren knew what they really wanted was for her to find a nice young man and settle down, just like her sister. Apparently they couldn't understand why their thirty-two-year-old daughter, as they so charmingly phrased it, wanted to be a cook.

"Jonathan Windsor stole that recipe," Lauren said insistently. She wrapped a soft towel around Michael as Eileen lifted the little boy out of the tub. "And stealing is against the law."

"I'm sure it's a very serious crime," Eileen said wryly. "Quick, grab the phone. It's our duty as law-abiding citizens to report this heinous crime to the food police."

Lauren's eyes narrowed. "That's not funny, Eileen. Look at this guy. I'll bet he's never even turned on an oven, let alone baked anything inside one. I swear, I'm going to sue him. Will you represent me?"

"I'm a tax attorney, Lauren. Not a litigator. Besides, I'm taking at least a year off from work, maybe longer."

Lauren folded her arms stubbornly across her chest. "What am I going to do? I simply can't let this jerk get away with this theft."

"Jerk!"

Lauren and Eileen simultaneously glanced down at Michael.

"That isn't a word a nice little boy like you should be saying," Eileen said calmly.

Michael looked directly at Lauren, smiled mischievously and shouted, "Jerk. Jerk, jerk, jerk, jerk."

"Wonderful." Eileen sighed as he continued singing in a staccato rhythm. "Michael's learned a brand-new word he can say clear as a bell just in time for my dinner party. My husband has invited the most influential and conservative doctors from the hospital tonight. Now Michael will have something memorable to say to everyone."

Lauren winced at the look her sister gave her. "Sorry," she mumbled, vigorously rubbing the boy's wet head. She pulled the towel away, and his hair stood up in short, wet spikes. Lauren thought he looked adorable. Until he started his singing again. She glanced over at Eileen and noticed her sister's deep grimace.

"For heaven's sake, Eileen, lighten up. He's only three years old," Lauren admonished. "Your guests won't be arriving until seven. Maybe Michael will forget his new word by then."

"Don't count on it." Eileen pushed the hair out of her face with the back of her hand and sighed again.

"You're right, Lauren. I'm overreacting. But tonight is so important to Rob. I want everything to be perfect."

"It will be," Lauren said. She gave Eileen's arm a reassuring pat. "I brought over a fabulous selection of pound cakes I baked this morning: lemon, orange poppy seed, marble and double chocolate fudge. Plus I personally selected the freshest strawberries from the produce market. They'll look great served in that crystal bowl Dr. Percy and his wife gave you for a wedding gift.

"For the main course I made chicken breasts with the sun-dried tomato sauce Rob likes so much. All you have to do is cook the pasta. And the hors d'oeuvres are really spectacular. Oh, my goodness. I was so enraged over this article I left everything in a box on the kitchen counter. I'll be back as soon as I put the food in the refrigerator."

Lauren ran out the door, turned her head without breaking stride and shouted, "Start planning my lawsuit."

When she reached the kitchen Lauren unpacked the cardboard box containing the desserts, main course and canapés for Eileen's dinner party. She arranged everything neatly on the counter, then opened the refrigerator to store the perishable items.

Her face broadened into a wide grin as she beheld the numerous half-empty cartons of take-out food from nearly every establishment in the area. Eileen was a woman of many talents, but cooking was not among them. Lauren felt a guilty prick of conscience because she secretly took great pleasure in the fact that her sister was a dismal cook. It was wonderful having a skill Eileen didn't, even if her parents had difficulty acknowledging culinary creativity as a proper talent.

As the older sister Lauren had been expected to assume the leadership sibling position, but even as children it had quickly become apparent that Eileen was far more capable of fulfilling that role. She was brighter, more organized, more intuitive.

And so Eileen became the star child and Lauren the not-good-enough child. Lauren honestly never believed that her parents deliberately set out to make her feel inferior, but they were guilty of being insensitive to the individual differences that made her and Eileen unique individuals.

As grown women the need to compete had vastly diminished, yet Lauren still felt the occasional pang of inadequacy if she compared herself to her flawless sister.

So she tried very hard to avoid making any comparisons. Unless she was the one coming out ahead!

Lauren was still shifting cartons around in the refrigerator when she heard someone enter the room. She turned around and met the kind blue eyes of her brother-in-law, Dr. Robert Dalton.

"I'm glad to see the calvary has arrived," he said in an amused tone. "Eileen was really nervous when I left for the hospital this morning." He ran an appreciative eye over the food spread out on the countertop, then leaned down and kissed Lauren's cheek in greeting.

"Hi, Rob." Lauren smiled at her brother-in-law. He was a tall, slender man with sculpted features and a warm, friendly manner. Lauren had always liked him. "Eileen's upstairs with Michael and Ashley."

"I'll go up in a minute." Rob selected a cherry tomato stuffed with goat cheese from the assortment of endive boats, stuffed snow peas, dilled baby carrots and caviar potato canapés. He popped the tomato in his mouth and closed his eyes. Lauren watched his attractive face contort into an expression of pure bliss. "Incredible. You've outdone yourself again, Lauren. Thank you."

A blush rose to Lauren's cheeks. There was something intimate, almost erotic about the way Rob had savored his tomato. Maybe she should offer to teach Eileen how to cook a few simple gourmet dishes. Rob snatched up three more tomatoes, flashed her a charming grin and left the room.

Eileen appeared a few minutes later. "What enticing creations have you been feeding my husband? He never even blinked an eye when Michael called him a jerk."

Lauren groaned. "One slip of the tongue and I'm condemned for life." Lauren held out a container of vegetable appetizers as a peace offering. "Try a cheesy cucumber slice. Maybe you'll forgive me before my nephew turns twenty-one."

"Pass me one of those caviar potatoes and I'll forgive you when Michael's eighteen." Eileen munched appreciatively on her potato. "I hope you'll be joining us for dinner. There will be not one, not two, but three unattached male doctors in attendance. Please say you'll stay."

"I have to work." Lauren leaned against the counter and tasted one of the endive boats. "Besides, Mother would go into cardiac arrest if she found out I met three eligible doctors. I believe the mere possibility of having both your daughters married to physicians automatically qualifies one for the Mothers' Hall of Fame."

"Mother isn't that bad," Eileen said in a halfhearted tone as she opened a cabinet and removed an oblong silver tray. She set it on the counter, and the two women began arranging the colorful vegetable appetizers.

"She's a mother," Lauren remarked cheerfully. "She was empowered with the ability to be irritating the moment she gave birth. It usually doesn't bother me, but I've had a very hectic week, and seeing my recipe published by this Jonathan Windsor character was the icing on the cake. I simply can't deal with Mother on top of everything else."

Eileen toyed with the neatly arranged vegetable tray. "If it would help I could spend a few hours this weekend doing some research into copyright statutes at the law library."

A strong sense of gratitude filled Lauren, nudging aside her previous thirst for revenge. "I appreciate the offer, but I'm sure it would be a waste of time. I've had my moment of anger, it's pointless to dwell upon it. As Dad always likes to say, 'What goes around comes around.' Someday soon something equally infuriating will happen to Jonathan Windsor. I'm just disappointed that I won't be there to witness the moment."

"Not necessarily."

Lauren was definitely intrigued by the glint of speculation in Eileen's glowing blue eyes. "You have an idea?"

"You're forgetting about the hospital auxiliary's cooking contest I'm coordinating. It's the biggest fundraising event of the year, and I believe we still have a few openings in the dessert category."

Lauren's brown eyes widened in understanding. "And I'm one of the judges in that category. What a brilliant idea! The scoring is based on technique and presentation as well as end result. All the baking must be done in front of the judges. Boy, I'd love to see Mr. Jonathan Windsor bumbling around the kitchen, melted chocolate and almond paste flying everywhere. How do we get him to enter?"

Eileen's mouth tilted wryly. "If he doesn't really bake, as you suspect, I doubt he would return an application if I sent him one."

"Then I suppose we'll have to complete the application for him." Lauren smiled conspiratorially. "After that, we'll see how anxious he is to share *his* cheesecake recipe with the world. There will be a preliminary meeting for all the contestants next Saturday to schedule cooking times and answer questions. If we can't find Jonathan's home address in the phone book, we can mail the meeting notification to his office. The address was included in the magazine article."

"Sounds good to me." Eileen's bright grin suddenly turned into a frown. "Of course, Jonathan might not come to the meeting or the contest."

"It doesn't matter. Sending him a letter notifying him of his expected presence is satisfying enough. I'll count it as an extra bonus if he has the nerve to show up."

"Okay. Mr. Windsor's letter will be sent in tomorrow's mail."

Lauren let out a delighted laugh and saluted Eileen with an elaborate swish of the wrist. "Bon appétit!"

Jonathan Windsor removed his reading glasses, leaned back in his black leather chair and rubbed the slight indentation on the bridge of his nose. He glanced down at the letter in his hand and frowned. He had read it three times, yet it made no sense. A cooking contest for the hospital auxiliary?

Shaking his head in bewilderment, he consulted the name and address neatly typed on the corresponding envelope his secretary had clipped to the letter. Naturally it was possible there were two Jonathan Windsors living in the area, but there was definitely only one Jonathan Windsor at the Madison Seafood Company.

"Linda, would you come in here for a moment please?" Jonathan asked, as he caught a glimpse of his secretary walking by his open office door.

Linda stuck her head inside and peered at him over the top of huge brown-rimmed glasses. "Having problems with that new accounting software again?"

"No." Jonathan stood up and strolled out from behind his desk, holding the mysterious correspondence in his left hand. "Does my mother have anything to do with this letter?"

Linda pursed her lips while she studied the contents of the correspondence. Well into middle age, Linda had worked for the Madison Seafood Company all of her adult life and had been promoted to her current position when Jonathan took charge of the company a year ago. Her title of secretary might be a bit old-fashioned, but she said it made her comfortable, and Jonathan was more than happy to comply with anything that pleased Linda.

He considered her one of the company's greatest assets. She was smart, efficient and loyal. They had a solid working relationship and an ever-growing friendship. He trusted her implicitly with all of his business secrets and most of his personal dilemmas.

"I've heard about this contest," Linda finally replied, placing the letter on Jonathan's desk. "Plenty of folks around town are really excited about it. The event should raise a lot of money for the hospital. All the cooking is going to be done in the kitchen of that fancy La Maison restaurant."

Jonathan made a small sound of disgust. He wasn't interested in the cooking contest. "Do you think this is another one of my mother's harebrained public relations schemes? After that ludicrous article appeared in *Washington Today* magazine, I thought she understood I would not tolerate any more of her interference."

Linda clucked sympathetically. "I'm sure no one took that article seriously, Jonathan. It was supposed to be a fluff piece, all flash, no substance. And you looked very handsome in the picture."

"It was a gross distortion of fact," Jonathan said, shaking his head in disbelief. "I very rarely have time to go sailing, I'd hardly classify myself as an environmentalist and I've never even tasted chocolate Amaretto cheese-cake."

Linda propped one hand on her slender hip and sent Jonathan a condescending stare. "Well, maybe if you had spent more than fifteen minutes on the phone with the man writing the article instead of leaving the details to your mother, you might have been happier with the results."

Jonathan held up his palms in an unmistakable gesture of surrender. "Point taken, Linda. At least give me credit for learning from my mistakes. But I want to get my facts straight before confronting my mother. Eileen Dalton is listed as the chairwoman for this event. Can you locate her phone number for me please? I'd like to give her a call."

Linda glanced down at her wristwatch. "Eileen won't be home at this hour. Her son attends the same nursery school as my granddaughter. The children are on a field trip to the petting zoo today, they won't be back until four. Why don't you take a drive into town and talk to Lauren Stuart? She's one of the judges. I'm sure she'd be glad to help you straighten all this mess out."

"Do you know Lauren Stuart?"

"Oh, my, yes. She's a charming girl. She and Eileen are sisters. Eileen is married to that nice Dr. Dalton, but Lauren is still single. I've known the family for years. Good people. Lauren is an extraordinary pastry chef. She teaches cooking classes for the adult school continuing education program and does all the baking for that darling little coffee shop on Main Street, Just Desserts. I walk an extra half-mile each evening so I can splurge Friday afternoons on a gorgeous pastry or slice of gooey, fattening cake."

Jonathan visibly relaxed. After hearing that Lauren was unmarried, he had instinctively stiffened at Linda's suggestion of driving into town, suspecting a matchmaking ploy. He had been dodging his mother's efforts at finding him a suitable wife for so long it became second nature for him to become wary of an introduction to an unattached female. But he reasoned Linda's motivation for driving into town to meet this woman was grounded in her irrepressible sweet tooth, not a quest to find him the perfect mate.

"I suppose I could take an early lunch," Jonathan conceded.

"That seems like a sensible idea." Linda turned to leave, hesitated, then spun back around. "Ahhh, Jonathan, since you're going to be at the coffee shop anyway, could you bring me back a pastry? I especially like the cream-filled kind with the chocolate and vanilla icing."

"I'm Lauren Stuart. What can I do for you?"

A small, compact woman emerged from behind the tall glass-enclosed pastry case. She was dressed in baggy black slacks, a white tailored shirt with the sleeves rolled up past the elbows and an oversized flour-covered apron.

Jonathan admired her dark brown eyes, pert, upturned nose and full mouth. Her deep honey-colored hair was pulled back and tied with a bright red ribbon, but wispy bangs fell across her forehead softening the effect. She moved with unconscious grace and efficiency, though her quick bounding steps ceased the moment their eyes met.

Jonathan recoiled at the nasty glare she sent his way. Lauren Stuart looked like she wanted to bash him over the head, preferably with a heavy, blunt instrument. It was not the female reaction he normally received.

"Hello, Ms. Stuart. I'm Jonathan Windsor," he introduced himself.

She didn't offer her hand, and her piercing brown eyes clearly conveyed her disapproval.

"What do you want, Mr. Windsor?"

The cool, barely civil tone of her voice surprised him. Yet Jonathan attributed her sharp manner to being annoyed at this unexpected interruption. The small shop was nearly overflowing with customers, and a line was rapidly forming behind him.

"I can see you are very busy, Ms. Stuart, so I won't take up much of your time. I'd like to ask you a few questions about the upcoming cooking contest being sponsored by the hospital auxiliary. I understand you're one of the judges?"

"I don't take bribes, Mr. Windsor."

Jonathan laughed. "I'm relieved to discover you are so honest." He saw her brown eyes widen and her mouth open, but he cut her off before she could speak. "Apparently there has been some sort of mix-up. I received a letter today, but I never registered for the contest."

Her eyes darted briefly to the floor, then turned up and glared at him. "I'll instruct my sister Eileen to remove you from the contestant list. She's coordinating the event." Lauren's lip curled up into a sneer. "We understand completely if you don't have time to waste on charitable causes, Mr. Windsor."

"I didn't ask to be removed from the contest, Ms. Stuart. I was merely interested in discovering how I came to be a part of it," Jonathan said pleasantly.

"I don't understand, Mr. Windsor."

Her eyes were still angry, but they no longer met his with a challenging stare. Her body language clearly indicated she was not being entirely truthful with him, and Jonathan felt pleased that she wasn't a very accomplished liar. He was also fairly certain his mother was somehow involved in this scheme, so he immediately decided to drop the matter. It would hardly be fair to drag Lauren into the middle of yet another battle between him and his strong-willed mother.

"Don't worry about it, Ms. Stuart. I look forward to seeing you next Saturday." His easy smile brought a flood of red color to her cheeks. Jonathan thought it made her look even prettier. "If it isn't too much trouble, could you wrap up a dozen of those cream pastries for me? I promised my secretary I'd bring her a treat from the shop."

He stared at her intently while she silently filled the bakery box, rang up the sale, then handed him the pastries and his change. Their fingers briefly touched during the exchange, and a flair of desire tugged at Jonathan. He glanced up quickly, hoping to see a similar reaction in her eyes, but Lauren turned her back on him and marched away.

Disappointed, but not entirely discouraged, Jonathan left the shop, completely mystified and totally intrigued by the small woman with a large chip on her shoulder.

Two

Lauren blew out her breath, trying to will away the knot in her stomach. She still couldn't believe she had just spoken with Jonathan Windsor. In the flesh. Her heart was pumping as though she'd just spent twenty minutes on the dreaded stair-climbing machine. Feeling wired and edgy, Lauren paced behind the counter as she waited on the next customer in the crowded shop. Seizing the first opportunity a half-hour later, she escaped into the kitchen.

With slightly trembling fingers, she picked up the phone and dialed Eileen's number, cursing softly when the answering machine picked up. Leaving a terse, urgent message to call at once, Lauren hung up the phone.

She changed her mind three times before finally deciding to roll out tart crusts while waiting for Eileen to return her call. Mechanically Lauren removed the chilled slab of marble from the refrigerator along with the dough she had made earlier in the day.

She expertly floured the marble board and rolling pin then vigorously attacked the dough. "This is going to taste like shoe leather," Lauren muttered as she forced herself to temper her aggression.

Jonathan Windsor! A far too pleasant memory invaded Lauren's mind, and she sighed deeply. She had been both shocked and dismayed to discover him standing calmly in the middle of the shop, asking to speak to her. Lauren had recognized him instantly and could scarcely believe the picture she had seen of him in that magazine hadn't done him justice.

The photograph had captured the lines and details of Jonathan's nearly perfect features, but it had missed the magnitude of his charismatic presence. Nearly every head in the shop, old and young, male and female, had turned when Jonathan passed through the doorway. He was a living, breathing embodiment of a stylish, sexy, self-confident male in his elegant, well-cut light brown suit.

And he had been so pleasant! A charming smile, a friendly laugh, a kind, but not deferential manner. Lauren felt the uncomfortable coils of guilt creeping around her conscience. Perhaps she had been a bit too hasty in her quest for revenge. There was apparently more to Jonathan Windsor than met the eye and Lauren feared beneath the physical perfection was a decent man.

The jarring ring of the phone startled her, and Lauren dropped the round piece of dough she had just cut out.

"Hello? Oh, Eileen, thank goodness it's you. You'll never guess who was in here asking about the cooking contest. Jonathan Windsor!"

"Are you sure it was him?" Eileen's voice sounded slightly alarmed.

"Yes, it was! I recognized him immediately, even without his sailboat."

"I guess everything went well if you're cracking jokes." Eileen's voice shifted into calmer tones.

Lauren frowned at the receiver. "Oh, it went swell. I was cold, nasty and insulting. Heck, I made the Gestapo look warm and friendly by comparison. Jonathan on the other hand displayed genuine good humor and impeccable manners." Lauren chewed furiously on her lower lip, then hastily blurted out, "Eileen, he wanted to know who signed him up for the cooking contest."

"What did you tell him?" The concern was back in Eileen's voice.

"Nothing. I told him nothing." Lauren paused dramatically, clutching the receiver tightly with her flour-covered fingers. "Eileen we didn't do anything, um, illegal, did we? After all we did enter him in this contest without his permission."

"We haven't broken any laws." The strong conviction in Eileen's voice calmed Lauren's agitation. "Did he seem angry about the contest?"

"Not exactly. He said he wanted to discover how he became a contestant. When I offered to remove his name from the participants list, he declined and said he would be at the meeting on Saturday."

"Then you got what you wanted, Lauren. Remember, melted chocolate and almond paste flying around the kitchen?"

"I vaguely remember saying that." Lauren twisted the phone cord around her index finger. It snapped down and slapped against her thigh. "It seems like a hundred years ago."

"Sounds as though Jonathan Windsor made quite an impression on you. What was he like?" Eileen's voice was laced with curiosity.

"Drop dead gorgeous," Lauren replied honestly. "But it's more than his perfect looks. He's classy and sexy but very approachable. Gosh, he even smells expensive."

"What?"

"Forget it. I've got to go, Eileen. I've just ruined the crust for my lemon tarts, and I have to make another batch of dough. I'll call you later tonight." Lauren rubbed her temple vigorously. "And Eileen, next time we come up with one of these brilliant schemes, do me a big favor. Please talk me out of it, okay?"

Jonathan opted for the longer, scenic route back to the office. Although the waters of the Chesapeake Bay were different from the rugged coast of Maine where he grew up, Jonathan felt a keen sense of nostalgia at being near salt water. He opened both the driver and passenger windows so the moist wind could blow completely through the car.

He drove slowly, enjoying the tranquillity of the view; the rolling expanse of water, the colorful shoreline, the white sails and boat hulls dotting the fluid sea. As he drove further along on the deserted road, he could hear the lapping of water against the rocky shore mingling with the indignant shrieks of the swooping gulls.

Jonathan downshifted into a sharp turn, the strong muscles of his forearms rippling beneath his suit jacket. The sleek Jaguar responded smoothly, its powerful engine purring. The expensive sports car had been a bribe from his widowed mother, but Jonathan wasn't adverse to accepting it. He had grown up with wealth and held a deep appreciation for the finer things in life.

When his mother had begged him last year to move to Maryland and assume control of the seafood company her grandfather had founded, she'd assumed a financial incentive was necessary. It wasn't, but Jonathan knew his mother wouldn't understand. In her world money was central and omnipotent.

The move to Maryland had been a good one for Jonathan. After years of dabbling in various business ventures, he at last had discovered a position that utilized both his talent for management and knack for anticipating market trends. He left the details of the day-to-day running of the company to the experts who understood the seafood business while he concentrated on keeping overhead low and profits high.

The box of pastries on the seat next to Jonathan slid to one side as he took another sharp turn. He touched the box, and thoughts of Lauren entered his mind. His pulse started beating in a quick, jumpy rhythm. What a surprise she had been! He glanced in the rearview mirror and smiled. The excitement of the encounter was still in his eyes.

She had made her dislike of him abundantly clear, yet he had experienced a strange desire to take her into his arms and kiss her until the hostility left her dazzling brown eyes. Jonathan had never before given much credence to the power of sexual attraction, but then again he had never before experienced it so profoundly. And it puzzled him.

Lauren was nothing like the type of women he usually dated and was a far cry from his image of the perfect mate. He wanted, no, he needed, a woman who would be able to effectively deal with his headstrong mother. As he had gotten older, Jonathan had learned to appreciate the true value of family harmony. It would be unbearable to spend the next forty-odd years of his life constantly refereeing feuds between his wife and his mother.

Jonathan had been dragged to enough new-age art exhibits and had slept through far too many operas not to realize shared interests were essential for any successful long-term relationship. He wanted a woman who participated in and enjoyed all types of sports and who had an affinity for sailing.

He'd always favored sophisticated, self-possessed women and had long been searching for a female with an imposing presence, one who exuded dignity and breeding, yet underneath exhibited a sense of untapped sexuality. Given a choice, he preferred mystery and subtlety in a woman.

Jonathan's lips curled. Lauren possessed all the subtlety of a runaway train. She appeared to despise him, for no obvious reason, and seemed to get a real charge out of displaying her dislike. He'd bet she hated sailing and probably loved opera. The only sensible course of action was to dismiss Lauren entirely from his thoughts, but he was honest enough to admit to himself it wouldn't be easy.

He did manage however to shift his mind away from Lauren as he expertly maneuvered his car into the tight parking space in front of the Madison Seafood building. It was an unassuming corporate headquarters by city standards. A two-story brick structure with a dusty gravel parking lot and a few scattered bushes to soften the effect. His mother complained constantly that the building was a disgrace, but Jonathan had selected the site himself when he'd taken control of the company, insisting it was essential to his cost-cutting plan.

The building was near the company's various oyster- and crab-processing plants, the price was reasonable and the interior space more than adequate. The company shipped its seafood products all over the country. Sales were made by phone, fax and even the Internet now that their website was up and running. Various members of the marketing team did most of their customer-service work by phone with periodic visits to the customer's place of business. Clients rarely came to the office.

If clients did travel to Maryland they were always more interested in touring the processing plants. They wanted to see the seafood they were buying, not a bunch of desks and phones. Jonathan felt it was a ridiculous waste of money paying for fancy, expensive offices when functional space was all that was required.

"Is that for me?" Linda's eyes widened with anticipation when she spied the neatly tied pastry box in Jonathan's hand.

"It sure is," Jonathan replied with a grin. He placed the box in the center of Linda's cluttered desk. "Knock yourself out."

Linda lifted the lid of the box and squealed. "Oh my goodness! I said bring me back *a* pastry, Jonathan, not a dozen. I'll gain ten pounds if I eat all this."

"So put them next to the coffee machine. I'm sure the sales crew will polish them off in no time."

"The sales crew!" Linda looked appalled. "They would never appreciate the quality of these delightful treats. They eat packaged snack cakes and those horrible deep-fried donuts."

Jonathan smiled. Linda was right. The sales crew's diet did resemble a twelve-year-old boy's idea of good nutrition. Their desks were usually littered with an interesting assortment of pizza boxes and empty fast-food bags, and the office often smelled like french fries.

Linda carefully creased back the lid of the pastry box and studied the contents intently. Her hand moved toward one of the sweets, hesitated, then veered toward another. Rejecting her second choice, she finally picked up her third selection and inhaled deeply.

Curious about these treats Linda clearly felt were extraordinary, Jonathan reached into the box and grabbed one. He took a jaw-splitting bite. A gush of rich French cream squirted out the sides of the pastry and coated his fingers. He paused before licking it off as the flaky crust and cream inside his mouth melted simultaneously, leaving him with a taste sensation bordering on sensual ecstasy.

"This is very good," he declared, sucking the cream from his fingers. He popped the remainder of the pastry into his mouth, then reached for a second.

"They are positively addictive," Linda said, chewing slowly. It was obvious she was savoring every mouthful. "I told you Lauren was a genius. I've tasted many a pastry in my day, and nothing can compare to her creations."

"She certainly has talent," Jonathan agreed, eyeing the box with longing. Giving in to his taste buds one final time, he snagged a third pastry. "I suppose that accounts for her temperamental attitude."

"Lauren temperamental?" Linda shook her head in bewilderment. "I've always found her to be a warm, friendly girl."

"Guess I caught her on an off day," Jonathan said. He watched Linda carefully scotch-tape each side of the box closed and firmly resisted the temptation to ask for another pastry. "I'm fairly certain this cooking contest was all my mother's doing. I think Lauren was nervous about covering up for her."

Linda clucked her tongue sympathetically. "Jonathan, your mother could make the queen of England nervous."

"It has been known to happen."

"Well, I'm glad you got everything straightened out. I'm sure the hospital auxiliary won't have a problem finding someone else to take your vacated spot. The contest is regarded with great prestige among certain locals. I've heard the gourmet club is really pressuring its members to be daring when choosing their recipes."

A slight, reckless smiled appeared on Jonathan's handsome face. "Actually, I told Lauren I would participate in the contest."

"What?" Linda's voice was laced with disbelief. "Jonathan, you can hardly boil water. How do you expect to participate in a cooking competition?"

Jonathan felt a creeping panic set in, but then his innate self-confidence asserted itself. "I don't have to win the contest, just make a respectable showing. How difficult can it be? I've got almost two months before the competition to practice."

Linda raised a skeptical eyebrow. "Why are you doing this?"

"Civic duty?" Jonathan winked at Linda's sour expression. Clearly his secretary was unconvinced. And she refused to be charmed. Because he respected her and needed her help, Jonathan decided to be honest.

"Okay, I'll admit it. I'm a coward. I'm not in the mood to go ten rounds with my mother over this silly contest. Mother had a reason for entering me in this competition. Heck, she might have even shared her reasons with me and I just wasn't paying attention. I tend to tune her out when she starts lecturing me on how I should conduct my life."

"I think you're crazy," Linda said, her eyes shining with disapproval. "I know several people who have entered the contest, and they are all very serious about winning. But if you are determined to make a fool of yourself, I'm not going to try and stop you."

"Thanks."

Jonathan shot Linda a quelling look, but she merely laughed.

"You had better find a copy of that *Washington Today* magazine article," Linda commanded. "The contest letter you received said you were going to bake a chocolate Amaretto cheesecake, and the recipe was included in that article. I'll make out a list of all the ingredients and baking supplies you'll need. I suggest you start practicing tonight."

"Yes, boss." Jonathan bowed to his secretary. "With a bit of practice, I'm sure I can hold my own in a cooking competition." Linda gave a scornful snort and Jonathan couldn't resist adding, "Who knows, if I put my mind to it, I might even win."

* * *

Lauren was running late. Again. Baking the lemon tarts for Mrs. Miller's party had taken longer than Lauren had originally planned since she'd ruined the first batch of dough and had had to make a second. Thankfully the second group of tarts had baked perfectly, but they were not ready yet.

The final missing element of the dessert was the delicate candy violets that decorated the center of each individual lemon tart. On a day that seemed to get progressively worse, Lauren decided she shouldn't have been surprised to discover the two new teenage girls working at the shop had found the last box of candied violets and, after sampling a few, had devoured the entire supply.

In an effort to avoid revealing the mishap to Mrs. Miller, Lauren had volunteered to personally deliver the pastries. But first she had to purchase the missing candied violets. And only one small specialty shop, located on the opposite side of town, stocked the confections.

Lauren drove her compact car into the remaining parking space in the small lot behind the row of newly renovated specialty shops and jumped out of the car, pulling her purse behind her. The delectable smell of rich chocolate assaulted her senses the moment she passed through the door of the gourmet sweet shop.

"Hi, Molly." Lauren called out a quick greeting to the owner, pleased that she was busy helping a customer. Normally Lauren enjoyed chatting with the effervescent Molly, but today there was no time for idle gossip.

Marching quickly past the rows of neatly displayed chocolate molds, Lauren rounded a corner and nearly collided with another shopper.

"Oh, I'm so sorry," she began, but her apology was

abruptly cut short when she lifted her eyes and saw who it was. "Good evening, Mr. Windsor," she managed to say coolly.

"Hello, Lauren."

Jonathan looked good. Very good. He had removed the suit jacket and tie he was wearing earlier in the day, and the soft blue color of his oxford-cloth shirt did wonders for his green eyes. His smile was both pleasant and seductive.

A strange rush of desire surged through Lauren. She enjoyed hearing her name roll so familiarly off his tongue, like they were old friends or even old lovers. Lauren drew a shuddering breath and deliberately broke eye contact. How humiliating to be so uncontrollably attracted to him!

Knowing it would be a mistake to look too closely at the tall, tanned, muscular man standing before her, Lauren instead cast her eyes down to the two baskets he held. They were filled to the brim with a wide assortment of items; mixing bowls, spatulas, three different sizes of springform pans, several boxes of chocolate wafers, imported chocolate, and two tubes of almond paste.

Lauren's head shot up in annoyance. The baskets contained many of the components needed for baking a chocolate Amaretto cheesecake. *Her* cheesecake.

"Come here often?" Lauren asked with a sarcastic edge to her voice.

"Isn't that supposed to be my line?" Jonathan joked. He cleared his throat when Lauren didn't even crack a smile. "Actually this is my first time shopping here. My secretary recommended it."

"Really? Where do you usually buy your almond paste? I thought Molly's was the only place in town that carried it."

Jonathan blinked. "I guess you've caught me, Lauren," he said in a deep voice.

She lifted a brow in mock surprise. Finally an honest answer, she thought, waiting to hear the rest. "Caught you, Mr. Windsor?"

"Yes. I usually get my supplies via mail order." He smiled charmingly.

His confident expression infuriated her. She knew he was lying. I'm going to hit him, Lauren, decided. I'm going to pick up that large copper pot from the shelf and swing it at his perfect smile with its perfect dimples and wipe that perfect expression off his perfect face.

She actually placed her hand around the handle of the pot before catching herself. Had she completely lost her mind? Letting out her breath in a loud huff, Lauren gave Jonathan Windsor her phoniest smile.

"Sorry I can't stay to chat anymore, but Mrs. Miller is expecting me to deliver the dessert for her party this evening and she'll be frantic if I don't get there on time."

She nodded her head dismissively and tried pushing past Jonathan, but he blocked the small aisle.

"Miller? Hannah Miller? She's a neighbor of mine."

"How nice." Lauren widened her phoney grin. She turned sideways and slid around Jonathan, sucking in her breath so there was no chance of brushing against him.

Apparently unperturbed by her dismissal, Jonathan followed closely on her heels.

"If you finish early at the Millers you should stop by my place. It's only a few houses away from theirs, number two-fifty-six. We could have a drink or maybe even dinner."

Lauren hated the thrill that swept through her, along with the strong sense of anticipation. This was utterly ridiculous. This man was clearly not to be trusted. She refused to acknowledge her attraction to him. It was equally baffling and unwelcome.

"I have a very busy evening planned," Lauren forced

herself to reply through set teeth. "Good-bye, Mr. Windsor."

"The offer stands, if you change your mind. And please, call me Jonathan."

Lauren opened her mouth to speak, but closed it abruptly when she saw the clock on the wall. She would never make it to the Millers' house on time if she didn't leave immediately. And she was afraid if she spoke her mind now, it would take a full twenty minutes before she finished.

Yanking three boxes of candied violets off the shelf, Lauren stalked away from Jonathan without uttering another sound.

This time Jonathan managed to control the masculine primal instinct that shouted at him to pursue her. Instead he contented himself with watching the gentle sway of Lauren's hips as she rushed away from him. She was certainly one intriguing female.

Jonathan felt sixteen years old, his body humming with sexual tension. Somehow Lauren evoked a primitive, wild desire in him, unlike any he had ever known. And he hadn't even kissed her yet.

He wasn't really sure why he had invited her to the house. The words had just popped out impulsively. Lauren was strangely irresistible, rather like her pastries. One bite and you were hooked.

Jonathan grinned. His resolve to purge Lauren from his thoughts had lasted only a few hours. The fact that he truly believed she was not the right woman for him was apparently not a good enough reason to stay away from her. Actually Lauren's not so subtle brush-off only succeeded in heightening his interest.

She wasn't the sophisticated, cultured, stylish type of woman he wanted to get involved with, but she also wasn't anything like the dull, passionless women with impeccable bloodlines, education and connections his mother was always pushing at him.

Lauren's dislike of him hadn't been so blatant this time. Who knows what her reaction would be the next time they met Jonathan thought as he chuckled softly. Turning his attention back to the shopping list, he continued to fill his basket, his mind no longer completely focused on the task.

THREE

I am clearly losing my mind, Lauren decided as she huddled behind the steering wheel. Her compact car was parked in a secluded spot on Jonathan Windsor's deserted street, affording her an excellent view of his mailbox.

She had been staring at that mailbox for fifteen minutes, debating what to do. *I should leave,* Lauren admonished herself. Immediately. Yet even as the thought nagged at her mind, Lauren started the car engine.

Instead of driving away she eased her foot down slowly on the accelerator and inched the car forward, hoping to catch a glimpse of the house. It was impossible. No matter which way she twisted and craned her neck, all she could see was trees.

The house was set too far back from the road, with only the long winding driveway visible. The thick green leaves and artfully tended foliage hid the dwelling completely from view.

Lauren stared at the mailbox and shook her head. It was made of attractively weathered gray wood and shaped like a barn. It reminded her of a mailbox she had admired in a country antique shop down in St. Michaels a few weeks ago. It didn't fit the wealthy, sophisticated image of Jonathan Windsor.

Without giving herself time to reconsider her actions,

Lauren gunned the engine and turned into Jonathan's driveway. No alarms sounded, no guards appeared to challenge her entrance. Still, her heart was pounding with excitement and nerves as she negotiated each bend through the dense trees. The heavy green leaves blocked what remained of the evening light, but when she reached the end of the drive, Lauren burst forth from the darkness.

"I don't think we're in Kansas anymore, Toto," she muttered breathlessly. She slammed on the brakes, and the car screeched to a halt. Then she lifted her head and simply stared, needing a few moments to take in the splendor of the view.

The Georgian-style colonial, situated at the top of a grassy knoll, was made of stone and brick. It stretched on endlessly, a magnificent example of detailed work-manship, appointments and materials of a bygone era that had all been tastefully restored. In front of the house was a cobblestoned circular courtyard accented by meticulously groomed shrubbery, strategically placed teak garden benches, and an elegant fountain.

The total effect was stunning. Lauren was enchanted. It was absolutely the most beautiful home she had ever seen and far more in keeping with her perceived image of wealthy Jonathan Windsor.

Lauren's quiet appreciation of all this splendor was abruptly shattered by the sound of a barking dog. She glanced about guiltily, searching for the animal. Suddenly a blur of golden fur appeared at the top of the knoll. Spotting the intrusive car, the animal charged down the hill at full speed, barking furiously.

Lauren sat immobilized for a few seconds, then frantically reached for the handle to roll up her window. How stupid of her! She had probably tripped some silent alarm when she'd turned into the driveway.

Naturally a place like this would have a security dog,

perhaps more than one. Cat-lover Lauren figured it was probably one of those fierce Dobermans or maybe even a German shepherd.

Locking the door for good measure, Lauren waited nervously for the large dog to reach the car. It didn't take long. With mounting apprehension she followed the animal's progress, but it raced around behind the car and out of view.

Lauren twisted her head around, then screamed in fright when the dog jumped up on its hind paws and braced itself against the door on the driver's side. The animal's large head pressed against her window, its loud barking echoing in Lauren's ears. She cringed.

"Chesapeake, get down!"

Lauren glanced out the front windshield and heaved a sigh of relief. She saw Jonathan advance toward the car at a leisurely pace. Apparently the dog also saw its master because the golden shaggy tail began wagging in a frenzy of excitement, even as the animal remained plastered against Lauren's door.

"Come on, Chesapeake, get down," Jonathan admonished. He stood patiently by the hood of the car and waited expectantly. Eventually the dog obeyed the command and Jonathan patted its big head affectionately.

Lauren slowly released her tense grip on the steering wheel and watched the interplay between Jonathan and his pet. Chesapeake rolled over on her back and gazed adoringly at her master with soft brown eyes. He rubbed her stomach furiously for a moment, and the animal shuddered in ecstasy.

Lauren giggled and grudgingly admitted the dog no longer appeared quite so menacing when it was sprawled with such abandon out on the driveway.

"Chesapeake makes a lot of noise, but she is perfectly harmless," Jonathan said in a conversational tone. He came forward to Lauren's side of the car, placed an arm on the roof and casually leaned down.

Lauren smiled faintly, but decided to remain safely encased inside her automobile. "What kind of dog is she?" she asked, raising her voice to be heard.

"Technically she's a mutt. Half-golden retriever, half-labrador retriever. She's rather exuberant but very affectionate and friendly. If you get out of the car, I'll introduce you," Jonathan said with a coaxing smile.

Lauren was starting to feel a little foolish. She was acting like a terrified child. It was only a dog, after all. Okay, a very large dog, but supposedly a friendly animal.

She unlocked the door and Jonathan opened it, reaching in to help her out. His hand was tanned and strong—it made her own look petite and delicate by comparison—yet his grip was gentle.

"I'm very glad you stopped by," Jonathan whispered.

An odd joy pulsed through Lauren at his welcoming smile. There was no mistaking that he was pleased to see her. Jonathan looked enormously appealing in his snug-fitting faded jeans and ash gray T-shirt. Lauren liked the way the ends of his wheat-colored hair brushed against the collar. It made him look boyish and sexy.

Feeling the need to resist the attraction, Lauren turned her attention to the dog.

"Nice doggy," Lauren said hesitantly. She gingerly stroked the animal's back. The fur felt soft and smooth. "You sure are a pretty girl."

Chesapeake responded to Lauren's tentative greeting with an enthusiastic tail wagging. Then the dog raced over to a cluster of bushes, retrieved a half-chewed tennis ball and dropped it at Lauren's feet.

"Chesapeake likes you," Jonathan said. "That's her favorite ball."

"I'm flattered." Lauren stooped down to pick up the

ball, but pulled back when she saw how wet and gooey it was. "I suppose Chesapeake expects me to touch it?"

"She wants you to throw it," Jonathan replied. Lauren hesitated, and Jonathan shrugged his shoulders philosophically. "It's only a little dog slobber."

Wrinkling her nose, Lauren slowly lifted the ball with her fingertips. Chesapeake immediately began dancing with excitement. Fearing she might be knocked over, Lauren quickly threw the ball. Her tenuous grip, combined with the slippery surface, produced a short, choppy throw. Chesapeake bounded after the ball with great excitement and returned with it in less than a minute.

"You throw like a girl," Jonathan said with a good-natured smile. He scooped up the ball and hurled it through the air. It sailed over the trees and out of view.

"I am a girl," Lauren retorted, telling herself she was not impressed. The hard muscles of Jonathan's forearms bulged in a very attractive, very masculine way when he gripped the ball. Lauren found it difficult to control her staring. "Besides, I've never owned a dog. We always had a cat when I was growing up."

"Cats!" Jonathan's voice was laced with disdain. "How can you possibly compare a cat favorably to a dog?"

"Cats are wonderful pets. They're intelligent, affectionate and practically self-sufficient." Lauren sent Jonathan a teasing glance. "And they don't slobber."

"A minor advantage," Jonathan said as he wiped his hand on his jean clad thigh. "Come on up to the house and we'll discuss this some more."

Lauren stepped back. "I didn't plan on staying. I noticed the number on your mailbox as I was driving down the street. I impulsively decided to indulge my curiosity since I couldn't see the house from the road." She turned her head and gazed up at the mansion. "It is truly spectacular."

Jonathan grinned sheepishly. "Don't be so impressed, it's only a loaner. My uncle built the place back in the early 1930s. He moved out to Arizona a few years ago, but didn't want to sell the house and lose the waterfront access. When I came to Maryland he asked me to stay here and look after the property. It's a convenient drive to the office, and I love being so close to the water. I've really enjoyed living here."

"Who wouldn't?"

Their eyes met and Lauren felt a connection forming, a bond of goodwill and comradeship. It surprised her. She reminded herself that she had come to Jonathan's house to confront him about stealing her cheesecake recipe, not because she was interested in pursuing any sort of relationship with him, friendship or otherwise. The sensible route would be to state her business and leave.

Yet Lauren was unable to resist a chance to view the inside of the beautiful house. After disclosing her reason for being there, she might never get another opportunity.

"I guess I can stay for a few minutes," she said.

They made the long walk up to the house in silence, with Chesapeake trotting between them, carrying the tennis ball in her mouth. When they reached the front door, Jonathan politely held it open. Chesapeake ran inside first, and Lauren heard the rhythmic tapping of claws on the marble floor as the dog raced across the vast entrance foyer.

She somehow managed to control her gasp of awe as she stepped inside. A grand center hall staircase of highly buffed oak, accented with cream-colored trim, wound its way majestically upward, eventually disappearing from sight. A crystal and brass chandelier hung low

over a claw-footed mahogany table positioned in the
center of the foyer that sported a silver Revere bowl
spilling over with fresh roses. The green of the stems
and red of the blossoms were echoed in the intricate
pattern of the Oriental rug that covered part of the
white marble floor.

Anxious to see more, Lauren eagerly followed
Jonathan through the various first-floor rooms. There
was a library lined with custom cabinets filled with
leather-bound books. It had warm cherry paneling. A
comfortable club chair and matching ottoman stood
invitingly beside the fireplace. The media room over-
looked a groomed garden and was furnished on a grand
scale with oversized country French-style sofas and
chairs and a huge custom-designed case filled with a
large-screen television, a VCR, stereo and CD player.

The vast dining room was a departure from the traditional style. Instead of one long dining table, it contained multiple tables strategically positioned around
the room on several complementing area rugs, creating
a cozy, intimate atmosphere.

The strong conservative colors of navy blue, hunter
green and garnet red were used on the walls and furniture throughout the house, and were often paired
with a vibrant amber gold, producing a soothing, elegant effect. Window treatments, consisting of swags and
jabots in the same rich jewel-tone shades, allowed in
daylight, emphasizing the unique style, shape and size
of the various windows.

The attention to detail was flawless. The rooms were
luxuriously furnished with fine furniture and heir-
looms, yet still managed to look comfortable and functional. Lauren could hardly wait to see the kitchen,
imagining a combination of high-tech appliances and
gadgets subtly incorporated into a traditional design.

But Jonathan halted the tour before they reached the kitchen.

"If we hurry outside to the west terrace, we can catch the sunset," he said. "The colors reflected off the water are spectacular."

"I'd rather see your kitchen," Lauren said bluntly. She felt her cheeks flush with embarrassment when he sent her an odd gaze, but she didn't withdraw her request.

When they stepped through the doorway, she immediately understood Jonathan's deliberate omission of this room on the tour. The kitchen was a creative vision of country French mixed with a dash of city chic, but the full magnificence of the large room was impossible to appreciate in its present condition.

Every inch of generous counter space, along with the entire surface of the jutting center island, was crammed with dirty mixing bowls, measuring cups, baking pans, cookie sheets and spatulas. A handheld electric mixer stood upright, the steely blades clogged with cream cheese. Crowded next to it was a food processor half-filled with melted chocolate, a nearly empty bottle of Amaretto liqueur and a dozen broken egg shells. The faint aroma of burnt chocolate and almonds hung ominously in the air.

"Sorry about the mess," Jonathan apologized. "I was practicing for the cooking contest."

"It looks like a hurricane blew through here," Lauren said. "Did you actually bake something or just demolish the place?"

"I made a cheesecake," he replied. He crossed the kitchen and opened the refrigerator. "It hasn't been chilling very long, but I think we can try a piece."

Lauren's eyes narrowed. She didn't voice any objection, however. She perched herself on one of the high-backed stools cozily arranged around the center island and studied his every move.

Balancing the cake in one hand, Jonathan swept several mixing bowls into an already overcrowded double sink, then placed the cake on the counter. After three attempts he managed to release the cake from the springform pan. With a dazzling smile of triumph, he lifted the cake for Lauren's inspection. She experienced a flush of annoyance as she beheld the perfectly shaped creation.

"It looks very plain." She clicked her tongue critically. "I assume you usually pipe a whipped cream edge and mound chocolate shavings in the center, or perhaps you try for a more sophisticated presentation?"

Lauren gazed at him intently while she spoke, trying to keep the annoyance from her voice. She was goading him deliberately, pushing to see how far Jonathan would carry the pretense. Did he have trouble meeting her eyes, or was that merely her hopeful imagination? Lauren scrutinized him closely, certain she detected a slipping of his natural self-confidence.

He ignored her question and cut two generous slices. Lauren accepted her serving with rigid fingers. Noting with catty delight that the chocolate crust crumbled as she cut into it with her fork, she took a bite. The bitter taste of chocolate exploded in her mouth the moment it hit her tongue.

"Oh, my." Lauren gasped, her eyes tearing. While searching frantically for some way to get rid of the horrible taste, she spied the paper towel dispenser near the sink. Jumping down from her stool, she sprinted toward it, ripped off several paper towels and spit out the cake. "This tastes disgusting. What did you do to the recipe?"

She turned toward Jonathan accusingly and watched in amazement as he valiantly struggled to swallow the piece of cake in his mouth. His throat muscles worked furiously, and Lauren could almost see the confection slide its way down to his stomach.

"I followed the directions to the letter," he said in a hoarse tone. "I don't know what went wrong."

Lauren wet a clean paper towel and rubbed it over her tongue vigorously, hoping to remove some of the unpleasant taste. She tossed the used towel into the overflowing garbage pail at the end of the counter, then paused to lift out an empty box.

Lauren immediately recognized the elegant gold stamp on the edge of the box of expensive imported Swiss chocolate. She was not surprised that Jonathan had chosen one of the most exclusive chocolate brands to make this cake, but he had made a serious error in selection. The recipe she had spent weeks perfecting called for *semisweet* chocolate. Jonathan had used *unsweetened* chocolate.

Oh dear, what a *horrible* mistake. Feeling a smug sense of justice Lauren returned the empty chocolate box to the garbage, placed her used paper towel on top and turned to Jonathan.

"I know everyone entered in the contest is committed to producing a winning recipe," she said with a sly smile. "I sincerely hope your final entry will at least be edible since the cake you produce will be served at the formal reception at the country club that evening. I expect many of the hospital's doctors will be in attendance, but I highly doubt anyone will be bringing a stomach pump."

Jonathan looked distressed. "I don't understand what went wrong," he repeated. "I measured everything very carefully. I set the oven at the correct temperature. I even moved the rack to the middle shelf. I didn't burn the cake." He rummaged through the mess of pans and dirty bowls on the cluttered counter. "Do you have any idea why this tastes so awful?"

Lauren hesitated for a moment. Then she saw him pick up a chocolate-spattered copy of *Washington Today* magazine and study it intently. Her momentary pang of guilt vanished.

"Haven't a clue," Lauren lied breezily. "I can see you have a lot of baking and . . . um . . . cleaning up to do tonight, so I won't keep you."

"I was hoping we could have dinner," Jonathan said, blocking her retreat. "If not this evening, maybe later in the week."

Lauren blinked. She'd never seen anyone move so fast. His nearness caused her heart to thump in a quick erratic rhythm. Refusing to surrender to this unwelcome attraction, she drew herself up to her full height. The top of her head barely cleared Jonathan's shoulder, but her stiff spine gave her confidence a boost.

"After tasting your prize-winning original cheesecake, Jonathan, I feel compelled to recommend that you spend all your free time in the next few weeks preparing for the contest."

With a vivacious smile, Lauren quickly left, insisting to herself as she practically sprinted to her car that she did not feel the tiniest bit of guilt or regret.

"I'm coming, Eileen, hold on a minute," Lauren shouted. Half-dressed, she emerged from her bedroom, crossed the cluttered apartment living room and opened the front door.

"You didn't even look through the peephole." Eileen began the lecture the moment the door opened. "Honestly, Lauren, you know very well a woman living alone can't be too careful."

"Yes, Mother," Lauren replied, making a face at her younger sister. She was in no mood to be preached to, especially when she was in the wrong.

"Sorry." Eileen was instantly contrite. "I've had a frantic morning. The hospital called Rob at five this morning to assist with emergency surgery. He arrived home just as I was leaving." She strode gracefully across the room, neatly sidestepping the piles of magazines, books and papers strewn about on the floor. "Can I use the phone? Things were chaotic at home, and Rob looked absolutely panic-stricken when I left.

"Ashley was screaming her head off. She's cutting two new teeth and barely slept last night. Michael refused to get dressed and insisted he wanted to watch a very inappropriate adult movie on cable TV. I kinda handed the kids off to Rob and bolted out the door."

"Sounds like it was the only sensible thing to do," Lauren said with a laugh. "Use the phone in the kitchen. It will take me a few minutes to finish getting dressed."

Lauren returned to the bedroom, stood before her open closet and contemplated the contents with dismay. No stunning fashionable clothes had materialized since she had last sorted through it ten minutes ago. Since she was already partially dressed in a navy blue suit she had worn in her former days as an accountant, Lauren decided she might as well put on the rest of the outfit.

She buttoned the high-necked blouse, donned the fitted jacket and added a short length of fake pearls. She stepped back and tilted her head. Creases formed in Lauren's forehead as she studied the effect in the full-length mirror. It was perfect. For a nun.

Eileen walked into the bedroom, and Lauren's spirits plummeted further. Her sister's long legs and slender torso were artfully displayed in a silky tailored dress of vibrant blue. She looked sophisticated and professional. Lauren felt dowdy and middle-aged, especially standing beside her perfect sister.

"That outfit is a bit severe," Eileen suggested gently. "I don't think you need to dress so conservatively for this meeting. You and Chef Henri will be the only judges in attendance. The main purpose of the meeting is to acquaint the participants with the rules and procedures of the cooking contest and to give them a tour of the kitchen where the competition will take place."

"I know the purpose of the meeting," Lauren snapped. She blew out her breath, then grinned apologetically. "I guess Ashley isn't the only one who didn't get much sleep last night. Help me pick out something to wear, Eileen. Please?"

Eileen gazed at her sister with kind eyes. "There isn't any special reason why you are suddenly so concerned about your appearance, is there?"

"What did Rob say when you called him? Are the kids okay?" Lauren asked, deliberately avoiding the question. She *was* concerned about her appearance and frankly it annoyed her.

Lauren knew she was an attractive woman, perhaps not as beautiful as her sister, but certainly pretty in her own right. And she had qualities that were even more important than looks.

She was an intelligent woman who had reached a measure of accomplishment in her chosen profession and was striving for even greater heights. She possessed a fine sense of humor and a quirky appreciation for the absurdities of life. She had fought hard over the years for every bit of her self-confidence, and she wasn't about to let it slip away over an unexplained attraction to a devastatingly handsome man who liked to steal her cheesecake recipes.

"Everything is under control at home," Eileen said, answering Lauren's question. The hangers clicked in a military rhythm as she sorted through the clothes in Lauren's closet. "Rob told me the baby was sitting in her high chair chewing on a frozen bagel and Michael was watching a *Sesame Street* videotape."

Eventually Eileen pulled out a gauzy skirt and matching silk blouse. Lauren frowned at the choice. "I don't think that's appropriate. It's too provocative."

"It's very pretty. Besides, these colors look wonderful on you." Eileen crawled around in the bottom of the closet and retrieved a pair of matching sandals with two-inch heels. Tossing them at Lauren she added, "Hurry up and finish dressing. We don't want to be late."

They were late, but nobody seemed to mind. The intimate dinning room of La Maison restaurant was filled with a lively crowd of people, their noisy conversation drifting about the room. The atmosphere reminded Lauren of a cocktail party. Everyone looked eager and excited.

"Is he here?" Eileen whispered in Lauren's ear as they stood on the fringes of the crowd and surveyed the room.

"I haven't spotted him yet," Lauren admitted, knowing exactly who it was Eileen had in mind.

Lauren's eyes scanned the room. Her breath caught in her throat when they unexpectedly met Jonathan's. He was engaged in conversation with several middle-aged women, who appeared to be hanging on his every word, but he paused to smile at her, and Lauren saw the warmth and friendliness in his eyes.

"Lauren! Eileen!"

Startled, Lauren turned and watched the restaurant's chef, Henri, come barreling toward her and her sister. Henri was a stocky man with shoulder-length blond hair usually pulled back and worn in a straggly ponytail. His stylishly baggy pants were jet black, the same color as his open-throated shirt. He sported a neatly groomed

pencil-thin mustache and a diamond stud in his left ear
the size of a large pea.

Lauren had always believed it was a strong testament
to Henri's culinary skills that the conservative Maryland
town of Salisburg had so eagerly embraced the flamboyant chef.

When he arrived at her side, Henri held Lauren's
hands and kissed both her cheeks in greeting, then repeated the dramatic gesture with Eileen.

"Shall we begin, ladies? I have delayed the restaurant
opening by two hours today, but I must have my kitchen
all to myself soon so I can begin creating tonight's spectacular entrées. I have spoiled my customers over the
years. They now expect only the best."

"And you only serve the very best, Henri," Eileen
said. "Everyone in town knows that. I promise this meeting won't take long. The hospital auxiliary greatly ap-
preciates all you have done. Allowing us to use La
Maison for the contest has added a dimension of elegance and quality to our little fund raiser that will guar-
antee its success."

Henri preened under Eileen's compliments, and
Lauren covered her mouth to hide her smile. Eileen's
social skills had always been impressive, but she was at
her best when stroking male egos.

Lauren, Eileen and Henri took up positions on the
makeshift dais. They waited patiently while everyone
found a seat.

"Jonathan's here," Lauren whispered out of the corner of her mouth to Eileen.

"Where?" Eileen's head snapped up from the note
cards she had been studying.

"Aisle seat, third row back. He just gave up his chair
to Mrs. Whitt."

"Mmmm. Handsome, rich and a gentleman." Eileen
smiled teasingly. "Mother will be thrilled."

Lauren's eyes turned fierce. "He's also a thief."

"A momentary lapse in judgment," Eileen said airily. "Just think, Lauren, you can reform him."

Lauren gritted her teeth. "I'm glad you think this is all so amusing. Just wait until I expose Jonathan as a fraud to the entire town."

Eileen raised an eyebrow. "What exactly are you plotting?"

"I don't have to plot anything," Lauren insisted. "All I have to do is give him enough rope to hang himself."

"I'm starting to feel like I'm in a bad community-theater play." Eileen's knuckles turned white as she tightened her grip around her note cards. "Don't you think you're carrying this a bit too far?"

"It's my recipe and my revenge. Now give your speech, Eileen," Lauren commanded, "or else I'll tell Henri you think his crêpes suzettes are soggy."

FOUR

Anticipation surged through Jonathan as he watched Lauren. She sat primly next to chef Henri, her hands clasped demurely in her lap, her eyes fixed on the woman addressing the crowd.

Everyone laughed, and Jonathan turned his attention to the woman who was speaking. She had introduced herself as Eileen Dalton, chairwoman of the event, and Jonathan remembered that she was Lauren's sister.

He could discern little family resemblance between the two women. Normally he would have been drawn to Eileen, the tall, leggy blond with the slender waist and shapely legs, but for some inexplicable reason he found the curvaceous Lauren, with her brilliant smile and sparkling brown eyes, more to his taste.

Jonathan's gaze stayed pinned on Lauren. She glanced briefly in his direction. He flashed her a killer smile and she quickly looked away. Lauren's expression never altered, but Jonathan could see her hands were no longer resting quietly in her lap. She was twisting and pulling on her fingers, a sure sign of nerves.

Good. At least he knew she wasn't indifferent to him. Jonathan hated to admit it to himself, but his ego had suffered a few dents when Lauren had refused his dinner invitation. And her attitude had clearly indicated she wasn't exactly holding her breath and waiting for him to ask her out again. In fact, the possibility of rejection loomed large, but Jonathan felt compelled to try.

Lauren's previous rejection presented a challenge to his male ego and pride. The thought of matching wits with her and emerging victorious made Jonathan feel edgy with anticipation. And the vibrant, unexplained chemistry that flared between them made the entire situation even more enticing.

There was a smattering of applause and Jonathan realized Eileen had finished her speech. He hoped she hadn't imparted any essential contest information. He hadn't heard a word.

Several people raised their hands and asked questions. Lauren answered one of them. The slightly husky tone in her voice might have been a touch of nerves, but it sounded sexy and alluring to Jonathan's ears.

Eileen announced that the final phase of the morning meeting was going to involve a tour of the restaurant kitchen led by either herself, Chef Henri or Lauren. The crowd began breaking up into three smaller groupings. Jonathan maneuvered his way across the room and placed himself in Lauren's group. He smiled at her and was jolted as male hormones rushed through his body when she answered his smile with a tiny one of her own.

There were oohs and ahhs from several people when Lauren led the group into the kitchen. Jonathan was not overly impressed. It was a kitchen; what was there to get so excited about? There were large stoves with lots of burners, huge ovens, a shiny assortment of bowls, pots and pans stacked on several tables, some even hanging from the ceiling.

A wide variety of electrical appliances—blenders, mixers, choppers—was provided, along with all sorts of utensils, long knives, wooden and metal spoons of all shapes and sizes, whisks, spatulas, and many other items that looked so strange Jonathan decided he didn't want to know what they were used for. The things he did appreciate were the spotlessly clean, sleek chrome counters.

"Each contestant will be assigned a work area since some people competing in different categories will be cooking at the same time," Lauren said. "All categories, main course, desserts, soups, et cetera, will compete in the same assigned section of the kitchen and will be awarded points by the same panel of judges. But only one contestant per category will be cooking at a time, so you will be judged individually as you create your dish."

This comment brought a murmur of excited whispers from the crowd.

"The contest officially begins at eight A.M., but many of you won't start until later," Lauren continued. "Chef Henri and I have coordinated the preparation time of each dish so we can serve a formal buffet of all the entries later that evening at the country club.

"Each food category has five judges, and we will be observing your preparation closely. In this competition, technique and style definitely count. We will be supplying the food ingredients needed, so if you have any changes to your recipes, please make certain you submit them to Eileen as soon as possible. You are encouraged to use the restaurant's equipment, but you may bring any special pans or bowls needed to create your masterpieces."

"Can I bring my lucky spatula?" one woman called out.

Lauren laughed. "Lucky spatulas are welcomed." She extended her arms about the room. "Feel free to explore and ask questions. We want this to be an enjoyable experience for everyone."

The crowd needed no urging and immediately began

poking and probing through the kitchen. Jonathan observed one earnest-looking man taking copious notes. Lauren was cornered by a pair of women, but he waited until they were finished before approaching her. He wanted her all to himself.

"Hello," he said.

"Good morning, Jonathan."

He stepped close to her and caught a whiff of sweet perfume. His lower body tightened, responding automatically to the sensual female scent. Jonathan was glad he was wearing pleated trousers instead of tight jeans. It was bad enough he couldn't control his own desire; he would be at a decided disadvantage if Lauren knew it.

"I've never seen a professional kitchen before," Jonathan said. "Is this like the one you use at Just Desserts?"

"No. This is much larger."

There was an awkward silence. Lauren leaned her hip against the stainless-steel counter and tapped her fingernails against the shimmering surface. The noise grated on Jonathan's ears, but he didn't move away.

"Are you looking forward to the contest?" she finally asked in a tight voice.

"Sure." Jonathan moved in closer. The pace of the fingernail tapping increased. He smiled.

"Has that always been one of your goals in life, Jonathan? To win a cooking contest?"

"In all honesty I can't say it's among the top ten things I'd like to do before I'm forty." Jonathan shifted his feet and tilted his head down so he could see Lauren's face. He wasn't sure why she was so prickly, but the flush of passion on her cheeks was having a stimulating effect on him. "I'm participating in this contest for the sheer joy of competition."

Lauren made a strangled sound in the back of her throat.

Jonathan decided he was probably laying it on a bit thick. "Hey, don't get me wrong. I like to win as much as the next guy. Maybe more. But the adrenaline rush from a tough challenge can be nearly as satisfying as a victory."

"Ahhh, yes. The innate male competitive spirit." Lauren's smile was sugar-sweet. "It is such an intrinsic part of the complex male mind, reflected in the need men have to clutch the remote while watching TV so they can control the channels or why they'll never stop to ask directions when they're lost even though they're running out of gas and have driven by the same service station three times."

"I never get lost," Jonathan insisted. "And I don't watch much television."

"Doesn't matter." Lauren's phony smile disappeared. "You still like to win, don't you, Jonathan? At any cost?"

Somehow the conversation had turned serious, and Jonathan knew he was in trouble because he didn't understand the innuendos. Lauren apparently was a woman who had a knack for turning the simplest conversation into a major statement. She also had some warped ideas about men. And a few embarrassingly true insights.

Shifting the direction of the conversation, Jonathan utilized the knowledge he'd acquired playing college football and employed the best defensive move he knew. A strong offense. "Have dinner with me tonight, Lauren."

"No."

That was it? A short single syllable. No hesitation, no explanations, no polite show of regret. Not even a half-believable excuse.

A small muscle twitched in Jonathan's jaw. She was

looking at him as if he'd lost his mind, but he forged ahead, propelled by ego and fascination. "How about dinner tomorrow night?"

"I'm catering a wedding reception tomorrow afternoon. I'll be comatose by six."

Well, at least she'd offered an excuse that time. A fairly good one, too. In his gut Jonathan knew the wisest course of action would be to turn and walk away, but his brain was having trouble making his feet cooperate.

Instead he conjured up a friendly smile and tried again, not understanding why he felt so driven to chase after a woman who was both wrong for him and apparently not at all interested in dating him.

"Why don't we make it next week? I have a board meeting on Tuesday evening and a softball game on Wednesday, but the other weeknights are free."

Lauren waited so long to answer Jonathan swore he could feel drops of nervous perspiration forming on his forehead.

"Since you're a contestant and I'm a judge, I think it's best to keep our relationship on a strictly business level. Cordial, of course, but professional." Lauren moistened her lips and smiled mysteriously. "I wouldn't want to compromise the integrity of the cooking competition."

Jonathan's faced hardened for an instant. He wasn't accustomed to being dismissed by anyone, least of all a woman. This was a new and not at all pleasant experience. Struggling to regain control of the situation, he experienced a brief momentary lapse of sanity in which he envisioned himself pulling Lauren hard against his chest and kissing her roughly. Passionately. Deeply.

Fortunately, he managed to control this wild, primitive impulse. As he fought to settle his emotions, he caught the vivid gleam of expectation in Lauren's eyes. Oh, she was a crafty one. Clearly she was waiting for him to lose control. It was exactly the encouragement he needed.

He took a deep breath and pulled himself together. With a spark of challenge in his eyes, Jonathan turned up the wattage on his smile and leaned closer to Lauren. Her eyes turned into round saucers as he advanced. Stopping a mere whisper from her lips, he muttered throatily, "Then I'll bid you a cordial good day, Lauren."

He nuzzled her cheek softly with his own and barely brushed his lips against hers in an imitation of a sensual, tender kiss. Their lips grazed slightly, soft and light as a feather.

He heard her breath catch, then hold. Next her eyes drifted shut. Jonathan let his lips linger near hers for as long as he dared. Then he abruptly pulled away.

Her eyes fluttered open. He read with triumph the puzzled, mesmerized passion that suddenly appeared in her deep brown eyes. Feeling justified, he sauntered casually away, suspecting Lauren's eyes were burning a hole in his back with each step.

When Jonathan reached the other side of the kitchen, Lauren finally let out her breath. Slumping against the counter, she clutched onto the slippery chrome for dear life. *Ohmigosh.* The gentle touch of his lips, the warm, pleasant feel of his breath on her face, the faint scent of his aftershave, the purring sound of his sexy voice had all combined in precisely the right mix to totally swamp her senses.

She still felt fluttery in the stomach and weak in the knees. *And he hadn't even kissed her!* At least Lauren didn't think he had kissed her. She wasn't exactly sure. Running an unsteady finger across her lips, she took a shuddering breath and closed her eyes.

"Do you want me to throw a bucket of cold water on you?"

Lauren's eyes popped open, and she stared into her sister's grinning face. "Very amusing, Eileen."

Lauren nervously scanned the kitchen, hoping no one else had witnessed Jonathan's antics. Fortunately everyone seemed preoccupied with other things. "This is so embarrassing. I can't imagine what came over him. I know I made my feelings crystal clear. I am not interested in dating him."

"Right."

Lauren turned sharply toward Eileen, deciding she did not like the impish twinkle in her sister's eye. "I mean it. I have no idea why he started acting like an amorous, predatory male. He must have an ulterior motive. I'm certain this behavior is part of some devious, underhanded scheme he has concocted."

Eileen raised an eyebrow. "Maybe Jonathan is attracted to you. Maybe he's interested in getting to know you, establishing a relationship with you. How about that for a scheme?"

"No way. Those spoiled, charming, playboy types are never interested in women like me." Lauren's eyes narrowed. "Jonathan proved he can't be trusted by stealing my cheesecake recipe. I would be stupid to take anything he says or does at face value. I have to be on my guard at all times when dealing with him."

Eileen burst out laughing. "Oh, Lauren, will you listen to yourself? We're talking about a cheesecake recipe, not the plans to build a nuclear reactor. Don't you think you're being a bit melodramatic?"

Lauren managed a slight smile, despite feeling affronted. "Perhaps I am overstating my case," she reluctantly admitted. "But Jonathan's distrustful behavior indicates a major character flaw. We have no idea how deep it goes. For all we know, he could be embezzling funds from the seafood company he runs."

"Jonathan's family owns the Madison Seafood Company."

Lauren's lip twitched. She'd forgotten he owned the company. Of course after that *kiss* it was understandable that her mind was slightly rattled. "Okay, maybe he isn't an embezzler. But the facts don't change. He stole my recipe. As Dad would say, I trust Jonathan about as far as I can throw him. I absolutely refuse to feel anything but distrust and contempt for him," Lauren stated firmly.

She nodded her head decisively to emphasize the point, all the while secretly wondering who it was she was trying harder to convince, Eileen or herself.

The phone was shrilling loudly when Jonathan entered his house later that afternoon. He raced across the marble foyer with Chesapeake barking and yelping at his heels. He managed to reach the cordless phone on the third ring, rescuing it before the answering machine was activated.

"Jonathan, is that you? It's Mother."

"Hello. How are you?"

"The same as always. But what's the use complaining? Nothing ever seems to change."

"How true." Jonathan rolled his eyes and made a comical face at his dog. "Are you coming to the board meeting on Tuesday night? I can give you a lift if you'd rather not drive."

"I haven't decided yet."

"Okay." Jonathan cradled the phone on his shoulder and wandered into the kitchen. He listened with half an ear as his mother rattled on about the upcoming board meeting, then switched to a variety of inconsequential subjects. Jonathan knew it was just a smoke screen, part of his mother's normal pattern of attack.

Eventually she would run out of small talk and state the real reason for her phone call.

Jonathan yanked open the refrigerator door, pulled out a can of soda and meandered into the den. He interjected a few "Oh really" and "Is that so" comments into the conversation, then dropped onto the deep-cushioned sofa. He propped his feet on the opposite coffee table, popped the soda tab and took a swig.

"By the way, Jonathan, did I mention Virginia Quinn's niece is visiting Salisburg for a few days next week?"

"How nice." Jonathan's head lifted off the couch in warning.

"Yes, it is. Virginia is so looking forward to seeing her niece again. I met her last year at the country club's golf tournament. She's a delightful young woman. Tall, blond, very pretty. She's an attorney. Works for the FAA in Washington. It's a very prestigious position. I think you should take her out to dinner. It really is the polite thing to do. Are you free on Thursday?"

"No sale, Mother." Jonathan grimaced into the receiver. Wouldn't she ever learn? "I'm not interested in meeting Virginia Quinn's niece, or Betty Parker's daughter or Mary Bradley's second cousin or any other young woman you can beat out of the bushes. Anyway, I'm too busy preparing for the hospital auxiliary's cooking contest to do much socializing these days."

"Cooking contest?"

"Don't be coy, Mother. You know exactly what I'm talking about." Jonathan lazily stretched his back muscles and adjusted his position on the couch. "I've decided to participate in the contest, although I can't imagine what you were thinking when you entered me in this competition. After tasting the breakfast I cooked for you that one Mother's Day, I thought you would have realized I can barely make toast."

"You were nine years old when you made that meal, Jonathan. I'll never forget how proud you looked when you carried the tray into my room. And I ate every bite of that breakfast, although it gave me the worst case of indigestion I've ever experienced. But I don't understand what you're talking about? I was unaware the hospital auxiliary was sponsoring a cooking competition."

Jonathan cleared his throat. What the hell was his mother up to now? How could she say she was unaware of the competition when she'd clearly entered him in the contest? Deciding he was not in the mood for an argument, Jonathan said, "Let's just drop it, Mother."

"Fine." A few seconds of silence followed. "Won't you reconsider dinner with Virginia's niece?"

"Trust me, Mother. In my current mood you don't want me dating the female relatives of your friends. Remember what happened the last time?"

"Please, don't remind me." Jonathan heard his mother's long, dramatic sigh. "I shudder at the memories. Gladys Wilson still avoids me at our Wednesday afternoon bridge game. I simply cannot fathom what possessed you to take Gladys's daughter to a bowling alley on a date."

Jonathan shrugged. "You told me to take her somewhere unique. I guessed right when I assumed my date had never been bowling. In her opinion it was definitely unique." He smiled mischievously. "As long as I live I'll never forget the expression on her face when she had to exchange her handmade Italian leather pumps for a pair of red and blue bowling shoes. It was priceless."

Jonathan started laughing at the memory.

"With an attitude like that, it is no wonder you're not married. I'm starting to have serious doubts you'll ever find a suitable wife."

His mother's exaggerated, suffering tone brought another smile to Jonathan's lips. "I've told you before, Mother, when I find a woman who can make Chesapeake obey a simple command, I'll marry her on the spot."

"Stop being ridiculous. Your dog is a disgrace. She rarely listens to any commands because you've spoiled her beyond belief. I doubt a veterinarian or even a dog psychologist could make that animal obey. Which reminds me, have you been watching those dog-training videos I sent?"

"Sure. I'm getting lots of useful advice." Jonathan glanced across the room at the neatly stacked tapes still encased in cellophane wrap.

They talked for a while longer. He decided it was time to end the conversation when his mother began a third plea for a dinner date with the blond attorney from Washington. Hell, the woman could give lessons on tenacity to a pit bull.

"I've gotta run, Mother. I'll call you Tuesday morning. Take care."

After hanging up, Jonathan headed for the kitchen, knowing he needed to practice baking the chocolate Amaretto cheesecake. Seeing how dedicated and serious many of the contestants were at the morning meeting had really emphasized his own lack of focus. On top of that, he knew he was at a tremendous disadvantage since he also lacked basic cooking skills. He would need to work twice as hard just so he wouldn't make a complete fool of himself in the competition.

Jonathan stretched his arms, arching his back as he reached into the cabinets and retrieved what was left of the baking supplies he'd bought earlier in the week.

"I can do this," he muttered under his breath. "I'm a reasonably intelligent person. I know how to follow directions." He opened the magazine to the correct page and started lining up the recipe ingredients. "And if I need a shot of motivation, all I have to do is picture the expression on Lauren's face when she presents me with the first-place award."

"Excuse me. Do you know where I can find the latest edition of *Writer's Market?* I checked the reference shelf, but the book isn't there."

"I have it right here." The librarian seated behind the wide, oak desk smiled briefly at Lauren, then turned and retrieved the heavy volume. "Do you want a copy of *The Literary Marketplace* too?"

"I'll come back for it," Lauren decided, shifting her briefcase, purse and notebook awkwardly in her arms.

"No need. I've got it."

A muscular forearm clothed in expensive wool shot by Lauren's cluttered arms and accepted the book from the helpful librarian. She turned to thank her benefactor, but the smile froze on her lips.

Jonathan stood gazing down at her with his usual sexy grin. Dressed in a perfectly tailored light gray suit, crisp white shirt and discreet silk tie in burgundy and gray tones he was the picture of a successful businessman. He held the heavy book easily in the palm of his large hand.

"Thanks, but I can manage on my own." Lauren gritted her teeth and managed to rearrange all the stuff she was carrying in one arm. Then she grabbed for the book with the other. It was childish, and mildly foolish, but she felt self-conscious. A weak, fluffy-headed female who couldn't even carry her own books.

"I said I've got it," Jonathan repeated.

Lauren saw determination flash in his beautiful green eyes. She deliberately tightened her hold on the book and stared up at him. His nostrils flared. He did not relinquish the volume. Standing this close, she could feel the heat of his body and sense the power of his leashed strength. She gritted her teeth and yanked hard, but the book didn't budge.

Lauren opened her mouth, then closed it without uttering a word. It was a standoff. She didn't want to back down, but neither could she engage in a tug of war in the middle of the very public library. As it was, the librarian was already looking at them oddly. Or rather she was looking at Lauren as if she'd just been beamed down from a space ship. Jonathan received a sympathetic glance of understanding.

Deciding if she retreated now she just might live to fight another day, Lauren let go of the book. Abruptly.

Jonathan barely moved a muscle. He acknowledged her defeat with a curt nod of his head, hoisted the book on his shoulder and stalked toward a table on the far side of the room. Lauren had no choice but to follow.

"Thank you," she muttered ungraciously when he placed the book on the empty table.

"My pleasure." The deep, smooth tone of his voice sent a shiver down Lauren's spine. Jonathan flipped the book open to the title page and leisurely examined the table of contents. "This isn't exactly light reading."

"It's research," Lauren said, wishing he wouldn't stand so close to her. The woodsy-smelling cologne he was wearing was causing a fluttery, breathless feeling in her chest. Maybe she was allergic to it? "I'm writing a cookbook, and I need to replenish my list of prospective publishing houses."

"You're writing a book? That's fascinating." Jonathan sat on the edge of the wooden table. "I always admire people who have creative talent. Probably because I don't have any myself. When will your book be published?"

"As soon as I find a publisher smart enough to realize how terrific it will be," Lauren replied.

The warm glow of his enthusiasm settled unexpectedly in Lauren's heart. When it came to her cookbook writing she was used to reactions of disbelief and dire predictions of failure. Even the best her family could come up with was some reluctant tolerance and grudging acceptance. It was a new experience for someone to actually *admire* her goals.

"If you write as well as you bake pastries you shouldn't have any trouble finding a publisher," Jonathan declared.

Lauren sent him a peevish look. "Clearly you know nothing about publishing." She reached into her briefcase and pulled out a letter. "Today I received the ultimate definition of a paradox, peculiar to the publishing industry, a positive rejection letter. The editor who wrote this letter expresses both his enthusiasm for my book proposal and regret at being unable to make an offer to publish the book at this time."

"Why?"

"Apparently this publishing house has already committed to printing several different cookbooks for the next two years and was unable to add any more to the schedule. The editor kindly suggests I try some of the houses that deal exclusively with cookbooks. He's listed several publishers, but I need the names of editors and addresses before I can mail out my proposal. Hence my research trip to the library."

"How long have you been trying to sell your book?" Jonathan asked.

"Over a year. I've made about every mistake imaginable, but the one thing I have learned is that publishing is not a business for the fainthearted. The competition is enormous, the rejection nearly constant. Still, I'm not giving up. Failure is simply not an option."

Jonathan leaned over and whispered, "It appears you possess plenty of that innate female competitive spirit. Congratulations."

Lauren's indignant reaction was instinctive, but when she saw the friendly, teasing grin on Jonathan's face she hesitated. "I guess I went a little overboard the other day."

"A little." Jonathan's smile broadened. "Do you really know a lot of guys who like to channel-surf and drive around in circles?"

"I've met a few." Lauren swallowed hard. "Okay, I'll let you express yourself, without censoring, on the complex female mind. But limit your comments to two examples."

"I'd never stoop to making stereotypical comments about women living up to the expectation of being born to shop or needing to begin preparations for an evening out the day before in order to be ready on time."

"Thank heavens you are so enlightened."

"Hey, I know that men need to press their advantage every chance they get. After all, we can go to a public restroom without a support group. Or open all our own jars. And we don't mooch off everybody's desserts."

"I get the idea."

As they shared a quiet laugh, Lauren's nerves began to hum with warning. He was being charming, and she was finding it difficult to remember how much she distrusted him. Drat. If they kept this up for much longer she might let her guard down too much and actually start liking him. The very thought irritated her.

Lauren settled herself in the wooden chair and arranged her books and papers on the table. Maybe he would take the hint and go away if she acted busy enough. She started scribbling notes on her pad. After a few moments she spared him a quick glance.

"I'll leave you to your work," Jonathan said the moment she looked his way. "I have an appointment with the library director, and I don't want to be late."

"Need to take care of all those overdue fines?"

"Actually I've been asked to join the library board of trustees." He glanced down at his watch. "I'd better get going. I have to learn more about the position and how much time it will require before I accept."

Lauren was silent. It was hardly the answer she'd expected, and was an unpleasant reminder that some misguided members of the community held Jonathan in high regard.

Well, that esteem was about to undergo a major change, Lauren realized as she watched him wave goodbye and saunter across the library. If Jonathan remained a contestant in the cooking competition he would invariably reveal himself to be an untrustworthy fraud. And Lauren fully intended to do everything possible to make certain that happened.

On Wednesday night she pulled into the already crowded high-school parking lot at precisely 8:35 P.M. according to the digital clock on her car dashboard. Annoyed with herself for being late for her cooking class, she dashed inside the school and headed for the second-floor home-economics classrooms.

Fortunately she had taught this continuing adult education group before and knew many of the women came to class to sharpen their cooking skills but also to enjoy a night away from their normal routines. Thanks to the relaxed atmosphere of the class, Lauren knew she would have a few minutes to organize her notes before starting the lesson.

After a dismal start to the week, her natural sense of optimism had returned, along with some good news. Several months ago she had approached the manager of Salisburg's local PBS station with the idea of hosting a weekly cooking show. She'd figured a show might gain her exposure and credibility as a chef, and it could improve her chances of getting published. The television station manager, George Kilmer, had been intrigued by the concept and had asked Lauren to compile a detailed proposal outlining her ideas and requirements for the show.

Lauren had slaved over the proposal for weeks, but the end result was worth all the hard work. George had been impressed by her creativity and dedication. Of course the tin of chewy, double chocolate nut cookies she had baked and submitted along with the proposal hadn't hurt either.

Lauren had met with George Tuesday morning, and he'd informed her he was definitely sold on the show. However drastic federal cutbacks over the past few years had shrunk the station's production budget considerably. They would need to secure corporate sponsorship to pay for production costs. George optimistically assured Lauren he had several solid leads on sponsors and believed they could begin production as early as next month.

The extra work and longer than usual hours she had been keeping should have exhausted Lauren. To her dismay, she found that while her days had been busy and productive, her nights had been filled with either restless wakefulness or disturbingly erotic dreams. All centering on Jonathan.

His attractive male image also occupied a large part of her thoughts during her waking hours. Remembering Jonathan's boyish smile and broad shoulders could easily start her heart thumping. It was a vastly annoying situation.

"Good evening, everybody." Lauren spoke in a breathless, apologetic tone to the class. "Sorry I'm late."

"Don't worry about it," Mrs. Shaffer answered. "We're used to it. Besides, we knew you wouldn't stand us up."

Lauren hoisted her briefcase onto the desk as the rest

of the class loudly seconded Mrs. Shaffer's opinion. She smiled and started to relax. Okay, so she tended to be late for things. At least the class was good-humored about it.

She shuffled through her papers, searching for her notes for tonight's class. Triumphant, she eventually pulled them out, distractedly listening to the class members murmuring, a collection of high-pitched female voices blending with a single deep male baritone. A male baritone? Good grief, was she starting to hear Jonathan's voice in her waking hours too?

Lauren's head shot up, and her eyes curiously searched the room. Her heart gave a funny little skip, and the papers she clutched in her hands floated gracefully down to the floor. *Jonathan! What in the world was he doing here?*

FIVE

Lauren's mouth opened, but she couldn't speak. Shock had stolen her voice.

Jonathan was leaning casually against the counter of one of the classroom's kitchen configurations, his legs crossed at the ankles and his arms folded across his broad chest. The pale peach-colored knit shirt he wore would have seemed ridiculously feminine on most men, but it was classic and masculine on him. He looked lean and handsome.

"Hi, Lauren, it's good to see you again. I'm really looking forward to class tonight."

Jonathan's words snapped her out of her trance. His voice held an overly polite edge that made her itch to reach out and shove him off the counter. Anything to throw him off balance, the way he seemed to so easily throw her.

"I see we have a new member of the class," she murmured, swallowing the words she *really* wanted to blurt out. "Ladies, I'm sure some of you already know Jonathan Windsor. Apparently he'll be joining us this evening."

Jonathan pushed away from the counter as several women approached him. Lauren caught a flash of white teeth and an impression of dimples when he smiled at them. The women crowded around him and started chattering, sounding very much like a swarm of bees. It was all rather surreal. The class was behaving as if they were thirteen-year-old girls and Jonathan was a visiting rock star. The newest teen idol spending a few precious moments with his local fan club.

The classroom door banged open unexpectedly and Susan Maxwell rushed into the room.

"I got stuck in traffic," she announced breezily to Lauren.

Barely breaking stride, Susan rushed over toward the crowd and successfully elbowed herself into a prime position directly next to Jonathan.

Stuck in traffic? In Salisburg? On a Wednesday night? Lauren gave up trying to puzzle out that odd statement after noticing that Susan was dressed in a clinging silk dress, matching black stockings and high heels. *High heels? For cooking class?*

Lauren knew Susan hadn't originally arrived in that outfit. She usually favored baggy sweatpants and oversized T-shirts for class. Lauren decided Susan must have raced out of the classroom and gone home to change the moment Jonathan entered the building.

And Susan wasn't the only student exhibiting a drastic change in her personal appearance. Lauren noticed many of the women in the class were decked out in full makeup, with freshly brushed hair and newly applied lipstick. What was going on? Had the mix of all the different perfumes in the room blended together to create a toxic, lethal scent that killed off female brain cells?

A smile threatened at the corners of Lauren's mouth. It was ridiculous. Totally absurd. A few of these women were single, but many were married, some were grandmothers. Yet here they were, practically drooling over Jonathan, acting like a bunch of adolescent boys with a girlie magazine. Lauren's sense of humor kicked in, and she allowed herself a good chuckle.

Jonathan glanced over at her. He must have heard her laugh, although Lauren couldn't imagine how he could hear anything but the titillating conversation of his numerous admirers.

Above the mounds of teased, coiffed, blue-rinsed heads they stared at each other. Jonathan gave her a sheepish, embarrassed grin, shrugged his shoulders and lifted his hands in a gesture of bewilderment.

Lauren dropped her eyes in surprise. Jonathan's opinion echoed hers exactly. How was this possible? He was her enemy. The thief of her hard work, the exploiter of her talent. Yet here they were, sharing a private joke together, finding humor in a situation that the majority thought was perfectly normal.

Deliberately shaking off the feeling of closeness, Lauren loudly cleared her throat. No one paid any attention. She rapped her knuckles sharply on the wooden desk. Not one head turned toward her. Realizing she'd have to forgo the subtle approach, Lauren resorted to shouting.

"Your attention please. Everyone. Attention." She clapped her hands together. "We need to get started right away or we'll never get our pastries baked tonight."

A few disinterested gazes were sent her way. Lauren repeated her command, then launched into her cooking demonstration to emphasize her point. She deliberately spoke louder and faster than normal.

Finally realizing that she meant business, the members of the class scrambled for seats. There was a major scuffle as two rivals literally dove for the seat next to Jonathan. After a silent tug-of-war, Mary Jo Reese emerged victorious. Due no doubt to her superior size.

Lauren started her lecture over, but after a few minutes decided she shouldn't have bothered. Only a handful of students were taking notes, the rest were trying a variety of coy, flirtatious moves to capture Jonathan's eye.

Quickly skipping to the finer points of making the delicate fruit tarts, Lauren announced it was time to break into smaller groups and begin the hands-on baking. No one moved. Lauren searched the room curiously, realizing that everyone was either openly or subtly staring at Jonathan, as if he were the last set of sheets at the January white sale.

"I'll make the kitchen assignments tonight," Lauren stated firmly, figuring it was the only way to avoid a class riot. "Mrs. Lawford, Mrs. Fukes, Mrs. Gray and *Mr.* Windsor can begin working at station number one. Everyone else will be grouped alphabetically."

There were a few grumblings, but no out-and-out rebellion. Susan Maxwell looked like she wanted to throw one of her spiked heels at Lauren's head, but managed to keep her disappointment under control.

"Remember to keep the phyllo dough covered with waxed paper and a clean, damp towel so it won't dry out," Lauren instructed the class. "Don't be afraid of it. Despite its fragile appearance, phyllo is actually quite strong if handled and stored properly."

She repeated most of the advice previously stated in her lecture since apparently no one had been listening. "Peel off one layer of dough at a time, brush it liberally with butter, cut it into two-inch strips, then arrange the strips in an unstructured circular design on a generously buttered baking sheet. Sprinkle each layer with a mixture of sugar, cinnamon and nutmeg before adding the thin slices of fruit. Be sure to experiment with different fruit combinations and amounts of sugar and spices. We'll taste and compare notes when the tarts are baked."

Eventually the class was humming with activity as the students began creating their pastries. Lauren circled the classroom slowly, offering advice, answering questions and doling out praise. All the while she was acutely aware of the boisterous conversation and laughter coming from Jonathan's group. Lauren stopped there last.

"Any problems?" she asked.

"No. Everything is coming along swimmingly," Mrs. Lawford replied. "Jonathan volunteered to slice the apples."

"Great," Lauren replied, telling herself the sudden tightness she felt in her chest was due to stress and not the intimate sexiness of the smile Jonathan sent her way. Lauren walked over to him.

"I'm surprised to see you here tonight," she finally murmured, hoping no one else in the class was aware of the tension between them. "I thought you had a softball game on Wednesday night."

"I decided to skip the game and attend your cooking class." Something dark and sensual flickered in the depths of Jonathan's eyes. "I'm flattered you remembered my softball game."

"Don't be," Lauren snapped.

"Lauren, the phyllo dough is all dry around the edges," Mrs. Lawford interrupted. "Can we still use it?"

Lauren shifted her attention away from Jonathan and went over to help Mrs. Lawford.

"Everyone is all thumbs tonight," Mrs. Lawford remarked when Lauren joined her. "Jonathan is having a peculiar effect on most of us."

"So it seems," Lauren commented, stressing by her no-nonsense tone that she was not among those women affected.

"I'm not surprised one bit," Mrs. Lawford said with a smile. "He is such a handsome young man. So polite and well mannered. You can tell he's been raised right, despite all his money."

"Jonathan is definitely unique," Lauren commented as she carefully tried to separate the stiff edges of the phyllo dough. It crumbled in her hands. Lauren bit her lower lip; then, lacking the patience and steady hands to continue, she picked up a large knife and hacked off the dried edges. "Try it now."

Mrs. Lawford gasped. Color flooded Lauren's cheeks. What was she doing? Acting like some crazed slasher and scaring poor Mrs. Lawford to death, that's what she was doing. Get a grip! Embarrassed by her lack of control, Lauren smiled apologetically at Mrs. Lawford and placed the knife gently in the sink. Out of sight.

"Jonathan's done a remarkable job with Madison Seafood. The business was sinking fast before he took over," Mrs. Lawford said hesitantly. She seemed to be watching Lauren closely for a reaction, and when no further violence was forthcoming, the older woman continued.

"A lot of families in town now have a steady income and job security, things they only dreamed about a year ago. Both my boys work for Jonathan, and he's promised my oldest grandson a job during the summer. Jonathan's hard work made a difference for folks in this town. And we sure appreciate it."

Mrs. Lawford's comments momentarily confused Lauren. She'd always thought of Jonathan as the spoiled, rich, outrageously handsome man who had stolen her cheesecake recipe. It unsettled her to hear that someone regarded him as a decent man, a respected, ethical member of the business community.

"It really tickles me to see how sweet he is on you," Mrs. Lawford confided to Lauren. "You make a lovely couple."

Lauren sucked in her breath loudly. "No, no, Mrs.

Lawford,'' she stammered, nearly choking on her tongue in her haste to get out the words. "You are mistaken. Jonathan and I are not a couple. No way. No sirree."

"Oh, dear. Now I've embarrassed you. I'm sorry." Mrs. Lawford lowered her voice to a respectable whisper. "But why else would Jonathan be here? Not for the cooking lesson. And certainly not to see Susan Maxwell in that indecent dress." Mrs. Lawford clucked her tongue. "Poor Susan hasn't been the same since her divorce last winter."

Lauren moved on to answer questions from another group, but Mrs. Lawford's comments lingered in her mind. Should she consider viewing Jonathan's unexpected classroom appearance with emotions other than distrust and annoyance?

He had been so charming and pleasant at the library the other day. Was it possible he'd come here solely to see her? After all, he had invited her out to dinner. Twice. Any normal woman would be flattered by such determined persistence.

Flattered? Who was she kidding? The room was filled with women willing to donate an organ just for the opportunity to bake pastries with Jonathan Windsor.

Lauren turned a sharp eye toward the object of her thoughts. The women were beginning to converge on him again, this time bringing along their baked goods for him to sample. Jonathan democratically tasted each one, showering smiles and praise on his little harem. He charmed and flirted with all, yet favored none.

Lauren's confusion grew. Had she misjudged him? Or was she letting the fact that he could swamp her senses with a single, intimate glance cloud her judgment?

Distracted, she began the final phase of class, critiquing everyone's fruit tarts and soliciting suggestions for next week's demonstration.

"I'd really like to learn how to make a chocolate souffle," Mrs. Fukes called out. "My husband ate one for dessert last year at a fancy restaurant in D.C., and he still talks about it."

"How about a class featuring strawberries?" Mrs. Lawford asked. "The fruit will be in season very soon, and I'd like to try something new."

"I've always been partial to cheesecake. Why don't we have a class devoted to the preparation, baking and decorating of cheesecakes?" Jonathan innocently proposed.

"That's a brilliant idea," Susan Maxwell chimed in brightly. She sat pertly in her chair and gave Jonathan a smile so sweet it made Lauren feel nauseous. "I vote for cheesecake."

"Any other ideas besides souffles, strawberries or cheesecake?" Lauren asked the class, struggling to keep her whole face from tightening up.

She shook her head at her foolishness. Jonathan was not "sweet" on her as Mrs. Lawford had so innocently suggested. He really had come to class for the cooking lesson. And apparently hadn't learned what he needed to know. She wondered idly if he was still making the cake with the wrong kind of chocolate or if he had gone beyond that mistake and was having other difficulties with the recipe.

When no one volunteered any alternatives, Lauren knew she was going to have to act fast or risk teaching Jonathan the secrets of baking *her* prize-winning cheesecake.

"I thought next week we could tackle the intricacies of puff pastry," Lauren tossed out casually. "We can always save the cheesecake idea for another class, perhaps during next year's fall session."

"Puff pastry!" Susan Maxwell sprang to her high-heeled feet. "We've been asking you to teach puff pastry since the second week of school. You always said there was too much time needed to chill and rest the dough to properly teach a ninety-minute class."

"With enough advanced preparation, I'm sure I can put a lesson together," Lauren replied, inwardly groaning at all the extra work that would be involved.

It was a close vote, but she believed the added possibility of having Jonathan attend class in the fall semester swung the final ballot in her favor.

The class broke up into small groups, chattering enthusiastically as everyone started gathering up their belongings. Jonathan remained seated, leafing intently through the notebook on his desk. His harem of admirers gradually backed away, but a few die-hard fans refused to leave.

Lauren waited for Jonathan's objections, doubting he would let this go without putting up a fight. She could see his jaw clench, could make out the dark glitter in his narrowed eyes, but he recovered, or suppressed his anger, quickly. A part of her couldn't help but admire his control.

She shoved her notes haphazardly into her briefcase, hoping for the right moment to slip away from class. But Jonathan managed to stand and free himself from his legion of admirers. He zeroed in on Lauren before she could escape.

She braced herself for an argument, but he merely smiled at her.

"I'm sorry you rejected my idea for next week's class." A ghost of a smile graced the corners of his mouth. "Still, I can only applaud how neatly you avoided my suggestion." With a touch of old-fashioned gallantry, he enfolded her hand and lifted it to his mouth. Lauren drew in her breath and held it.

At this close proximity, it was impossible to ignore his magnetism. It wasn't just that he was heart-stoppingly handsome. Or so overwhelmingly male. There was something unique and intangible about him that made a person feel he or she would do anything, and everything, necessary to please him.

Jonathan dipped his head, and his lips glided slowly, sensually across the top of her hand, just above the knuckles.

Lauren suddenly felt hot.

"Round one to the pretty lady with the unforgettable brown eyes and quick wit," Jonathan whispered softly. He released her hand, and it dropped down to her side. "Good night."

Lauren's breath shuddered out of her loudly. She stared mutely at Jonathan's retreating back and broad shoulders, her mind a disjointed jumble and her heart pumping so fast the blood was pounding in her ears. *What in the world was he up to?*

"I've put out the last of the crab balls and fresh salmon, Ms. Stuart. Is there anything else you'd like me to do?"

Lauren walked past the inquiring waiter and examined the buffet with a critical eye. The multitiered table, with its blossoming flowers and oddly shaped mirrored trays still looked attractive despite the fact that most of the food was gone.

"Everything is fine, John," she told the anxious waiter. "Instruct the staff to continue clearing the dirty glasses and dishes. The party should be breaking up shortly, and the guests will begin leaving within the hour."

The efficient John hurried away, and Lauren let out a sigh of relief. The cocktail reception celebrating the engagement of Jennifer Lewis and Ronald Williams was an unmitigated success. It was the first large party Lauren had catered at the country club, and Lauren was pleased with the result. Since the hosts of the evening, the prospective bride's parents, were friends of Lauren's mother and father she had felt an extra measure of pressure to produce a flawless party.

Allowing herself to relax for the first time all evening, Lauren mingled with the guests. While still keeping a supervisory eye on the staff, she exchanged greetings and pleasantries with the numerous party-goers. She knew many of the people in attendance and felt fairly comfortable in the crowd.

Still, she kept searching for one particular face, that of a tall, broad-shouldered, lean, golden man with a sinful smile and a dishonest nature. Lauren suspected Jonathan might be included in the guest list since the groom-to-be traveled in Salisburg's loftier social circles. Thus far she hadn't seen him, but she'd been busy working.

Staking out an unobtrusive position behind a towering potted plant, Lauren diligently scanned the glittering crowd with all the enthusiasm of a newly commissioned spy. This was all part of her new and improved strategy for handling Jonathan. No more surprise meetings.

She was tired of always being caught unawares. For once she'd really like to turn the tables and be the one with the element of surprise working in her favor. Besides Lauren reasoned if she was adequately prepared she could deal more effectively with him.

With the tips of her fingers, Lauren gingerly parted the green foliage at the base of the plant she was standing behind and peered out. A woman in a hideous eggplant colored dress glided past. Following fast on her heels was a dark-haired man who weaved slightly while

he walked. Lauren made a mental note to make certain
the weaver wasn't driving when he left the party.

"Lose something?"

Lauren shrieked. The deep, silky masculine voice and
warm breath on her neck not only startled, but scared
the hell out of her. She whirled around, trying to ignore
the way her heart was pounding.

Jonathan's green eyes, alive with humor, met hers.

She took a deep shuddering breath. "It's very rude
to sneak up on people." She tried to sound stern but
was too breathless to have much impact.

"Sorry. I didn't realize I was sneaking. You were too
absorbed in . . . um . . . what exactly were you doing?"

Lauren flushed. "Supervising the staff." She rubbed
her palms against the skirt of her silk cocktail dress and
struggled to recapture an element of dignity, knowing
she'd survived more embarrassing moments than this,
although at the moment it was impossible to recall any.
"I'm catering the party tonight."

"Where did you learn your supervisory skills?"
Jonathan asked. He selected a cracker spread with a
generous amount of pâté from the small dish he carried
and popped it into his mouth. "The Amazon jungle?"

"No, the rain forest." Lauren's mouth quirked. "The
same place I learned to make that lizard pâté you are
enjoying so much."

"It's delicious." Jonathan grinned, but Lauren noticed he had a little trouble swallowing. "This food
tastes great, especially compared to the chewy shrimp
and soggy canapés the club usually serves."

"Some people like those shrimp. Several people
asked me if we were going to be serving them tonight,"
Lauren replied, feeling ridiculously pleased that
Jonathan had complimented her work. She rarely received those kinds of ego strokes.

"I guess there is no accounting for taste in this

world," Jonathan said with mock thoughtfulness. "How else can you explain the popularity of shag carpeting?"

"Or pierced eyebrows?"

"Or disco music?"

"Hey disco isn't all bad." Lauren laughed. "It has a great beat and you can dance to it."

"Geez, dancing." Jonathan rolled his eyes. "The only decent aspect of that activity is being able to hold a woman tightly in your arms as you shuffle around the floor."

"You must be a real blast at parties."

"I have my moments."

They moved out from behind the plant, but still remained on the edges of the crowd. Jonathan set his dish down on a nearby table and procured two fresh glasses of champagne. He handed Lauren one of the drinks.

"I hope tonight's catering triumph will secure your position as the club's first choice for purveyor of superior cuisine." Jonathan raised his champagne glass. "To your success. May this be the first of many."

Lauren raised her glass fractionally then took a small sip of champagne. The bubbles tickled her nostrils and she wrinkled her nose. She glanced over at Jonathan, slightly embarrassed by her unsophisticated gesture. He either didn't notice or didn't care because he took a casual sip of his drink, then gave her a heated, intimate look over the rim of his glass.

Lauren nearly dropped her own glass. With a slightly unsteady hand, she gulped a mouthful of champagne, then started coughing loudly. Jonathan immediately moved forward to help, but instead of thumping her on the back as most people would have done, he gently kneaded the sensitive spot between her shoulders. A shiver ran down Lauren's spine and she coughed louder.

Jonathan exchanged Lauren's fluted champagne glass for a tumbler full of ice water as a waiter conveniently passed by them.

"Try this," Jonathan suggested kindly.

Eyes tearing, Lauren accepted the water, but decided against drinking any. Using every ounce of mental and physical power she possessed, she managed to get her cough under control. She ventured a small sip of ice water, took a lung-filling breath of air and wondered if her face was beet or fire-engine red.

"Better?" Jonathan asked sympathetically.

Lauren nodded her head vigorously. Fearing to speak lest she bring on another fit of coughing and draw even more unwanted attention to herself, Lauren kept her mouth shut. Yet she was finding it increasingly difficult to ignore the curious heads turned their way, especially when one of those heads belonged to her mother.

"Excuse me," Lauren croaked. Out of the corner of her eye Lauren noticed her mother moving purposefully in their direction. "I need to go to the ladies' room."

"Don't rush off." Jonathan reached out and grabbed her hand. "I have a business proposition I'd like to discuss with you."

Lauren stared down at the strong fingers holding onto her own and couldn't help but remember what happened the last time Jonathan had grabbed her hand. "Business? Do you want me to cater a party for you?"

"No." Jonathan laughed. "It's a bit more involved than a party."

"The reception will be over at eight," Lauren said hastily. Her mother, along with her feelings of panic, were both moving fast. "I'll try to talk to you then."

Lauren disappeared into the crowd, believing she'd made a clean getaway until she felt a tug on her sleeve.

"Hello, dear."

Lauren's shoulders sagged. Taking a restorative breath, she turned toward her mother with a smile that was overly bright and slightly forced. Julia Stuart was a tall, striking woman in her late fifties who looked ten years younger. She possessed a simple, natural elegance that Lauren had always envied and an innate talent for consistently looking as though she'd just stepped off the pages of a fashion magazine.

No matter what the occasion, Julia Stuart was always wearing the perfect outfit, a flattering hairdo, just a hint of makeup and expensive yet understated jewelry. What annoyed Lauren most, however, was knowing that her mother did not fuss with her appearance, but managed to achieve this elegance with minimum effort.

"Enjoying the reception, Mom? I saw Rob and Eileen earlier." Lauren's eyes searched the room frantically as she prayed for a glimpse of her sister.

"Your father and I are having a lovely time," Julia replied. "After weddings, I think engagement parties are my favorite affairs. Jennifer and Ronald look so happy. And Jennifer's mother can barely contain her pride and excitement. It's a moment every mother dreams about, seeing her daughter so content and settled." Julia smiled charmingly and nodded as an elderly couple strolled by them. "I noticed you were talking with Jonathan Windsor. How well do you know him?"

The ice in Lauren's glass rattled. *Where was Eileen?* "Jonathan is a contestant in the hospital cooking contest, Mother, not a prospective bridegroom."

"Goodness dear, there's no need to be hostile."

"Sorry." Lauren grinned weakly. "I'm a little tired. It has been a very hectic night. Actually it has been a very hectic week."

"You work too hard," Julia insisted. She hooked her arm through Lauren's. Effectively captured, Lauren was forced to make the circuit around the room, trying to keep the distress she felt from showing on her face.

"Jonathan Windsor is an attractive man, Lauren, I'll grant you that, yet I couldn't help but notice how he was ogling several of the women here, you in particular. It is obvious, dear, he's the type of man who has difficulty making a permanent commitment to one female. My advice is to avoid him completely."

Lauren ceased walking. "That's incredible, Mother. You've managed to dissect Jonathan's character and offer me stellar advice without ever actually exchanging a word with him. How do you do it?"

Julia appeared baffled. "I've always had excellent instincts when it comes to people, dear, especially men. Didn't I tell Eileen the moment I met Rob I knew they were destined for each other?"

"Yes, Mother, you did," Lauren answered with a sigh. *Please Lord, spare me the Eileen and Rob story. I swear I'll scream if she launches into the long version.*

"I get emotional every time I remember it." Julia's eyes took on a faraway gleam. "There I was, all alone. Stranded. Frightened. Twilight was upon me and I was starting to panic. It was getting dark quickly, the road was filled with ominous shadows. Then suddenly Rob appeared. A kind, compassionate stranger. He saved me."

Lauren let out an exasperated sigh. "You had a flat tire, Mother. Less than a mile from your house. You weren't lost in the Alaskan tundra. Besides, if you had left the car immediately after the tire blew out, you could have easily walked home before it became dark."

"You are missing the point entirely. Do you know how many cars drove past me?" Julia challenged.

Lauren shrugged, knowing the number generally varied with the degree of her mother's irritation.

"At least a dozen," Julia huffed. "And no one

stopped. Heavens, no one even slowed down. Except Rob. I knew the moment he pulled over that he was a gentleman. He was so sweet and helpful to a flustered old woman, and I was grateful for his assistance. It demonstrated to me what a compassionate and caring man he was, what a good and unselfish soul."

"Yes, yes, Mother. Rob is truly a prince among men."

"Oh, Lauren." Julia looked beseechingly at her older daughter. Then suddenly her expression brightened. "I've just had a lovely thought. Why don't you join Daddy and me for dinner tonight. We have reservations at the Harbor House. I know that's one of your favorite places."

The sunny smile her mother bestowed upon her triggered major alarm bells in Lauren's head. "Tonight isn't convenient."

"Oh, bosh, it's Saturday. I'm sure you don't have any other plans except for working on your cookbook." Julia discreetly pointed to the other side of the room. "Do you see that nice young man standing next to your father?"

Lauren obediently turned and observed the attractive dark-haired man with little interest. "Yes," she answered, knowing all too well what was coming next.

"His name is Douglas O'Brien. He's one of your father's new associates. He'll be joining us for dinner this evening. Daddy thinks he shows great promise in the insurance field." Julia leaned in close and lowered her voice to a confidential tone. "Douglas is single."

"No!" Lauren rolled her eyes in an exaggerated motion. "I never would have guessed. And you want me to meet him, Mother? I'm shocked!"

Julia pursed her lips. "A simple no thank you is all that is required, Lauren. I don't know why you persist in acting so melodramatic."

"Probably for the same reason you keep trying to

find me dates," Lauren admitted. "An excess amount of affection combined with an underlying need to control the situation."

"I'm only concerned with your happiness, dear," Julia said quietly. "Douglas is a very intelligent, charming man. I thought you might enjoy his company."

"He's awfully cute, too," Lauren added, deciding to call a truce with her mother. It was the least she could do since she had no intention of ever dating Douglas O'Brien. "He's a big improvement over the last guy you tried to set me up with. That character had big ears, a weak chin and sold ladies lingerie out of his car. Good old Steve what's-his-name."

"Steve Rand, Barbara Castle's nephew." Julia's lips twisted. "Barbara assured me her nephew was bright, accomplished and handsome as sin, and I naively trusted her. Believe me, dear, you weren't the only one disappointed in Steve."

"Perhaps it would be better if you let me choose my own men," Lauren suggested. "I am a far better judge than you of what type of males interest me."

"You are so busy with your work and your cookbook you don't have time to look for a man. Besides, if Jonathan Windsor is an example of your type, then I will be redoubling my efforts," Julia said stubbornly.

Lauren decided she was going to ignore the belligerence in her mother's voice. And leave her with the incorrect impression that she was interested in Jonathan Windsor. Attempting to set the record straight would only prolong the conversation. Spotting Eileen chatting in a small group near the buffet table, Lauren expertly steered her mother toward them.

At the first opportune moment, Lauren flashed a meaningful glance at her sister and slipped away. Then Lauren literally ran into Jonathan.

"I've been looking for you," he said, placing his

hands casually on her shoulders to steady her. "The guests are starting to leave. How soon can you get away?"

"I have to check with the hostess and cleanup crew." Lauren wriggled away from his touch. It was vaguely disturbing. She consulted her wristwatch. "I should be ready to go in about a half-hour. I can meet you somewhere for coffee."

"Let's make it dinner," Jonathan insisted. "I'll wait for you in the bar."

Lauren watched him walk away and wondered why she hadn't instantly rejected his dinner invitation this time. Probably because he had mentioned a business proposition. And because the I-refuse-to-be-brushed-off look in her mother's eye tonight could mean spending an evening eating clams with her parents and their handpicked choice for her newest beau. It was, Lauren decided, a classic case of what her father called being caught between a rock and a hard place.

SIX

Jonathan drove slowly, checking his rearview mirror constantly to make sure that Lauren was following close behind. He would have preferred that she accompany him in his car, but she had insisted upon bringing her own vehicle. He wasn't about to argue with her; he was still shocked that she had agreed to come to dinner so readily.

Using his car phone, Jonathan called the restaurant and made dinner reservations. It took a firm tone of voice and some name-dropping, but eventually he was able to wangle a table at the most exclusive French bistro in the area. Even though this was going to be a business dinner, Jonathan didn't see any reason why they shouldn't enjoy some first-class food.

Watching the road signs diligently, he located the restaurant without any problems. He swung his car sharply into the parking lot, spraying gravel everywhere. Leaping out, he waited impatiently while Lauren pulled carefully alongside him without disturbing a single pebble.

Jonathan opened her car door. She exited unassisted, and he stared with masculine appreciation at her shapely legs. She was wearing a bronze dress made of soft material that clung to her body in all the right places. It was sensual, but far from immodest. Jonathan thought she looked classy and sexy.

"I hope you left a trail of bread crumbs to get us back to Salisburg," Lauren said with a cynical frown when she stood beside him in the crowded parking lot. "I have no idea where we are."

"Au Petit Café is a bit off the beaten track," Jonathan admitted. "I've heard rave reviews about the food, though."

Lauren cast him a cautious look, but made no further remarks as she accepted his proffered arm. As he held the door open, she preceded him into the restaurant. Despite all the cars in the parking lot and the near impossibility of securing last-minute dinner reservations, the small foyer was empty. But Jonathan could hear the faint sound of humming voices, the discreet clinking of cutlery against china and the hushed strains of classical music coming from the main dinning room.

A tuxedoed maître d' entered the foyer. He eyed them speculatively, then struck a theatrical pose.

"Do you have a reservation?" he asked in a superior, nasal voice.

Lauren coughed softly, shielding her mouth behind her hand. Jonathan strongly suspected there was a smile hidden beneath those delicate fingers.

Jonathan gave his name and the maître d's snotty attitude slipped a fraction. With a flourish, he motioned them through a pair of French doors. They were immediately plunged into darkness.

It took a few moments for Jonathan's eyes to adjust to the dimness. He had deliberately chosen this place for its quiet atmosphere and expensive, gourmet menu, but as he stumbled over a wine stand, Jonathan wondered if it would have been smarter to go somewhere less romantic.

They came to a cozy alcove, and the maître d' pulled out the table. Jonathan placed his hand in the small of

Lauren's back to help guide her into the circular booth.
She took two steps forward, then stopped.

"Is anything wrong?" he whispered in her ear.

"I want my own chair," she said flatly.

Puzzled, Jonathan squinted into the semidarkness
and saw the deeply padded circular booth. It looked
intimate and very private.

"Bring the lady a chair, please," Jonathan requested,
feeling more sure by the minute that choosing this restaurant had been a big mistake.

One of his sales associates, Alex Page, had eaten here
a few weeks ago and raved about the place. His praise
should have put Jonathan on the alert to steer clear of
the restaurant. Alex was a terrific salesman but a bit of
a pompous ass. Naturally he'd been enamored of all
this foolish pretense.

With an audible huff of disapproval, the maître d'
snapped his fingers and a chair was brought to the table. After Lauren was seated, Jonathan slid into the
booth. Alone. He felt conspicuous, but was determined
to make the evening a success despite its less than aus-
picious beginning.

Lauren smiled at the waiter who handed her a menu.
At least Jonathan thought he saw her smile. It was so
damned dark he couldn't be certain.

Lauren sat back, put her elbows on the arms of the
chair and propped the pretentiously large menu in her
lap. There was a long silence.

"Jonathan?"

"Yes?"

"I can't read my menu. It's too dark."

The instant her words were spoken a waiter appeared.
He produced a thin flashlight and shined it on Lauren's
lap. Startled, she jumped, then burst out laughing.

"Maybe we should request a table near the kitchen,"

Lauren suggested with a giggle. "We might catch a glimpse of light each time the door swings open."

"This is ridiculous," Jonathan muttered. He observed the slight flame of the single lit candle in the center of the table with disgust. Addressing his request to the waiter he said, "If you can't turn on the lights then bring us more candles."

"Five or six should do the trick," Lauren added snidely.

The maître d' rushed over. "Is there a problem?"

"Yes." Jonathan spoke very softly. "It is so dark in here I can't help but wonder what you are trying to hide. Is the food so unappetizing that it is only palatable if you can't see what you are eating?"

The maître d' puffed his chest out. "Sir, I can assure you Au Petit Café's reputation for culinary excellence is unsurpassed."

"It must be for people to put up with all this pretension," Jonathan remarked dryly. "I want this table ablaze with candles. Understood?"

The maître d' nodded his head curtly. Within minutes there were a half-dozen strategically placed candles on the table. Jonathan craned his neck to look over the top of his menu, pleased that he could finally see Lauren's face. She was studying her menu as though it were an engrossing novel.

"I haven't seen so many classic French dishes since my days at the CIA," she said. Her lips curved slightly. "In answer to your unasked question, I was not a spy. CIA, as in Culinary Institute of America."

"I knew that," Jonathan lied. He folded his menu and placed it on the table. "Since you're the expert in French food, I think you should order dinner for us. I don't eat much red meat, but I like everything."

"Everything?"

Jonathan decided the gleam of sly speculation in

Lauren's eyes could mean trouble. "Let me clarify that statement. Fish, poultry, pasta, even beef are all fine, but stick to the basics. I don't want to consume animal glands or stomach linings or any other unusual body parts."

"Ah, a cautious man." Lauren smiled mysteriously. When the waiter returned, she placed their dinner order in rapid French.

Thanks to his high-school French teacher, Jonathan was able to translate enough of what Lauren said to know she had selected fish. His gaze drifted to her mouth. Her accent was charming. So were her lips. Full, smooth and red. He'd bet they tasted sweet, like fresh strawberries. Or warm honey.

"The wine list, sir."

"What?"

Jonathan reluctantly dragged his gaze away from Lauren and noticed the waiter standing stiffly at his side. The man held out a thick, three-ringed binder with a deep maroon cover. Jonathan accepted it with a sigh. He gave a cursory glance to the forty or so pages of wines listed in the massive volume and quickly chose a California Chablis hoping it would complement the fish.

The wine steward brought Jonathan's selection to the table, but Jonathan waved him off before the man could begin the decanting, cork sniffing, slurping, sipping, wine-tasting ritual.

"Just uncork it and leave the bottle," Jonathan demanded.

"Aren't you enjoying all the fuss?" Lauren asked as Jonathan poured them each a goblet of wine.

"Not especially," he answered, taking a small sip of his drink. "Next time we go out for dinner, I'll let you pick the restaurant."

"I like the Crab Claw down on Front Street," Lauren said defensively.

"That rickety old place built on pilings and overlooking the bay? I thought they closed years ago. My grandfather used to bring me there when I was a kid. Do they still spread newspapers on your table and throw the steamed crabs in the center?"

"Oh, sure," Lauren replied, running her fingers over the handle of her silver dinner fork. "It's very elegant."

"Point taken." Jonathan leaned back and folded his arms across his chest. "Tell me more about yourself. Did you always want to study at the CIA?"

"No, I originally wanted to be a stockbroker." Lauren smiled. "I did college on the five-year plan, switching my major so many times I had to stay longer to finish. Eventually I graduated with a business degree." Lauren's chin lifted defensively. "Not *summa cum laude*, like my sister, but I graduated. I wanted to live in New York City, and I thought it would be exciting to work on Wall Street."

"What happened?"

"I hated it," Lauren said with a laugh. "Sitting in an office twelve hours a day, constantly scrounging for clients, making endless phone calls. It was awful. Eventually I switched to the accounting department, but crunching numbers was so boring I moved to personnel just so I would have someone to talk to."

Jonathan nodded his head in sympathetic agreement. "What made you decide to try cooking school?"

"I went on vacation to a California resort with a girlfriend. It was a beautiful place, we both had a terrific time. The resort offered all kinds of activities for their guests, including cooking classes. I spent the entire vacation in the kitchen and loved every minute of it. When I returned to New York I knew what I really wanted was a career in which I could be more creative and less corporate."

"So has this new career lived up to your creative expectations?" Jonathan probed, trying to imagine Lauren dressed in a conservative stockbroker business suit with a white silk blouse buttoned to the neck. He just couldn't picture it.

"Definitely." Lauren's eyes sparkled. "I love experimenting with food and creating new recipes. Ever since I decided to write a cookbook—"

"How's that going?" Jonathan interrupted. "Have you heard from any of those publishers yet?"

"No, it is much too soon." A wistful expression crossed Lauren's face. "Waiting is the hardest part of the process. But I've come too far to get spooked now. It is such a relief to finally discover something I am both good at and enjoy doing."

"I know exactly how you feel."

Lauren's fork clattered onto her plate. "You do?"

"Sure." Jonathan shrugged and took a bite of his turbot with bechamel sauce. "I had a few 'stockbroker' years myself. I'm really fortunate I landed at the Madison Seafood company before I ran out of options."

Lauren cocked her head to one side. "Weren't you raised believing you were going to run that company someday? I always imagined you were born with the words 'crown prince of seafood' tattooed on your forehead."

Jonathan chuckled. "Wrong words. I believe the tattoo read, 'future governor of Maine.' " He spread a thin layer of butter on a hot, crusty roll. "My mother's family owns Madison Seafood. The profession of choice for generations of Windsor men has always been politics."

"Really?"

"The family viewed my defection with extreme disappointment. Instead of a law degree I went for an MBA." Jonathan's smile stiffened slightly. "It nearly broke my father's heart."

Lauren wiped the corners of her mouth with a napkin. "I'm sure he's forgiven you by now. Especially since you've made such a difference at the company."

"My dad died several years ago, long before I came to Salisburg," Jonathan revealed softly.

"I'm so sorry. I didn't know." She sighed. "It's so odd that no matter how old we are, we still look to our parents for validation of our success in life."

Not only her words, but the underlying element of sincerity in her voice struck a chord with Jonathan. Lauren seemed to understand the loss of a parent and the loss of the opportunity to prove his worth to his father.

He gazed into her sweet brown eyes and felt a peculiar sensation in his chest. It must be the fish, he told himself. Or the wine. Or all the butter he'd been slathering on his rolls.

Lauren smiled shyly, and Jonathan suddenly decided he needed to know if it really was the fish causing this strange sensation. He leaned forward without thinking, intent on kissing Lauren senseless. Kissing her until her arms wound themselves tightly around his neck, until she became breathless and started making sweet moaning sounds deep in her throat, until her entire body started quivering with escalating passion, until—

"Would you care for some freshly ground pepper, miss?" The fawning waiter stepped between them, poised and ready, an almost obscenely large pepper mill clasped in his hands.

"No," Lauren choked out. "No, thank you."

Jonathan put all his frustration into the glare he aimed at the waiter. His outrageous, completely inappropriate fantasy had been totally ruined, and he needed to vent his anger somewhere. The man wisely did not inquire if Jonathan wanted any pepper and slunk away.

Jonathan glanced over at Lauren. She was staring down at her plate, taking enthusiastic bites of the food and making a great show of eating her dinner. Jonathan forked up a bit of his fish, hardly tasting it. The moment was lost. Now all he had to do was make certain there was another before the evening ended.

Lauren kept shoveling the food into her mouth, reasoning if she could finish her dinner quickly, then she could leave and the evening would be over. She surmised she was making a spectacle of herself, judging by the odd looks Jonathan was giving her, and felt a twinge of anger. Well, too bad!

It was happening again. That quiet, shared moment of perfect understanding. In fact, it was expanding to include similar life experiences. To look at him now one would never guess Jonathan had struggled, as she had, to find a sense of worthiness and accomplishment in a career.

And something else was stirring too. A heightened sexual awareness that threatened to ignite into a full-blown fire at any moment. Lauren knew her carefully built resistance was starting to crumble, and the very idea of being vulnerable around this man terrified her.

Jonathan caught her eye and smiled. Lauren felt a dizzying surge of heat rush through her body. She managed to stop herself from returning the smile by gulping a large swallow of water.

A bold and striking woman with a thick mane of shining dark hair materialized suddenly at the table. Lauren gasped. The woman was gorgeous. She had huge, dark, heavily made-up eyes, high arched eyebrows and full, pouty red lips. She was wearing a chic low-cut black dress so tight it looked painted on.

"Jonathan, darling." The woman bent over and kissed him lingeringly on the lips. He seemed surprised, but not embarrassed.

"Hello, Celia." Jonathan's greeting was casual and friendly. He introduced the two women, but made no reference to how he knew Celia. Lauren wondered if the omission was deliberate.

Lauren smiled tightly at Celia, who glanced down briefly at her, then returned her full attention to Jonathan.

"Did you know I own this restaurant? Daddy bought it for me last month." Celia waved her hand around as if she were shooing gnats. "If I knew you were coming tonight, I would have instructed the chef to prepare something special for you and your little friend."

Celia spoke through full, lush lips. Her voice was low and breathy. Probably because her dress was so tight it cut off her air supply, Lauren decided with a twinge of envy.

"What happened to the flower shop your father bought you last year?" Jonathan asked.

"I got tired of it," Celia said with a dismissive sigh. "I think Daddy's still looking for someone to buy it." Celia pursed her lips together in such a perfectly shaped Cupid's bow Lauren was certain she had practiced the affectation many times in front of the mirror.

It was a repeat of Wednesday night's cooking class, although Lauren conceded Celia, with her fluttering, painted eyelashes, could easily outperform Susan Maxwell.

"I certainly hope your father finds someone who's interested in the flower shop soon. It was nice to see you, Celia," Jonathan said in a pointed, dismissive tone. "Thanks for stopping by our table to say hello."

Lauren could see Celia's eyes darken, first with surprise, then anger. She shot Jonathan a sullen glance, whipping her head to one side. The ends of her thick, dark hair flew across the table. Lauren wrapped her hand around her water goblet protectively and moved it out of the way.

"Call the waiter if you need anything," Celia said stiffly, flinging her hair in the opposite direction. This time Jonathan had to duck to avoid getting hit.

It was deeply quiet at their table after Celia stalked off. "That must be a very special cologne you wear," Lauren commented, unable to resist teasing him. "It attracts women like flies."

"Yeah, it's special all right." Jonathan gave a cynical laugh. "It's called *eau de money*."

His remark showed a rare, unexpected vulnerability that hit Lauren right in the heart. Reacting to the emotions engulfing her, she reached out to him, but pulled back her hand just before she made contact.

What was wrong with her? How could she allow herself to be charmed by him? She was forgetting the truth about Jonathan. He was a man who lacked a conscience. A man who felt no remorse at stealing another person's hard work.

Lauren cleared her throat and forcefully reminded herself this was supposed to be a business dinner. "You mentioned earlier that you had business to discuss."

Jonathan regarded her, a confused expression on his handsome face. "Ahhh, yes I do." He fiddled with the stem of his wineglass. "Cooking class was great Wednesday night, but I was hoping you'd be interested in giving me a few private lessons."

"Cooking lessons?" Lauren squeaked. "You want me to teach you how to cook?"

"Yes. Actually I'm interested in learning how to

bake." His eyes were warm with persuasion. "Will you consider it? I'll pay you whatever you think is fair."

Ahhh, money, the great weapon of the rich and privileged. Dangle enough of it in front of people and they forget everything. Like their integrity.

Still, an irrational sense of disappointment overtook Lauren. All he really wanted from her was cooking lessons. She swallowed sharply. How ironic. She was struggling to find the strength to resist him while he was attempting to find the key to manipulating her.

"I don't have any time to give you cooking lessons," Lauren stated flatly. Jonathan opened his mouth, presumably to argue, but Lauren cut him off. She didn't owe him any explanations, yet she figured she had better continue talking or else she might do something certifiably insane. Like agree to teach him how to cook.

"Aside from all my other work I've been collaborating with one of the local public television stations. We've developed a format for a new show featuring baking techniques and my original recipes. As soon as we secure corporate funding, production will start. That should happen sometime in the next few weeks."

"What a clever marketing idea," Jonathan replied. "A television show will build up name recognition and create a demand for your recipes. It could help you land a publishing contract."

"That's the plan." Lauren pressed three fingers against her left temple. The last thing she needed to hear was Jonathan's praise and admiration. It was starting to take the sting out of her outrage. "It has been a very *interesting* evening, but I'm rather tired. I think I'll skip dessert and—"

"Hello, Jonathan."

"Mother!"

"I had no idea you were coming here for dinner this evening. What a delightful surprise."

Lauren froze. Surprise didn't even begin to define the expression on Jonathan's face. She twisted her head around and caught a full view of the woman arriving at their table.

Jonathan's mother was dressed in a trim gray suit with a pale silk blouse and a complementing light-colored scarf pinned at the neck with a small expensive brooch. She wore her discreetly frosted hair in a short, simple style that flattered her angular features. There were a few honest wrinkles at the corners of blue eyes that gleamed brightly with speculation.

Lauren conceded Jonathan's mother was an attractive woman. Yet she decided he must have received his incredible good looks from his father. His mother was more of a handsome woman than a beautiful one. She was lean, graceful and aristocratic, and despite her rather plain features carried the look of old money with style and elegance.

Jonathan politely stood up the moment his mother reached the table. "Mother, I'd like to introduce Lauren Stuart. Lauren, this is my mother, Eleanor Windsor." Jonathan spoke with all the enthusiasm of a man facing a firing squad.

"It's nice to meet you, Mrs. Windsor."

"It is a pleasure to make your acquaintance, Lauren." Eleanor Windsor acknowledged the introduction, an overly bright smile of curiosity on her face. She sat down without being invited and rested her perfectly manicured fingers on the edge of the table. "Have you known Jonathan long?"

"Not really," Lauren mumbled noncommittally, struggling not to squirm under the intense scrutiny of Eleanor Windsor's examining gaze.

"How did you two first meet?" Eleanor pressed on.

"Jonathan surprised me one afternoon," Lauren said sweetly.

"Did he?" Eleanor looked charmed by the idea. She glanced approvingly at her son, then turned back to Lauren, assessing her with a shrewd, calculated stare.

Jonathan made a low sound in the back of his throat and slowly sat down. He reached for his glass and took a hefty gulp of wine.

"Do you live in Salisburg? Or are you just visiting?"

"I live here." Lauren smiled stiffly. She returned Eleanor's scrutiny, refusing to be cowed. "Actually I grew up in Salisburg."

"Did you?" Eleanor's eyes widened. "I'm surprised we've never met before. What did you say your family name was, dear?"

"Stuart," Jonathan answered in an impatient tone.

Lauren saw him flash his mother a warning gaze, which the older woman blithely ignored.

"Do you work for our company, Lauren?"

"Lauren is a chef, Mother," Jonathan interjected.

"My specialty is baking," Lauren added, not wanting Jonathan to think she needed rescuing, although she did appreciate the half-second respite from Eleanor Windsor's spotlight.

Eleanor looked mystified. "A baker?" She exchanged a quick, confused glance with her son. "Are you telling me she bakes cookies and such? For a living?" The inflection in Eleanor's voice made it sound like the most immoral, vulgar occupation imaginable.

"I certainly do." Lauren elevated her chin and tried to look unconcerned.

Jonathan shot to his feet and clasped his mother's elbow. "Time for you to go, Mother," he stated firmly.

But before he could safely march her out of the way, Lauren seized the moment and also jumped to her feet. If anyone was leaving, it was definitely going to be her. She was out of breath and off balance, but this was clearly the best chance she was likely to get.

She had already reached and exceeded her tolerance for the Windsor family that night. Better to go now before she lost her temper and started spouting some of the rude remarks furiously expressed in her head.

Lauren extended her hand toward a bewildered Jonathan. "Thank you for a fascinating evening," she said while shaking his hand delicately. Shifting her attention to Eleanor, she added, "It was delightful meeting you, Mrs. Windsor. Good night."

With a waxy smile on her face, she turned away and lifted her head regally in the air. She heard an indignant female gasp and a swell of rising murmurs among the restaurant patrons. Lauren had to call on all her inner reserves not to give in to the temptation to turn and look back at Jonathan and his arrogant mother. It would spoil the dramatic effect.

She had every intention of showing them all a thing or two about class. Striving hard to appear as the very epitome of grace under fire, Lauren pivoted neatly on her heel and, with the dignity and drama worthy of a royal princess, sailed majestically away from the table.

Directly into a waiter.

Carrying a trayful of dirty dishes.

The problem with dramatic exits, Lauren concluded while driving home, was timing. She was proud that she'd had the presence of mind to seize the moment and make good her escape, especially considering how annoyed she was at both Jonathan and his mother. Yet her moment of triumph had been ruined completely in a shower of dirty china.

Jonathan had rushed to her side the instant the collision had occurred, but she'd refused his help. Lauren remembered slapping his hands away and scrambling to her feet while hearing Eleanor Windsor ask in a deep, rich tone, "Gracious, what is wrong with the girl? Is she drunk?"

Ah, yes. It had been a real Kodak moment. Definitely one for the scrapbook. Lauren recalled brushing the hair back from her eyes, uttering a chilling good night to the various onlookers and fleeing the scene. Now that the adrenaline rush was starting to wear off, she assumed she'd be able to find the humor in the situation and enjoy a good laugh. Any minute now.

Lauren eased her car up to the traffic light and looked around the deserted intersection. There were two road signs posted, but she was unfamiliar with both route numbers. Terrific. On top of everything else she was lost. Without a gas station, convenience store or fast-food outlet in sight she had no choice but to try and ferret out the highway on her own.

Using the highly scientific selection method of eenie, meenie, minie, mo, Lauren opted to make a left turn. Biting her lips in vexation, she found herself pulling up to the same traffic light twenty minutes later, only this time she was coming from the opposite direction. She boldly made another left turn.

Physically and emotionally spent, Lauren arrived home an hour later. The red light on her answering machine was blinking furiously when she entered the apartment. Flopping onto the sofa, she kicked off her shoes, propped her feet on the coffee table and pushed the play messages button.

"Hi, Lauren, it's Eileen. Where did you rush off to in such a hurry tonight? Mom was looking everywhere for you. She was really upset to discover you had left the party. Anyway, I want to invite you over for Sunday brunch tomorrow. Don't worry I won't be cooking. Rob is going to make his famous buckwheat pancakes. Call me in the morning if you can make it. Talk to you later. 'Bye."

"Lauren this is Jonathan. If you're there, please pick up. It's ten forty-five, and I want to be sure you made it home without any problems. Please call me. My carphone number is five-five-five-two-five-two-five."

Lauren frowned and listened to the rest of the tape. Jonathan had left three more messages, each fifteen minutes apart. His voice sounded a bit more frantic with each subsequent call. Lauren was still debating whether or not to return his calls when the phone rang. Feeling too wired and edgy to deal with it, she let the machine answer and Jonathan's deep voice echoed through the living room.

"Lauren it is now eleven forty-five. I am on my way over to your apartment. I should be there in ten minutes. I need to be certain you are okay."

"No!" Lauren yelled and lunged for the phone, knocking it down in her haste. Fumbling with the cord, she yanked the receiver up to her mouth. "Jonathan? Hello, Jonathan? Are you there?"

"Lauren? Where have you been? I've been calling for an hour."

"I just walked in the door," Lauren said. She grimaced sarcastically. "I took the scenic route home."

"I've been so worried."

Lauren heard the concern in Jonathan's voice and hardened her resolve to combat the warm feeling it gave her. It seemed safer all around to stay angry with him.

"There was no need to be concerned." Lauren ran her hand through her hair and came away with a small, limp piece of lettuce. "I am perfectly fine."

"Please accept my apologies for this evening. My mother can be unusually difficult at times."

"Don't sweat it," Lauren remarked breezily. "No

harm done." Except to my dignity, she added silently. "I've already forgotten about it."

"I doubt that, but I'm willing to try and pretend it didn't happen." There was a brief pause. The rushing sound of traffic could be heard faintly in the background. "Of course, I'm mostly relieved to report that tonight's events placed in the top ten, but failed to win the award for worst date of my life."

"Really?" Lauren knew the smart move would be to hang up the phone. Now. "How could you possibly beat that dark restaurant, Celia, your mother and my graceful exit?"

"Easily. With wrestling."

"Pardon?"

Jonathan laughed. "You heard me. Wrestling. There was this date my mother arranged a while back that I absolutely could not talk my way out of, so I decided to exact a bit of revenge by escorting the young woman to a professional wrestling match in D.C."

"Professional wrestling?" Lauren wrinkled her nose. "The sport featuring those large men with no necks who dress in strange costumes, prance around the ring and shout at each other all the time?"

"Ahhh, so you're a fan."

"I most certainly am not." Lauren smiled and leaned on the edge of the couch. "Okay, I'll bite. Tell me about this date."

"I figured I had the foolproof way of helping my date, Marcy, decide she never wanted to see me again by taking her to this wrestling extravaganza. I thought she would practically trample me in her haste to get out of the arena. It was a wild, rough crowd that night, lots of barrel-chested men, rowdy teenagers and women in heavy makeup with big hair. Hardly the crowd that junior leaguer Marcy hangs out with on a regular basis."

Lauren couldn't resist. "What happened?"

"She adored it. She didn't stop screaming and shouting the most unbelievable suggestions to these hulking guys, who were tossing each other around like volleyballs, until we got ejected."

"Ejected?" Lauren could almost hear Jonathan's smile through the phone line. "As in thrown out?"

Jonathan gave an exaggerated, long-suffering sigh. "We had ringside seats. Marcy apparently didn't like the way the referee was calling the match so she tossed her beer into the ring and then took a swing at one of the wrestlers. The only positive note in the entire evening was when she regretfully informed me I was too straitlaced and conservative for her to consider dating."

"You're making this up."

"I only wish I were. It hurts a man's pride to be rejected in favor of a staged stunt show that masquerades as a sport."

Lauren pursed her lips. Jonathan's easy charm and quirky sense of humor were starting to get to her again. She was suddenly very glad the telephone was providing a physical barrier between them.

"Well, it's getting late and I have to get up very early tomorrow. Just another aspect of the glamorous, challenging life of a *baker.* So—"

"I really am sorry about tonight."

"I know." His quiet, sincere words of apology unsettled her even more. She had to get off the phone. "Good-bye Jonathan."

"Lauren—"

Lauren gently hung up the phone. She gazed blankly at the receiver for several moments, half-expecting it to ring again. It remained silent, and she felt strangely bereft. With a deep sigh, she trudged to the bathroom to take a shower, hoping a steady spray of hot water would calm her nerves and remove the smell of salad dressing from her hair.

The first bouquet of flowers, a whimsical arrangement of daisies, tulips and freesia arrived promptly at nine the following morning. Next came an unusual garland of daffodils, spring lilies and fragrant herbs bound into a long flower rope and tied on each end with wide silk ribbon.

This was followed by a sweet-scented bouquet of pinkish white- and dark blue-flowered lavender. And ten minutes later, two dozen perfectly formed long-stemmed sterling roses were delivered.

The roses were the only arrangement that had a card. It read, *Next time, dinner at the Crab Claw.*

Lauren stared down at the simple words for an inordinate amount of time, realizing Jonathan had succeeded in doing the one thing she feared most. He had captured her attention.

SEVEN

"It's so flat."

"I know." Jonathan ran a hand through his hair and gave his secretary, Linda, a distressed look. "It's hard as a rock, too."

They stood side by side in Jonathan's kitchen, staring down at the table that held his latest baking attempt.

"Maybe it tastes better than it looks," Linda remarked skeptically. She swiveled the plate and critically examined the cake from a different angle. "Let's cut a wedge and find out."

Jonathan shook his head. "Forget it. I already cracked a knife handle trying to saw it in half before you got here." Jonathan stuffed his hands into his pockets and sighed. "The only thing left to do is give it a decent burial. Preferably down a large hole in the back yard so some poor unsuspecting animal pawing through my garbage doesn't mistake it for edible food and break a tooth trying to take a bite out of it."

Linda grinned. She poked curiously at the cake with the tip of her finger. "What's that white, runny stuff on the top?" she asked cautiously. "Marshmallow?"

"It's whipped cream," Jonathan replied. "I'm supposed to artistically decorate the top of the cake, but I couldn't figure out how to work the pastry bag I bought at the baking supply store. I improvised with the canned stuff."

Jonathan shoved the cake into the center of the table. "It didn't look too bad when I finished, but the cream started getting soft and runny real fast. It just doesn't stay puffy very long."

Linda shuddered visibly. "Jonathan, you cannot use an aerosol can of whipped cream in a gourmet-cooking competition."

"I know." Jonathan's brow crumpled with anxiety. "What am I going to do, Linda? The competition is less than three weeks away."

"I warned you this wasn't going to be easy," Linda said in a censorious tone of voice.

The fact that she was right made Jonathan stifle the objection that automatically sprang to his lips. She had warned him. Yet he had ignored her advice and charged ahead, egged on by his ego and an unhealthy attraction to one of the contest judges.

You would think he'd be older and wiser by now when it came to women. He was an adult male. He should be able to ignore his body's hormonal reaction every time it came near Lauren, but somehow fate seemed determined to push him in her direction. And now he was about to make a complete ass of himself in front of half the town. Jonathan rubbed a hand over his aching forehead.

The regret he felt about his baking failure must have been evident on his face because he noticed the righteous light quickly fade from Linda's eyes.

"The contest isn't until the end of the month. Three weeks is plenty of time for you to learn how to bake one of these cakes," she offered encouragingly. "You just need practice."

"I need a miracle." Jonathan walked away from the table and picked up the coffeepot. He poured two mugs, then handed one to Linda. "I'm starting to buy chocolate and almond paste by the case so I don't have to run to the store three times a day for supplies. I have baked this damned cake at least a dozen times, and each attempt reveals a new problem.

"The cake I made yesterday morning was practically cemented to the inside of the pan. Eventually I managed to pry it free. It came out in ten pieces. Even Chesapeake had trouble swallowing it. The one I baked last night caught fire in the oven."

Linda made a noise that sounded suspiciously like a chuckle to Jonathan, then gave him an affectionate pat on the arm. "Don't get discouraged. A skilled and patient cooking instructor can show you what you're doing wrong and teach you how to avoid these problems. Have you had a chance to ask Lauren for private lessons yet?"

"She turned me down. She's too busy working on other projects." Jonathan took a sip of coffee. "But thanks for suggesting I ask her. It was a good idea."

There was a whole lot more to the story than his simple statement implied, and Jonathan could tell by the intense way his secretary was staring at him that Linda had picked up on that fact. But he wasn't going to attempt to explain something he couldn't even begin to understand.

Any sane person would have regarded his dinner with Lauren on Saturday night as a total disaster. The wrong restaurant, an uncomfortable appearance by a predatory female, an embarrassing incident with his mother, a slapstick ending more in keeping with a Marx Brothers' movie than a dinner date. Yet he couldn't remember when he'd felt a stronger connection to a woman or a greater sense of ease.

Common sense told him that getting involved with Lauren could mean big trouble. On so many levels it was obvious their attraction could lead nowhere. She was prickly, opinionated and hard to understand, but he had bonded with her in a way that made him anticipate their next meeting with excitement and fascination.

The only feeling of regret Jonathan carried was knowing that Lauren probably wouldn't agree to go out with him again anytime soon. And that bothered him. A great deal.

"Why don't you ask your mother's cook Regina for help?" Linda suggested. She strolled over to the open pantry and began studying the contents with great interest. "I'm sure Regina would be happy to answer your questions and demonstrate a few simple baking techniques."

"Regina is in Nova Scotia visiting her sister. She won't be back for two weeks." Jonathan gave a low growl of frustration. "I can't wait until she returns to learn all this stuff."

He grabbed the tin of cookies Linda was struggling to open and easily twisted off the lid. After offering her some, he took a handful for himself and set the decorative container on the counter.

They munched cookies and sipped coffee in contemplative silence.

"Maybe you could teach me," Jonathan said without much enthusiasm.

"Spoken like a man who's tasted my meat loaf." Linda laughed. "I doubt I could teach you anything more than a few bad habits. I've never aspired to cook any kind of gourmet-style food. The only cookbook I own is the Fanny Farmer book my mother gave me when I got engaged. She called it a kitchen bible, although I think my poor husband needed divine intervention to digest some of the meals I prepared."

Linda crunched on another cookie and smiled.

"Most of the pages in that cookbook are stained with my ambitious attempts, some are literally glued together. The book's so old the spine is split in half. The whole thing is held together with a large rubber band that I haven't removed in three years."

"Well, I'm encouraged to discover that cooking is a skill even intelligent people find difficult to master," Jonathan remarked, accepting Linda's rejection with a philosophical shrug knowing his secretary was right. All she probably could teach him were more bad cooking habits.

"Thanks." Linda frowned slightly as if she were trying to decide how to interpret Jonathan's last remark.

He placed their dirty coffee mugs in the sink and fought a sudden burst of irritation as he contemplated his other options. There weren't many. Who ever would have thought learning to bake one stupid cheesecake would turn into such a mammoth undertaking?

"I have half a mind to sponsor the cooking show Lauren mentioned the other night at dinner," Jonathan muttered as he bit into a crisp cookie. "If she worked for me I might have some control over how she organizes her schedule."

"What cooking show?"

"Lauren and our local public television station have developed a show that will feature on-camera demonstrations of her original recipes. All that's missing is the necessary funding to put the show on the air."

Jonathan felt a surge of pride. It was a smart, gutsy idea and he admired both Lauren's ingenuity and creativity.

"I think you should do it." Linda's eyes widened with growing excitement. "Madison Seafood has a steep advertising budget. As long as the production costs aren't too extreme, we should be able to sponsor Lauren's show by utilizing some of those funds."

"I suppose it's worth considering purely from a public relations angle," Jonathan conceded slowly. "We could provide some much-needed support for our community station while generating enough positive publicity to make even my mother happy."

Jonathan looked to Linda for her opinion and noticed a faint diabolical gleam of excitement light his secretary's eyes. It put him on instant alert.

"Why stop at sponsorship, Jonathan? As president of the company you should take a more visible role. I think you should co-host the show with Lauren."

Jonathan hesitated a long moment. The concept was so completely outrageous it gripped his imagination and held fast. He slowly swallowed the remaining piece of cookie in his mouth. It felt hard and scratchy as it worked its way down his throat. "I can't cook, Linda. Remember?"

"I know." Linda's grin looked wide enough to make her jaw ache. "It's perfect. You'll be making the food together, on camera, so Lauren will have to spend a lot of time teaching and coaching you on the food preparation. You'll learn how to cook, or specifically bake, while providing Lauren with an excellent opportunity to showcase her talent. It's a win-win situation."

Jonathan highly doubted Lauren would view the situation with the same degree of enthusiasm as Linda. "Lauren is a pastry chef. Her specialties are desserts. Won't it seem odd to have a seafood company underwriting the cost of her show?"

"Good point." Linda nibbled on her bottom lip. "The main focus of the show must be Lauren and her fabulous desserts, but there could also be a segment featuring an appetizer or main course item using a Madison Seafood product. It's a natural tie-in and terrific advertising."

"I suppose it could work," Jonathan said slowly, hardly believing he was seriously considering the idea.

Without being told, Linda retrieved the phone book from his study. "Do you want me to set up an appointment with the television station manager for tomorrow morning?" she asked, while pouring through the white pages.

"Yes." Jonathan's heart began to pound in an irregular rhythm. This whole notion was nuts. "I'd better meet the station manager and discuss all the particulars of the deal before whatever is left of my common sense kicks in and I abandon this whole crazy scheme," Jonathan muttered with a touch of sarcasm in his voice.

He noticed Linda biting her tongue as she dialed the phone. He felt grateful she was able to refrain from either agreeing or disagreeing with him because he truthfully wasn't sure which would have made him feel worse.

Lauren alternated between cursing and plotting as she drove the twenty miles from the public television station to her sister's house. She had just spent a fascinating, frustrating morning with George Kilmer, the station manager.

Their meeting had started out on a high note. George had found a sponsor for her cooking show, a company willing, nay eager, to underwrite the production costs. That was the good news. The not-so-good news was that the sponsor was the Madison Seafood Company. And the president and CEO of the company, one Jonathan Windsor, wanted to appear in the show as her co-host.

Lauren's initial reaction had been laughter. It had to be a joke, and because she believed she shared an insight into Jonathan's offbeat sense of humor, Lauren's amusement had been genuine. But when George produced a contract outlining the details of the agreement, Lauren had stopped laughing. Immediately.

She had left the station in a hurry, her mind filled with confusion. She hoped the drive to Eileen's house would give her the much-needed time to organize her thoughts so she could rationally discuss her feelings with her sister and develop a suitable counterattack.

Jonathan Windsor. He was like a bad penny who kept turning up when she least expected him. In her thoughts, in her dreams, in her professional world.

Lauren was honest enough to admit that she was partially to blame. None of this insanity would have ever started if she and Eileen hadn't registered Jonathan for the cooking contest. But she was way past having regrets about that less than brilliant move. They had created this beast and now she needed to discover how to cage it, tame it, or set it free.

The problem was that Jonathan was a study in contradictions. A sinfully handsome playboy who had women practically throwing themselves under his car tires to get noticed, yet he did nothing to overtly encourage them and attributed much of their attraction to his money and position rather than himself. A man who exuded self-confidence and success, who had struggled to find his own self-worth and deeply regretted not being able to share his eventual triumph with his father.

Lauren liked his ability to laugh at himself and admired his determination to pursue what he wanted full-out. Yet the bottom line remained unchanged. Jonathan's character was not to be trusted, and the strong, ever-growing attraction she felt for him needed to be contained. Lauren had never let her hormones rule her head and she wasn't about to start now.

Her past contained no torrid love affairs gone bad, no deep regrets nor distrust of men. But as she had matured and struggled to move from a self-centered girl to a self-reliant woman, Lauren had wisely used caution as her guide when it came to dealing with men.

She had almost become engaged during her final year of college but the timing had been wrong for marriage. Her "almost fiancé" had accepted a job with a West Coast computer company and after spending several weeks visiting him, Lauren knew she wanted to live on the East Coast, specifically in New York City.

They parted regretfully, yet amicably. There had been dates and a few relationships since, but nothing that put her stomach in knots and sent her heart racing like spending time with Jonathan did.

The street was unusually quiet when Lauren arrived at her destination. She parked her car next to Eileen's Land Cruiser and walked toward the back of the house. As she came closer she could hear shrieks of childish laughter coming from the yard and concluded Eileen and the children were taking advantage of the warm morning sunshine.

The baby gave her a wide, wet, gap-toothed smile the moment Lauren entered the yard. Ashley was sitting calmly in her toddler swing, her chubby legs pumping back and forth as the swing stood nearly stationary. Eileen was standing to the left of the baby, pushing Michael's swing high in the air.

Lauren could hear her sister's exaggerated grunts and groans each time Eileen pushed the swing. Apparently Michael also heard his mother because he giggled and laughed at each noise she made.

"Hi, everybody." Lauren strolled over to Ashley and tweaked the baby's nose. The little one gurgled happily and stuck her fist in her mouth.

"Good morning." Eileen greeted her sister with a smile. "You're out and about rather early this morning."

"I had a meeting at the station with George Kilmer," Lauren replied.

"Judging by the dour expression on your face I have to assume things didn't go very well," Eileen commented as she lifted Ashley out of the swing. Lauren opened her arms and Eileen passed over the squirming baby. Lauren nuzzled Ashley's neck and the baby squealed. She smelled soft and warm, like sunshine.

"Oh, some things went very well," Lauren said with a sigh. "Others were a bit more dicey."

"I'll get some iced tea and we'll talk about it," Eileen volunteered. She scooped Michael off his swing. "Watch the kids. I'll be right back."

"Hi Warren." Michael hugged Lauren's knees tightly, then dashed off toward the bright red and blue child-sized picnic table. The area surrounding the table was littered with bits of cereal, a slice of toast with a half-moon bite taken out of one side, several squashed grapes, an empty yogurt container and a strip of banana peel. Lauren smiled. Obviously the children had eaten their breakfast outside.

Lauren rested the baby comfortably against her hip and followed Michael closely, taking to heart her sister's request to watch the children.

"New brush." Michael held out a bright yellow hairbrush for Lauren's inspection.

"That's cool, buddy," Lauren replied, snatching a grape off a plate. She gave him a quick kiss on the cheek, then sat gingerly on the end of the picnic table, hoping it would hold her weight. Michael immediately stood up on the bench seat and jammed the yellow brush through Lauren's loose hair.

"Whoa, go easy on the scalp," Lauren yelped. "You're going to brush my head bald."

"Bald?"

"Yes, bald. As in no hair, like weird Uncle Harold."

Lauren winced while Michael continued grooming her. Fortunately he soon lost interest and went skipping over to the sandbox, waving the brush in the air. He happily brought a ladybug back a few minutes later, but screamed loudly when Lauren refused to let him feed it to his sister.

"Michael!"

The little boy froze at the sound of his mother's voice. The yard miraculously became quiet. Lauren marveled at the way her nephew's screams and tears disappeared the moment his mother spoke his name.

Lauren waited patiently as Eileen set a pitcher of iced tea, two glasses and a plate of cookies on the wrought-iron patio table. After Eileen clamped the baby's chair securely to the table's rim, Lauren carefully lowered Ashley into the chair and tied the safety strap.

Lauren held the box of cereal Eileen gave her and watched her sister spread a handful of Cheerios within easy reach of the baby. After Lauren and Eileen were sprawled comfortably in the cushioned chairs, Michael retrieved a half-eaten banana from his breakfast leftovers and climbed onto his mother's lap.

Eileen's arms closed loosely around her son, and Lauren's heart gave a little tug. How serene and loving they looked. Lauren experienced an odd flash of longing, wondering if she would ever cuddle a child of her own that way.

"So what's going on?" Eileen asked conversationally.

"George found a sponsor for my cooking show."

"That's terrific!" Eileen's brow furrowed deeply. "Why aren't you thrilled?"

"The sponsor is none other than Jonathan Windsor," Lauren remarked, not even trying to hide her agitation. "His seafood company is underwriting the show, and since his company is footing the bill, Jonathan apparently feels entitled to a few perks. He wants to be my co-host."

"That's sweet."

"It's annoying." Lauren glared at her sister with a mutinous expression. "A few weeks ago I never even knew who he was, and now every time I turn around, I bump into him. It is definitely starting to grate on my nerves."

"Yeah, it sure can be tough when a handsome man shows he's interested in you," Eileen said with a teasing smile. "Must be a real nightmare."

Lauren resisted the urge to throw something. "You are totally missing the point. I really don't know what Jonathan is interested in," Lauren complained. "I have doubts that it's me. Serious doubts."

She huffed out a breath and continued. "He crashed my cooking class because he wanted to learn how to bake a cheesecake, and when I outmaneuvered him he tried to entice me into giving him private lessons. I turned him down and the next thing I know he wants to co-host my show. I feel certain he expects me to teach him how to bake."

"I don't want to deflate your professional ego, but you are not the only woman in Salisburg who knows how to bake," Eileen remarked. She picked up a stray Cheerio and chewed it thoughtfully. "Present company excluded, of course."

"Then why is Jonathan so persistent?"

"Maybe he likes you," Eileen suggested, idly stroking Michael's hair. The little boy twisted off her lap and ran across the yard to the swing set.

"Now there's a terrifying thought," Lauren muttered, trying to repress the elation a part of her felt at the idea of being liked by Jonathan. Being desired by Jonathan. Being loved by Jonathan.

"Maybe he's suffering from a Henry the Eighth complex," Lauren offered. "I rebuffed his initial advances, so he now sees the challenge to chase and conquer. Historians say Anne Boleyn became Henry's wife and queen because she wouldn't have sex with him unless they married. Yet after the wedding Henry quickly lost interest in her. When Anne failed to give birth to a son, Henry had her beheaded and moved on to new challenges."

Eileen leaned back in her chair and crossed her arms. "So what are you telling me, Lauren? Are you secretly afraid you are going to lose your head over Jonathan?"

"Not just my head. Maybe my heart," Lauren whispered. She flushed with emotion and stared off into the distance. It was difficult to voice her fears. "There is something about Jonathan's sexy smile and the way his lips curl just before he laughs that makes me want to sidle up close to his broad chest and start rubbing against him like a cat.

"He has this effortless charm that at times nearly overpowers me. I can practically feel myself weakening toward him, Eileen. Heaven knows I don't posses an abundant amount of willpower. I can't stay on a low-fat diet more than twelve hours because chocolate is eliminated as a major food group.

"Whenever I look at any sort of *do's* and *don't's* list I always gravitate toward the *don't's*. My feelings for Jonathan are embarrassing, humiliating, and are going to get me into big, big trouble."

"Here, have a cookie." Eileen skidded the plate toward Lauren. "They're your favorite kind, chocolate chip. It will make you feel better. I remember you once told me that food is the real joy in life, so my advice to you is never let a man take away your appetite."

Lauren smiled. "Loss of appetite is *never* one of my problems." She nibbled unenthusiastically on a cookie while Eileen watched closely.

"Hey, you really are upset." Eileen stroked Lauren's arm sympathetically. "I think you need to view this as the glass is half full instead of half empty situation. Just let yourself get involved, Lauren. You might be wonderfully surprised where this relationship takes you."

"I can't get romantically involved with Jonathan. I don't trust him."

Eileen smacked Lauren's wrist. "The man pilfered your cheesecake recipe, Lauren. Stop acting like he robs banks for a living."

"Trust is too important a factor in any relationship to dismiss it so lightly," Lauren insisted. "Besides, this is probably a moot point. I'm convinced Jonathan wants to host this show so I can teach him how to make a cheesecake for the competition, not because he's hot for my marvelous body."

"Why in the world would Jonathan care about this cooking contest? I'll bet anything he had no idea it even existed until we signed him up for it."

Lauren wrinkled her brow. "I think he wants to win and will go to any lengths to achieve success. Kinda like those fathers at their kid's soccer games who act as if they bet the house on the outcome of the game, so their team had better win or else. It's a guy thing."

Eileen didn't look convinced. In fact she was looking at Lauren much the same way she did when Michael told his mother the baby was crying because she was sad, not because he had ripped a toy out of her hand.

"I brought the contract Jonathan worked out with the television station." Lauren reached down into her purse. "I'd appreciate it if you would review it before I sign. I want my rights spelled out in black and white so there are no surprises. Of course what I really need is a clause that will give me some control over the content of the show. It makes me nervous having Jonathan calling all the shots."

"Oh, goody, something to read that doesn't have talking animals and brightly colored pictures." Eileen rubbed her hands together, then reached eagerly for the document. "I'll see what brilliant legal codicils I can invent."

Lauren wandered over to the swing set to play with Michael while Eileen read the contract. The little boy's infectious laugh and carefree attitude helped settle the turmoil in her stomach. When Eileen called her back to the patio, Lauren felt calmer and more focused.

"I've penciled in the changes, but you need to have these sections of the contract retyped and initialed by both you and the station manager before they are sent to Jonathan," Eileen said. "Since you are the culinary expert it is reasonable to expect retention of creative control over format, style and content for each twenty-six minute episode."

Lauren blinked. "What exactly does that mean?"

"Jonathan can give all the orders or make as many suggestions as he wants, but you have the final word on what recipes are demonstrated on the show, how the demonstrations are formatted and how much on-camera time is devoted to every dish," Eileen said with a smile, clearly pleased with her ingenuity.

"Well, that rather neatly solves one problem," Lauren said. She cleared her throat and stared at her sister expectantly. "Now if you could only help me overcome this ridiculous infatuation I have for Jonathan, maybe I can start sleeping at night."

EIGHT

Responding to a phone call from George Kilmer several days later, Lauren arrived at the public television station early the following morning. She traipsed past the empty receptionist's desk and headed directly toward the door with the plastic plaque marked STATION MANAGER.

Lauren knocked first, then poked her head through the open doorway. She spied a slender man of medium height fiddling with an automatic coffee machine.

"Morning, George. Need any help?"

"Lauren?" George whirled around, knocking his elbow on the coffee maker. He frowned at Lauren, wrinkled his brow; then a smile of understanding lit his craggy features. "I didn't expect you until nine, but I'm glad you're here. Come in and sit down."

He indicated a wide-based chair on the opposite side of the desk that had seen better days. Lauren perched on the edge of the seat, crossed her ankles and drew them under the chair.

"I hope I'm not inconveniencing you by arriving so early, George."

"Not at all. Would you like a mug of coffee? It's freshly made."

"No thanks. I love coffee but I get really jittery if I

overindulge. Unfortunately I've already consumed my allotment for the day."

"Trying to cut back on the caffeine?" George grunted with sympathy. "It seems as though every week my wife is reading another medical study that warns against consuming too much of it. She is always harping on me to limit my coffee drinking. Drives me nuts. Heck, she even started brewing a decaffeinated brand at home. Horrible-tasting stuff."

He shuddered and Lauren smiled. She liked George. He had been managing this small public television station as long as anyone could remember. He was a bit unorganized, but Lauren couldn't hypocritically hold that small flaw against him. Besides, with his rolled-up shirt-sleeves and crooked tie, he reminded her of her father. George even had a receding hairline very similar to her dad's.

"So tell me George, what's the good word from Madison Seafood?"

"They faxed me the revised contracts late last night," George replied, settling himself in the squeaky chair behind the desk. He took a long sip of coffee. Lauren could almost hear his sigh of contentment. "Jonathan agreed to the changes you wanted. All you have to do is sign the contract and we are in business."

"Oh, George. This is wonderful news." Lauren jumped up from her chair and reached across the desk. She gave the startled George a quick hug. He seemed mildly embarrassed.

"I'm really happy for you, Lauren." George smiled fleetingly, took several more gulps of hot coffee and started riffling through the folders on his cluttered desk. "I know how hard you've worked to make this happen."

Lauren accepted the contract George handed her with shaky fingers. A host of feelings washed over her. Excitement. Apprehension. Pure terror. Signing quickly, she passed the document back to George and watched silently as he shuffled the folders on the desk, searching for the correct one.

Eventually he found the one he needed. Lauren let out her breath when he placed the document inside the folder. There was no room for any doubts now. It was a done deal.

George reached over and refilled his coffee mug, then stared about his office with a confused expression on his face. "Now where did I put those plans?" he mumbled, scratching the side of his head. Grinning sheepishly, he added, "Guess I shouldn't conduct business until I've consumed at least two mugs of coffee."

Lauren smiled. "My dad always told me never trust a person with a neat desk."

"Smart man, your father."

"Can I help you?" Lauren offered.

"No thanks. I know it's hard to believe, but I really have a system for organizing my papers. I know where everything is, I just have trouble finding things when I need them."

After several minutes of good-natured grumbling George discovered what he was looking for under a large stack of books and files precariously balanced on top of a cabinet. George pulled out a cardboard cylinder and removed a tightly wound sheet of thin paper from inside the canister. He rolled out the oversized set of blueprints on the credenza behind his desk and beckoned Lauren.

"One of our set designers already started working on the kitchen for your show," he said. "I want you to look these over and make any adjustments you think are necessary."

Caught up in the excitement, Lauren moved closer and studied the plans carefully.

"I think it would be better if we reversed the stove top and sink configuration and extended the island demonstration area by several feet. May I?" Lauren lifted a pencil questionably. After George's nod of consent she scribbled on the blueprint, illustrating her idea.

"That looks fine." George reached over and lifted a thick soft-cover book off the edge of his desk. "I got Freed's electronic store down on main street to underwrite the cost of the appliances. Take a few minutes to look through their catalogue and let me know which stove, oven and refrigerator you want.

"Most of the actual cooking will be done ahead of time, off air," George explained. "But you will be demonstrating the more complicated and interesting aspects of the recipe preparation in front of the cameras, and I want you to be comfortable with the equipment."

"I have better flame and heat control with gas appliances," Lauren said, flipping through the enormous book. She folded back the edge of several pages and jotted down model numbers in the margins. "Can you get a gas hookup in the studio?"

"I have to check with the set designer, but it shouldn't be a problem," George replied. "What I really need is Jonathan's approval so we can begin construction of the set."

"I'll bring the plans to his office," Lauren volunteered. She reasoned that, since she was going to be working with Jonathan, it was essential that she learn to interact with him on a purely business level. Taking the plans to his office would demonstrate her professional attitude and hopefully set the tone for their working relationship. *And give her the perfect excuse to see him again.*

"After Jonathan reviews the plans, tell him to give me a call. If he gives me verbal confirmation over the phone, I can order all the necessary materials for the set this afternoon," George said, placing the rolled prints back inside the cylinder and handing them to Lauren. "If we don't hit any snags we could begin taping our first show by the end of next week."

"Next week!" Lauren clutched the blueprints protectively against her chest. "That doesn't give me very much time to prepare, George."

"Relax," he said with a smile. "The show will be on tape, not live. I'm going to direct the first few episodes, and I'll schedule several hours of crew time so we won't have to rush."

George's calm manner assured Lauren. Slightly. Yet there was still a tremendous amount of work to be done if she was going to be ready to tape her first show by next week. Lauren glanced down at her watch. "I'd better hurry over to Jonathan's office. I'll call you later this week after I've organized the recipes for the first show."

"That sounds fine." George leafed anxiously through a computer printout on his desk, obviously shifting his attention to other matters.

Taking the none-too-subtle hint, Lauren said goodbye and hurried out to her car. She drove swiftly, but carefully, her mind cluttered with ideas. Concentrating on the show helped focus her mind away from her upcoming meeting with Jonathan. Lauren was relieved to realize she barely felt nervous when she presented herself to Jonathan's secretary.

"It is so nice to see you, Mrs. Martin," Lauren said as she greeted Jonathan's secretary. "I didn't know you worked with Jonathan."

"Oh, my yes," Linda answered. "I've been with the company for years."

"I don't have an appointment, but I was hoping

Jonathan could spare a few minutes to talk to me," Lauren said.

"I'm sure he'll make time for you," Linda replied. "Mrs. Windsor is with him now, but she should be leaving shortly. I'll let him know you're waiting."

Lauren's stomach muscles tightened, and she felt a strong burst of anxiety at the thought of meeting Jonathan's mother again. Some people just naturally made you nervous. Eleanor Windsor could have taught classes on the subject.

Hastily Lauren brushed back a stray wisp of hair from her temple and smoothed down the small wrinkle on the front of her skirt.

Linda led the way into his office.

"What a delightful surprise. You remember Lauren Stuart, don't you, Mother?" Jonathan moved forward and shook Lauren's hand. His touch and his tone were warm and friendly. "I just got off the phone with George Kilmer. I'm really pleased that you are going to star in the new cooking show our company is sponsoring."

"Thanks." Lauren turned and greeted Jonathan's mother. "Hello, Mrs. Windsor."

Eleanor Windsor acknowledged Lauren's greeting with a sharply raised eyebrow and a slight nod of her head. Her expression was cautious, her eyes cold, and she did not offer Lauren her perfectly manicured hand.

Lauren's fingers tightened around the cylinder of blueprints she held. Mrs. Windsor did not appear very happy. In fact she seemed like a woman easily capable of frightening a ravenous bear away from honey. Lauren took a small step closer to Jonathan. He immediately placed a casual hand on her shoulder.

Mrs. Windsor's eyes narrowed. "Is this true? Are you going to appear on this cooking show?" she asked with strong disapproval in her rich, well-modulated voice.

"Yes, I am," Lauren replied firmly. Her nerves were finally under control, and because she knew it would annoy Eleanor, she couldn't resist adding, "I'm surprised to find myself looking forward to it. Did Jonathan also tell you he is going to co-host the show with me? Isn't that great? I think your son and I will make a marvelous team."

Lauren raised her chin and fluttered her eyelashes at Jonathan. He looked shocked, but his face was tilted away from his mother, affording Eleanor a view of Lauren's expressions, not her son's reactions.

Taking shameless advantage of the situation Lauren pursed her lips in a secret, seductive smile. When she caught the look of martyred suffering Eleanor exchanged with Jonathan's secretary, Lauren knew she had scored a direct hit.

"Tell me, Miss Stuart, how did you manage to talk my son into sponsoring this little show of yours?" Eleanor inquired in a cold voice. She moved closer to her son, as if she were guarding him from an evil menace.

"Underwriting the cost of the show was my idea." Jonathan's gaze moved from her to his mother. "I believe I mentioned that fact to you already," he insisted, not even bothering to hide his exasperation.

"It must have slipped my mind," Eleanor said with a vague smile. She waved her hand in the air dismissively. "Inconsequential items often do."

Jonathan closed his eyes briefly. "Thanks so much for stopping by to visit. I know you have a lunch date at the club, Mother, so I won't keep you any longer. I'll call you later."

"Fine."

Lauren thought Eleanor looked anything but pleased at having to leave, but with Jonathan's assistance, she donned a lightweight coat and gathered her expensive purse close to her chest. "I'm having lunch with Mitzi Wells and Buffy Mason. I will give them your regards, Jonathan. They always ask about you."

"Good-bye, Mother," Jonathan said in a brusque tone. He hustled his mother and his secretary through the door and shut it firmly behind them.

"Mitzi and Buffy?" Lauren couldn't resist the jibe. "They sound like a pair of poodles."

"They're actually more like a team of pit bulls," Jonathan muttered. "And both are blessed with unmarried daughters."

"Ahhh, that explains part of your mother's disapproval of me. Compared to Buffy's and Mitzi's offspring I seem like a scullery maid."

"I'm really sorry. Mother usually isn't so snobbish, but I suppose she can sense my interest in you."

"It doesn't matter," Lauren said, deciding she wasn't going to acknowledge the little thrill his words sent down her spine. "Since we don't have a romantic relationship it is hardly an issue. Besides, your mother is merely enforcing my own mother's opinion. She agrees that we are all wrong for each other and warned me most emphatically against becoming involved with you."

Jonathan's brows knit together in a frown. "Funny, I don't remember meeting your mother."

"You didn't." Lauren grinned. "My mother is under the delusion that she has psychic intuition when it comes to men and her daughters. Unfortunately she has been right only one time in her life, when she matched my sister Eileen with her husband Rob, but her one success made Mother uncompromisingly dictatorial. I've finally given up trying to argue with her. It is a total waste of breath and energy."

Jonathan nodded his head in agreement. "There is nothing more vexing than a tenacious mother determined to guide her child. When dealing with my mother I usually agree with her outrageous demands, then go off and do whatever I want."

"Coward."

"You bet."

They shared a quiet laugh. Lauren relaxed and leaned against the edge of Jonathan's desk. With a smile still on her face she glanced up at him. The look he sent her was sexy and hypnotic. She realized that she was staring at him. He was staring right back. Lauren felt herself falling and struggled against being pulled in.

"The only way the cooking show will work is if we maintain a business relationship, Jonathan," she said in a small voice.

"I agree."

His ready response left Lauren suspicious, but she was willing to give him a chance to prove his sincerity. She looked around the office for an appropriate spot to display the kitchen blueprints. The sooner they talked business the better.

The spartan, functional furnishings in Jonathan's office were very much at odds with the wealthy business image Lauren had formed of him, and she found herself once again reluctantly intrigued. Utilizing the only appropriate place, Lauren leaned down and rolled out the blueprints on Jonathan's desk, then called him over.

Jonathan responded to her summons, draping himself over the desk. He appeared to intently study the blueprint over Lauren's shoulder. She could feel his warm breath on her neck. The air was charged with sexual awareness.

"Do you think there is enough counter space on this demonstration island? I tend to use a lot of space when I cook," Jonathan whispered in her ear.

Ignoring the shiver of excitement that turned her

first cold, then hot, Lauren shifted her head around, coming nose to nose with Jonathan. She squinted her eyes and poked her index finger in the center of his chest. It was firm as a rock, so she jabbed it a second time to emphasize her point.

"This is business, so cut the Romeo act."

Jonathan threw his arms up in a gesture of helpless innocence, but Lauren wasn't buying it.

"Jonathan, this strange attraction we appear to have for each other will not become an issue unless we allow it. I'd like to think we are both mature enough to ignore it and conduct ourselves in a professional, business manner."

"I've got news for you Lauren," Jonathan replied. "There is nothing strange about the feelings I have for you. They are powerful, intense and frustrating as hell. But maybe if we finally got this out of the way we could concentrate on business."

Jonathan's arms encircled her and before she could even blink, his mouth fastened on hers. Pleasure, pure and simple flooded her system, rippling through every single nerve ending. *Oh, yes.* His lips were soft and compelling, yet hungry and hot at the same time. Her eyes drifted shut as she absorbed the protective, masculine feel of him.

Lauren clutched at the solid strength of his arms and parted her lips, searching for more of the wondrous sensations. His tongue grazed the soft skin of her lower lip, brushed boldly against her teeth, then met and caressed her tongue. Lauren whimpered.

She pressed herself closer to Jonathan and felt the strength and hardness of his chest and thighs, a marked contrast to the gentle sweetness of his mouth. He dug the heels of his hands into her buttocks and lifted her against him. She unconsciously rubbed herself back and forth against his heated flesh as an intense feeling of urgency skittered through every pore of her body.

Jonathan drew back slowly, dipped his head against her neck and groaned softly, "Man, do I want you."

Lauren snapped her head back. Reality returned like a slap in the face. Everything was happening precisely as she had both feared and secretly desired. She felt hot, queasy and completely unable to cope with her conflicting and ever-changing feelings for Jonathan.

She pushed away and tried to slow her breathing. Turning her back on him, she announced in a husky voice, "This isn't going to work. I'll call George and let him know I can't do the show."

"No deal."

Lauren spun back around. Jonathan's eyes were dark with passion, but his expression was impossible to read. "You signed a contract, and I intend to hold you to the terms. Twelve episodes, Lauren."

"That's blackmail!"

"No, that's hardball." Jonathan regarded her shrewdly. "Any businessman who's achieved even moderate success knows how to play."

Lauren fumed silently, unable to think of a comeback that didn't sound childish or petty. She gripped her arms over her chest and pouted for a few minutes. Jonathan turned his attention to the blueprints, apparently oblivious to her annoyance.

"I think the set design looks fine, but I'm not the expert," Jonathan said in a neutral tone. "Are you satisfied with the set?"

Lauren nodded curtly. She took a step toward Jonathan. A very small step.

"I'll let George know we approve," Jonathan announced. "What's next?"

Jonathan's casual business attitude diffused some of Lauren's anger. And pricked her pride. He was acting as though their kiss had never occurred, while she could barely resist brushing her fingertips across her swollen lips and remembering the taste, feel and smell of him.

"We have to choose recipes for the program and organize our on-camera presentations," Lauren said stiffly.

"Whoa. I'm going to need major help in that department. Can you spare an hour or so right now? I'd like you to come to one of our processing plants. We can pick up some fresh seafood. Maybe inspiration will strike."

"I have to be at Just Desserts no later than two. I'm catering a dinner party for eight tonight."

"Great. That gives us plenty of time. We might even be able to grab a quick bite to eat." Jonathan took Lauren by the elbow and pulled her out of the office. "You can reach me at the Bay Street oyster house," he called to his secretary as they left.

Jonathan held onto Lauren tightly as they snaked their way through the maze of cars in the small parking lot.

"I'll drive," he announced, opening the passenger's side door of his dark green Jaguar.

Before she could catch her breath Lauren was settled inside the luxurious sports car with her seat belt fastened and the door locked.

Jonathan climbed behind the wheel, took a pair of aviator sunglasses off the dashboard of the car and put them on. Lauren swallowed hard. Goodness, he looked sexy. You would think covering up those beautiful green eyes would detract from his appeal, but the glasses made him look gorgeous. Harder. Dangerous. Forbidden.

Jonathan drove a tad recklessly and thirty miles over the posted speed limit. Lauren found it exhilarating.

Their unannounced arrival at the oyster house caused a great deal of excitement among the workers.

The place appeared to be overflowing with people, but Jonathan explained they were only operating at a quarter of normal capacity.

"It is tough getting good quality oysters this time of year, but I think it's important to provide steady employment for our workers. Our biggest season runs from late summer through the middle of January. That's when the demand for oysters reaches its peak."

Even running at limited capacity Lauren thought the oyster plant was a noisy, bustling place. It had a briny smell that was pungent but not offensive. Each section of the sprawling one-story structure they entered was teaming with activity and groups of busy workers.

There were thirty-foot-high mountains of fresh oysters still inside their shells kept in enormous refrigerated warehouses. These impressive mountains were slowly depleted as workers shoveled them onto moving conveyer belts. Jonathan and Lauren followed the progress of the oysters as they were washed, sorted, then brought into a huge room. Here workers stood against waist-high wooden work stations surrounding the perimeter of the room and opened the oysters with short blade knifes and a quick flick of the wrist.

The empty shells were thrown into the center of the room while the oyster meat was slipped into plastic containers. Some people wore headsets and rocked to the rhythm of the music from their cassette players as they worked, but most talked and joked among themselves, moving with amazing speed and dexterity. Lauren noted many of the faster "shuckers," as Jonathan called them, were women. Not surprisingly, he had an easy and natural rapport with these female employees and called several by name.

On the way to the administrative offices to meet the plant manager, Mel, they passed through a connecting tunnel of glass. Lauren gasped when she saw hills and hills of sun-bleached oyster shells dotting the landscape behind the processing plant.

"My goodness, what do you do with all those shells?" she asked.

"A certain amount are dumped back into the bay to reseed the oyster beds and keep the water environmentally sound. We also sell a fair amount to a paving company in North Carolina and, believe it or not, to a company in Mississippi who uses them to make chicken feed."

Lauren heard the pride of possession in Jonathan's voice as he patiently and knowledgeably answered all of her questions. It surprised her. This well-educated, wealthy man in his well-tailored suits owned what was essentially a very unglamorous processing plant. And was clearly delighted with it. Jonathan might be many things but he certainly wasn't a snob.

The plant manager, Mel, greeted them with a genuine smile and a hearty handshake. He insisted on personally selecting the oysters for them after Jonathan explained about the cooking show. Like a delighted grandmother passing out food at a Thanksgiving feast, Mel kept packing containers of various sizes into plain brown shopping bags. Jonathan and Lauren left carrying three heavy bags each.

"We have time to stop by one of the crab-processing plants, but I think I need to buy a bigger car first," Jonathan remarked as he rearranged the bags in his trunk, trying to fit everything inside.

"Let's save the crabs for another show," Lauren said. She buckled her seat belt. "I noticed several different brand names on the containers of oysters Mel gave us. How many companies do you own?"

"There is only one company, Madison Seafood," Jonathan answered. He gunned the engine and maneuvered the car through the light traffic. "We are a direct wholesaler, selling our products to restaurants and retail stores under our own name, but we also package oysters for our clients under their brand names."

Jonathan turned off the highway and after a few minutes Lauren recognized their route. "Why are we going to your house?"

"I have to refrigerate the haul in my trunk before it spoils," Jonathan answered. "I doubt I could ever get rid of the smell if I let those oysters sit too long in this warm weather."

It was deceptively quiet when they pulled up in front of the beautiful mansion. Lauren barely managed to open the car door and put one foot onto the driveway before Jonathan's dog came bounding down the hill. Greeting them with several high-pitched barks and much tail wagging, Chesapeake circled Lauren energetically.

"Nice doggy." She hesitantly patted the large dog gently on the head. Chesapeake whimpered and crowded against her, practically pinning Lauren to the side of the car. The large retriever was apparently overjoyed at seeing her again.

Jonathan smiled at Lauren. "She likes you." He lifted the shopping bags out of the trunk, and Chesapeake, intrigued by their interesting scent, quickly abandoned Lauren and started prancing around Jonathan.

"Now she likes you," Lauren remarked with a smile.

"There's nothing here for you, Chesapeake," Jonathan insisted in a deep voice. He stretched out his arms and hoisted the bags to shoulder level as Chesapeake danced around his heels and tried to poke her nose inside the shopping bags.

"Actually I think Chesapeake likes you much more than me." Lauren laughed. It looked as though the large dog was going to knock Jonathan off his feet, but he proved too nimble for his pet. Displaying grace, agility and excellent balance, Jonathan jumped, dodged and leaped away from the tongue-lolling dog as they walked up the hill toward the house.

"Would you please grab my house keys, Lauren? If I put the bags down Chesapeake will tear into them. They're in my left front pants' pocket."

"I'll take the bags," Lauren volunteered, knowing there was no way in the world she was going to start poking her hand in Jonathan's pants.

"They're too heavy," Jonathan said. "Ouch, that hurt. Chesapeake, cut it out! You stepped on my foot!"

"I don't believe this," Lauren mumbled. "The man runs a multimillion dollar company and he can't get a dumb dog to listen to him." Lauren took a deep breath. "Hey, Chesapeake, where's your ball? Huh, girl? Where is that gross, disgusting, half-chewed tennis ball? Can you find the ball? Can you bring it to me?"

Chesapeake's ears perked up. Tongue flopping with excitement, she ricocheted her head back and forth between Jonathan and Lauren, clearly torn between the promise of food and the promise of play.

"Come on, Chesapeake, find the ball," Lauren coaxed in an enthusiastic voice. The dog's tail began swishing with interest and after a final, fleeting glance at Jonathan, she took off toward the bushes at a fierce gallop.

Seizing the momentary respite, Lauren pulled the bags away from Jonathan. "Hurry up and open the door. If she finds that ball before we get into the house I might have to touch it again."

Jonathan laughed. "That was great." Lauren handed the bags back to him as they entered the house. Chesapeake streaked passed them, across the hall and out of sight, carrying the tennis ball in her mouth. "I thought you owned a cat. How did you know what to do?"

"Distraction works like a charm with my three-year-old nephew. I figured it was worth a try." Lauren helped Jonathan place the shopping bags on the kitchen counter. "My neighbors smack their dog on the snoot with a rolled-up newspaper, but I think it's petty to strike a defenseless animal. Of course a cat would never have fallen for such a lame trick. They're too smart."

"I've never hit Chesapeake, but I have to confess, there have been times when I was tempted." Jonathan shrugged out of his jacket, threw it casually over a stunning antique chair and loosened his tie. "Is your nephew Eileen's only child?"

"No. Although sometimes I think Michael wishes he didn't have to share his toys and his parent's attention with a little sister." Lauren rotated her shoulders. They felt a bit stiff. "The kids don't always get along, but I'm sure as they grow up they'll start sticking up for each other and learn to present a united front to their parents. Then Eileen and Rob will really have their hands full."

Jonathan cocked his head. "Is that how it was when you and Eileen were younger?"

Lauren laughed. "That's how it is now that Eileen and I are *older*. Like all siblings, we had our rough spots growing up. And there are sections of our teenage years that are best forgotten by my entire family. But today I consider Eileen my best friend. One of the reasons I moved back to Salisburg was so I could be near my sister."

"Family can make your life heaven and hell. All in the same day." Jonathan opened the refrigerator and starting stacking the containers of oysters. Lauren moved forward to help him. "I never minded being an only child when I was a kid. My father had a fairly large extended family and there were always plenty of relatives, young and old, to play and fight with."

"Cousins go home at the end of the day," Lauren remarked as she handed Jonathan a gallon-sized container. "Sisters never leave."

"True." Jonathan shut the refrigerator, then faced Lauren with a philosophical smile. "But siblings can share the parental microscope."

"Having a whiz-kid younger sister who seems to do everything perfectly can wreak havoc on your self-esteem." Lauren methodically folded the empty shopping bags and stacked them neatly on the counter. "I remember my friends going through those world-stopping teenage crises and declaring they wished they'd never been born. I never felt precisely like that. I usually wished I had been born into *another* family."

"That tough, huh?"

"Let's just say a dish of mouthwatering crème brûlée cannot begin to compete with making law review," Lauren said dryly.

"Well, maybe it shouldn't." Jonathan rested his shoulder against the refrigerator door and crossed his arms over his chest. "Personally I think the world would be an awfully dull place if lawyers ran it."

Lauren felt her throat constrict. *How did he do that?* He had this strange almost innate talent for saying exactly what she needed to hear. And he made it so easy for her to talk to him, she found herself blurting out things she never spoke to anyone about. Like her occasional feelings of insecurity and her twinges of jealousy over Eileen.

Lauren's heart started pounding. If she moved closer and lifted her chin, their faces would be separated by only a few short inches. And if she stood up on her toes and leaned forward until his lips were a whisper from her own—

Lauren yanked herself away from her daydreams. Stiffening, she turned away and sat down in one of the ladder-back chairs at Jonathan's kitchen table, needing to place a physical barrier between them. If not, she might react to the shiver of desire shooting through her system and do something totally humiliating. Like attack him.

Lauren viewed the shuddering passion in her stomach and tingling flush of sexual excitement in her chest as warning signs of imminent disaster. It was essential that she somehow avoid falling victim to these feelings.

There was no future in a relationship with Jonathan. Heck there was no present either. For all his decent qualities and major physical attractions, there was still the not so inconsequential matter of trust. Lauren was not so far gone on lust that she couldn't distinguish between what was truly important and what was trivial. Honesty was essential.

"We'd better get started," Lauren said brightly, fighting to hide the feelings of confusion and frustration that were swamping her. "I have to leave soon." She retrieved her purse and removed a pen and small note pad, then flipped to a fresh page. "Let's make a list of your favorite oyster dishes. I'm sure we can find several that would be appropriate for our show."

Lauren could tell from Jonathan's tight expression that the last thing he wanted to discuss was oysters. Her stomach flipped and flopped while she waited for him to answer.

"This list is going to be very short," Jonathan finally said.

"Why?"

He smiled deviously. "Because I never eat oysters. Frankly I just don't like them."

NINE

"How about some lunch?" Jonathan suggested, jumping up from the chair. Lauren seemed a bit stunned, and Jonathan figured a change of subject might help dull the look of dazed alarm in her eyes. "I should have enough lettuce and fresh vegetables to make a decent salad."

"Salad?"

"I like salad. When I was a teenager I ate so many hamburgers my mother swore I said moo every time I opened my mouth. It must have killed my desire for red meat." Jonathan rummaged noisily in the refrigerator. "Salad can be a very substantial meal if you select the right ingredients." He took a foil-wrapped loaf of bread from the freezer and tossed it into the oven. "I usually add a loaf of hot French bread and a stick of butter."

"Very nutritious."

"Works for me."

Jonathan lined up the raw vegetables and lettuce on the butcher-block table his housekeeper always used when she cooked his meals. He placed a large bowl on one side and started cutting, tossing the trimmed vegetables inside. He thought he was doing fine until he noticed Lauren biting her lip.

"You don't know how to cook, do you, Jonathan?"

Her voice was calm, with only a trace of accusation. Jonathan sighed resolutely. "How can you tell?"

"You're chopping that green pepper with a bread knife. And you didn't remove the pepper stem or seeds."

"Oh." Jonathan stifled a groan. He didn't know what to say so he continued chopping. With the wrong knife. But he did wash away some of the seeds and threw the part of the pepper he thought was the stem in the garbage disposal.

He removed the bread from the oven, tossing it nimbly between his fingers to keep from being burned. While cutting the hot loaf, he smashed and mangled most of the pieces, but he hid the worst-looking slices on the bottom of the serving basket.

Jonathan placed the large salad bowl and several different bottles of dressing in the center of the table then poured two tall glasses of iced tea. Lunch was served. He joined Lauren at the table and extended the bread basket toward her. She was ominously silent as she took a piece and placed it on the edge of her plate.

"I didn't expect you to be a pro," Lauren finally said, not unkindly. "I figured you probably had a few favorite dishes you enjoyed making and would feel comfortable preparing them on camera. And I'll admit the idea of having someone appearing on that show with me was appealing. I really wanted to do this, but I felt nervous at the thought of carrying the whole thing myself, especially since I have no experience in the medium.

"I even liked the idea of having you make a seafood dish, while I made the dessert. I thought it would add a nice balance."

Her expression was bland, but the hurt and confusion in her eyes was tearing Jonathan apart. He felt like slime. This wasn't a game to Lauren. This was her future. It was serious business. Hosting a cooking show when you didn't know how to cook *was* a ludicrous notion. Thinking he could force Lauren into teaching him how to make a cheesecake for that ridiculous contest by sponsoring her show was dumb. And selfish.

"Everything is going to work out, Lauren," he said gently. "I promise."

"Yeah, sure. Whatever."

She nodded, making a sound that was partly a laugh and partly a groan. Then, without saying anything else, she picked up her fork and stabbed at her salad.

They ate lunch in uncomfortable silence. Jonathan watched Lauren try to discreetly slip a piece of bread under the table to an eagerly waiting Chesapeake. The dog never left her side, but it wasn't just the promise of food. There was an air of innate kindness about Lauren that even an animal as pigheaded as his dog could sense.

Jonathan took a bite of salad, without tasting it and realized there was no sense kidding himself. He had gotten into this mess because he was drawn to Lauren, not because he cared about winning the cooking contest. And now he had to do everything possible to fix the problem he'd created. He owed her that much.

Jonathan cleared their lunch plates while Lauren remained at the table scribbling notes in her pad. When he finished loading the dishwasher, Lauren stood up.

"I need to get to the coffee shop so I can start cooking for the dinner party I'm catering tonight," Lauren said. "We can discuss the show in the car on the way back to your office."

"Good idea." Jonathan gave the counter top a half-hearted swipe with a damp sponge, flipped the sponge into the sink, then picked up his suit jacket. "Let's go."

He drove much slower than usual, deciding he needed to concentrate more on the conversation than his driving.

Lauren sagged against the headrest. "Originally I thought it might be fun to close the show by tasting the dishes we had just prepared, but that certainly won't work if you don't like the food," Lauren remarked dryly. She took a deep breath, then straightened her spine. "I like the idea of having some sort of signature ending—you know, something we do at the end of each show so people will remember us."

"I agree, on both points. A signature gesture would help make us unique, but it might ruin the effect if I start gagging after taking a bite of my oysters," Jonathan admitted, thrilled to hear the edge of power back in her voice. It hadn't taken Lauren long to regain that feisty determination he admired so much. "Do you like oysters? We could taste each other's dishes and make appropriate, complimentary remarks."

"Forget it." Lauren shook her head emphatically. "I'm not that brave. And I have a big deductible on my medical insurance."

"You ate the salad I made for lunch."

"True. And now I'm going to be picking pepper seeds out of my teeth all afternoon."

His mouth tightened and a muscle twitched in his jaw. She was treating him like a slightly backward kid. "Not everyone is a graduate of the CIA."

"Not everyone co-hosts a cooking show on TV either," Lauren exclaimed. "An insane notion that I feel compelled to point out was your brilliant idea, not mine. How are you going to demonstrate recipes and techniques if you don't know how to cook?"

"I'll keep it simple," Jonathan said. "And short. Very short." He gave Lauren a self-deprecating grin. "Of course you're missing the obvious solution. You can teach me how to cook. I'm good with my hands, and I learn fast."

Lauren muttered a short, sharp word under her

breath. "Maybe I should put up a web site. These days more and more people enjoy using the Internet. I might start generating enough interest in my cooking ideas and recipes to impress a publisher."

Jonathan regarded Lauren with impatience. And a faint edge of panic. If she bailed out of the show, he wouldn't have any reason to see her. Or any opportunity to spend time with her.

"This TV program is going to be great. We just need to put a positive spin on it," Jonathan said in an indignant tone. "We can easily turn my inexperience into an advantage. You'll look more professional when you demonstrate your recipes after people watch me stumbling around the kitchen like an amateur."

"I don't want to look good because you're so bad," Lauren said through clenched teeth.

Jonathan smiled and started to make a flip remark, but after a quick glance at Lauren held his tongue. There was more than a hint of aggression on her pretty face.

They stopped at a red light, and Jonathan heard Lauren blow out her breath. He turned to face her. Lauren's right shoulder was tensely angled against the passenger window, and she looked ready to bolt out of the car. Jonathan prayed it was a quick light.

He wanted to reach over and stroke her arm, but he was afraid she really would jump out if he touched her, so he reluctantly kept his hands to himself.

Lauren was silent for the remainder of the ride, but she came alive the moment Jonathan pulled along side her car.

"George told me he wants to tape our first show the end of next week," Lauren said as she tumbled out of the car. "The show is twenty-six minutes long. You'll do a six-minute presentation, I'll do twenty minutes. Since I'm preparing a dessert, your segment will be first.

"Use the oysters we got today to experiment with recipe ideas and prepare an appetizer or main course or soup, whatever you want. Try to be creative. Make sure you practice and time your presentation before you come to the studio.

"I'll need a detailed copy of your recipe for the screen graphics that will appear during the show and a second copy to send to the company who prints the program guide. Since I strongly doubt your recipe will be an original creation, be sure to credit your source."

Lauren leveled a look at Jonathan that left no doubts as to her seriousness.

"What am I going to cook?"

Lauren narrowed her eyes. "That is entirely up to you. As far as I'm concerned, you're on your own, buster."

The car door slammed shut. She was gone before he could peel his tongue off the roof of his mouth. Panic helped Jonathan finally discover his voice.

"We have to work together if the show is going to be successful," he shouted in a hoarse voice as she flounced away.

Lauren's step never faltered. She got in her car and just for good measure, slammed the door. The temptation to shout at her was almost overwhelming, but he held on tightly to the last remnants of his male pride. Besides, she couldn't hear him anyway.

Jonathan watched her drive away and all of the confidence bolstering his belief that he was capable of pulling this off slowly leaked away.

Man, he had really blown it this time.

Lauren kicked off her shoes and flopped down on the overstuffed couch in her living room.

"Are you sure I'm not keeping you from something

important?" Eileen, seated opposite her on the matching chair, inquired. "I know you're teaching a cooking class tonight. I don't want you to be late."

"I'm always late. The class will have a coronary if I'm on time." Lauren curled her feet up under her legs and regarded her sister skeptically. "Okay, spill it, Eileen. You've asked me three times if you're keeping me from something important, and three times I've told you I have at least a half-hour before I have to get ready for my class. What's up?"

Eileen noisily crumpled the cellophane from a package of gum she'd found on Lauren's coffee table. "I went to a hospital fund-raising committee meeting this afternoon."

"Oh?" Both Eileen's tone and expression sent the alarm bells ringing loudly in Lauren's head. Her sister was acting uncharacteristically nervous and evasive. "I'm not going to like this, am I?"

"Probably not."

"Hold on." Lauren bolted to her feet and traipsed to the kitchen. She returned with a wine bottle and two goblets. Grunting softly with the effort, she worked the already loosened cork free from the bottle, then filled the two glasses she had placed on the coffee table. Eileen silently accepted hers when it was passed over. Lauren took a healthy swig out of her glass before settling back down on the couch. "You were saying?"

Eileen looked down at her lap, then back up at Lauren. "The two major hospital auxiliary spring events are the cooking competition and a silent auction where we browbeat local merchants into donating goods and services."

"I remember." Lauren smiled lightly. "You shanghaied me into donating a romantic dinner for two, with the menu planned by the winner and the dinner cooked and served by me."

"Right." Eileen took a hasty sip of wine. "We held the auction last weekend. Actually your dinner was one of our more profitable items. It definitely generated the most interest among the participates. Which was a huge help, considering that the overall turnout wasn't quite what we had hoped for and ticket sales were low."

"But . . ." Lauren prompted, hearing the hesitation clearly in Eileen's voice.

"Well, as I already said, ticket sales were low, and some of the prizes were downright ridiculous. Janet Parker got the local service station to donate a lube job. Geez how exciting is that, I ask you? Anyway we started getting creative with the prizes, matching some of the donations together to make the items more attractive. It definitely made a difference."

Lauren's brows knotted together. "That shouldn't affect me. You already said that my dinner generated the most interest."

"Yes, yes it did. Especially after Mary Quinn paired your dinner offer with a romantic sailboat ride on the bay." Eileen reached for the wine bottle and refilled both glasses. "Won't that be a terrific evening?"

"It sounds perfect," Lauren replied slowly. "After the couple enjoys my fabulous gourmet meal they're going to take a sailboat ride on the bay. Probably by moonlight. Delightful."

"Well, not exactly." Eileen cleared her throat. "Apparently the sailboat is rather large, so the meal can be cooked and served on the boat."

"While it's moving?" Lauren asked in a horrified voice. Her wineglass tilted as she abruptly stood up and a puddle of rosé spread across the beige carpet. "Please tell me that you're kidding."

"Oh, no, that wine is going to leave a horrible stain." Eileen popped up and raced to the kitchen, returning quickly with a roll of paper towels and a bottle of club soda. She immediately started blotting the stain, attacking it with such fervor that Lauren suspected there was even more disastrous news to follow.

"I think you can stop cleaning my rug, Eileen. You're creating a bald spot." Lauren reached down and yanked Eileen to her feet. "Tell me more about this dinner I have to cook and serve."

Eileen smiled nervously. She paused, not quite meeting Lauren's eyes. "I've already told you. The boat owner will be responsible for sailing the ship. All you have to do is prepare the meal and serve it to the guests. On the boat."

"I don't sail. And I hate the water. Especially salt water. But you already know that." Lauren chomped down on her lip. "Eileen, how could you do this to me?"

"Come on Lauren, it won't be so bad." Eileen walked to the kitchen in search of a trash can with Lauren following closely on her heels. "The couple who won the dinner/sailing prize are the dearest pair. They're going to be celebrating their thirty-fifth wedding anniversary. Isn't that sweet? I met them after the auction, and they are very excited about their prize. You can't disappoint them. Besides they've already paid an obscene amount of money for this little dinner cruise." Eileen's voice drifted away.

"Of course I'll do it," Lauren grumbled, folding her arms and leaning against the door frame. She didn't like it, but she also knew there weren't many options. "I've already made the commitment. But I'll be a lot smarter next time and make sure I know exactly what I'm getting into before I agree to participate in any more of your charity events."

"Thanks so much," Eileen said, heaving an audible sigh of relief. "I knew I could count on you." Eileen washed her hands thoroughly at the kitchen sink. After a second she cleared her throat. "There is one small snag however. The winners are going on an extended cross-country jaunt, and they want to enjoy this little dinner cruise before they leave. Are you free tomorrow?"

Lauren threw up her arms in a gesture of mock annoyance. "Boy you sure don't give a girl much notice. Lucky for you I have a nonexistent social life. I was planning on working on my cookbook tomorrow evening, but if that's the only time to do this dinner, then I suppose my writing will have to wait."

"Great." Eileen perched on the edge of a kitchen chair. Warily Lauren joined her at the table, not liking her sister's jittery, evasive manner. There was an odd light glimmering in Eileen's eye. Something that made Lauren believe there was still more to this dinner fiasco she hadn't yet been told.

Eileen hesitated and then stated brightly. "Oh, and did I also mention that the owner who so generously donated the sailboat cruise is Jonathan Windsor?"

"What!" Lauren's head jerked up so fast she nearly got whiplash.

"Isn't that lucky? Now you won't have to spend the evening with a stranger."

Lauren put her hand over her eyes. "All I can say is that one of us has lost our mind. And it ain't me."

"I don't see what the big deal is," Eileen huffed defensively. "The two of you are already working on a cooking show together. Just think of tomorrow night as another business commitment."

Lauren heaved an exaggerated sigh, then stared hard at Eileen. Deciding her sister didn't look nearly guilty enough, she heaved another, bigger sigh. "I'm trying to avoid spending any more time than is absolutely necessary with Jonathan. I thought you understood that."

Eileen lowered her voice. "What are you trying to deny? That you find him attractive?"

"Of course I find him attractive. I have eyes, don't, I?" Lauren rubbed the back of her neck where the muscles felt like they were knotted into a pretzel. "I'm trying to prove to myself that I am mature enough not to act on these feelings, especially when I know that it's lust, pure and simple. We have no future, Jonathan and I, nor any chance of a future."

"You sound so sad and hopeless," Eileen said quietly. Lauren shot her a thoroughly disgruntled look and Eileen shrugged. "Why must you always concentrate on the negative aspects of a situation?"

"I like being maudlin. It's one of my finer qualities."

Lauren went to the kitchen counter and started fiddling with the coffee machine. She had a good reason to mistrust Jonathan, and she was hanging onto it with her last bit of strength. The exact reason for that couldn't bear much scrutiny, but Lauren decided basking in denial was better for her piece of mind than the alternative.

"How about some coffee?" Lauren poured two cups before her sister could reply and set them on the small kitchen table.

Eileen ignored the mug. "I'm really sorry about all of this," she offered meekly. "I didn't realize the sailboat cruise had been matched up with your dinner until after the prize was won. It was too late to change anything."

"I know it's not your fault. Exactly." Lauren propped her elbows on the table and cradled her forehead in the palm of her hands. "All I want to know is, why me? Why do these things always happen to me? They never happen to you." She lifted her head and gave her sister a searing look of outrage.

"It's not fair," Lauren continued. "Your life is nearly

perfect, so well organized and controlled. You're a first-class attorney, you have a terrific husband who adores you, two darling children, one boy and one girl, who are normal and healthy and as a bonus happen to be beautiful too. I want to switch. I'm tired of always being the one catching all the bad breaks. I want my life to be a whole lot more like yours and a whole lot less like mine."

Lauren looked at her sister with envy, gradually becoming aware of the vulnerability showing on Eileen's face.

"What a bunch of crap!" Eileen shook her head. "You have really done a number on yourself, haven't you, big sister? My life is perfect. Hah! What a joke! I think you need a healthy dose of reality, so I'm going to tell you exactly how this first-class attorney spent her perfect, well-organized and controlled morning with her two, one boy and one girl, beautiful children.

"I dragged my two darling children, who were whining and cranky, to the grocery store because we were out of diapers and milk and juice and bread and other essential food items.

"And while I'm standing in the frozen-food aisle, debating over which flavor ice cream to buy, I literally bump into Susan Jenkins. Do you remember Susan? We graduated law school the same year, even competed for a few of the same jobs after graduation. I remember feeling so triumphant when the firm selected me instead of her. A major professional accomplishment. But that was five years ago. Times have changed and Susan, who is single and childless, recently made partner at her law firm.

"So here I am, standing next to the perfectly groomed Susan, who looks like a professional *Vogue* model in her white designer power suit. I, on the other hand, am wearing a pair of Rob's baggy sweatpants because I haven't done the laundry all week and don't have any clean clothes of my own. Susan and I try to make the usual polite chitchat, but it becomes obvious fairly soon into the conversation that we have very little to talk about after exhausting the fascinating topic of the weather."

Lauren couldn't help herself. She started laughing.

"It wasn't funny," Eileen protested, but she smiled too. "At this point Susan looks in my shopping cart and smiles when she sees my two darling children. Remember, one boy and one girl? Ashley is a grinning, drooling little doll, with a smeared-cookie face. Beautiful. Michael, who is wearing last year's too-small Halloween costume because I lacked the energy to argue his choice of wardrobe for twenty minutes before we left the house, is a boy with an attitude. A bad attitude.

"He's mad at me because I won't let him open a second box of cookies. But, hey, since it's only nine-thirty in the morning and he's already polished off most of the first box, I figure I've got to stand firm on at least this one issue.

"Anyway, Susan tries to make friends with the children, and Michael responds by folding his arms across his chest, huffing in annoyance and turning his back. Typical male behavior. Embarrassed by my bratty kid I start making lame excuses like he's tired, hungry, high on sugar—whose fault is that? I wonder—and he's been brainwashed by extraterrestrials. Susan gives me a weak, doubting smile, but is willing to play along."

"Oh, Michael's not that bad," Lauren interjected.

"Of course he is," Eileen replied. "You don't spend enough time with him to fully appreciate how obstinate he can be." Eileen sipped her coffee, then smiled. "Getting back to my wonderful morning, Susan next shifts her attention to Ashley, my pride and joy, and I hastily start wiping the mess off the baby's face with a rather small, rumpled tissue I dig out of my pocket. I'm so busy trying to make my child look beautiful that I don't notice Ashley grasping for the shiny gold accent buttons on the sleeves of Susan's very white suit jacket.

"Next thing I know, Susan turns to me with a horrified expression on her face, mumbles something about being late for an important meeting and rushes out of the store. As she disappears down the aisle I can clearly see Ashley's perfectly formed chocolate fingerprints trailing down Susan's sleeve."

"Oh, Eileen, what a nightmare!" Lauren struggled to hold back another giggle. "Still, it wasn't your fault Susan overreacted. Ashley's a baby for goodness' sake."

Eileen shook her head. "You haven't heard the best part. Two hours after I get home Susan calls. I immediately apologized and offered to have her suit dry cleaned, but she insisted it was no big deal and then she started apologizing like crazy to me for leaving the store so abruptly. Apparently the man she's living with keeps talking abut getting married and starting a family, but Susan's been making excuses and putting him off because she wanted to make partner so badly. Spending just a few minutes with me and my children somehow emphasized the lack of family in Susan's life. She left the store so quickly because she felt overcome with emotion."

Lauren rolled her eyes. "What are you trying to tell me, Eileen. None of us are really happy with the roles we choose? Is all of womankind doomed to unhappiness, envy and bouts of emotional melancholy? Is Dad right when he lectures, 'The grass is always greener on the other side of the fence'?"

Eileen grinned. "I'm not sure about Dad and the grass, but I do know that there are way too many times you compare yourself to me and somehow find yourself lacking. Remember the time you came to visit me after

Michael was born and I was crying like a lunatic because the baby book said he should be sleeping longer at night?"

"Vaguely."

"Well, I remember it. What a horrible time. I was so overwhelmed by motherhood. I felt totally unprepared, and every chapter I read in that book made me feel more and more inadequate." Eileen sighed. "You gave me the best advice I've ever received that afternoon, Lauren. You told me to throw the book away."

Lauren smiled. "Now I remember. Michael was doing fine, but reading that book was making you miserable."

"Exactly. So now I'm going to return the favor. Follow your own advice, Lauren. Throw away the book, and stop being so hard on yourself. You are a really terrific person with many talents and many accomplishments. And problems. Just like me. You want to switch lives? Great. Just be prepared for a day like I had this morning 'cause that's typical."

Lauren's expression softened. Her sister was right. For too long she had been unfavorably comparing herself to Eileen's achievements and inevitably falling short. She needed to make a conscious effort to change her attitude. In the end it would be beneficial to both of them.

As for her evening with Jonathan, well, she'd just have to make the best of it. Lauren considered the possibilities. The kitchen on his boat obviously had to be inside the cabin somewhere, and if he was steering the boat he would naturally be outside so she really wouldn't have to spend much time with him. And this charming couple that Eileen seemed so enthused about would be on the boat too, so she wouldn't be alone with him.

If she kept her cool and did her job, she should manage to get through the evening without making a fool of herself, Lauren decided.

"Okay, Eileen you win the worst day of the week award. For today." Lauren's grin was skeptical as she thought about spending a whole evening with Jonathan on his sailboat. "I just hope I can somehow avoid winning this dubious honor tomorrow."

TEN

The sailboat listed suddenly to one side. Lauren gave an undignified yelp and clutched at the shiny chrome rail with both hands.

"If you plant your feet firmly on the deck you can shift your weight and easily retain your balance when the boat rocks," Jonathan called out.

"Easy for you maybe, Captain Bligh," Lauren retorted. "I don't enjoy water unless it's in my bathtub." She crouched down, wrapped her arm around the rail and hung on for dear life. "You know, Jonathan, I've never been on a sailboat. And I'm a terrible swimmer. Shouldn't I be wearing a life vest?"

Jonathan stared at her. "The boat is moored to the dock. If some freak accident occurs and you manage to fall overboard, I promise I'll throw you a line."

Lauren lifted an eyebrow. "I fail to see how holding on to the end of a rope will prevent me from drowning."

She tried to sound haughty, but doubted she achieved the desired effect. It was rather difficult to appear aloof and unconcerned when you were clinging like a half-wit to the rail of a boat. A stationary boat.

"Why don't you come to the stern of the boat and sit at the helm with me?" Jonathan suggested. "The Spencers—that lucky couple who won this fabulous prize—won't be arriving for quite a while. They want to capture every moment of this magical evening on film so they're sending a photographer to take pictures. He wants to scope out the location and take a few shots before the Spencers get here. If you move about the boat for a while, maybe you'll feel more comfortable having your picture taken."

"No thanks. I'm fine right here."

Lauren nervously repositioned her death grip on the rail and turned to stare at Jonathan. He was pulling and adjusting several ropes, she remembered he called them *rigging*. The muscles in his forearms tightened and swelled as he twisted the lines around a metal bar, then knotted it. Dressed in a navy blue polo shirt, stark white shorts and docksiders without socks he looked good enough to eat.

He moved with the grace and power of a natural athlete. As far as Lauren could tell he was doing an awful lot of hard work and barely breathing hard. Or sweating. Impressive.

She wasn't usually attracted to athletic men since she was such a dismal athlete herself. In fact, she had always been smugly satisfied to have been named the high-school senior with the greatest number, and most imaginative, reasons for needing to be excused from gym class.

Yet watching Jonathan's straining muscles was having a definite effect on her libido. The shorts he was wearing were sinfully sexy, displaying finely muscled thighs and calves that were tan beneath the covering of golden hair. Lauren couldn't seem to drag her eyes away from them.

She pressed her hand to her rapidly beating heart and tried to convince herself that nerves from being on this floating death trap were causing all the excitement in her chest. When that excuse didn't hold water,

Lauren tried reminding herself that she was completely out of her depth, physically and emotionally when it came to Jonathan Windsor.

That thought steadied her until Jonathan turned her way. He smiled briefly, and Lauren could feel her hands getting sweaty. *He was just so damn gorgeous.* Tall, handsome, self-assured. With an abundance of charm and a dash of good humor. Every woman's fantasy come to life.

Jonathan continued moving across the deck of the boat with the fluid efficiency of a mountain cat, each step bringing him closer. Lauren drew in a deep breath. Only fear of falling off the boat prevented her from backing up.

"What's the matter?" he asked when he reached her side. "Did I get some dirt on my shorts?"

"There isn't a speck of dirt anywhere on you." Lauren cleared her throat. "Why would you ask me that?"

Jonathan's eyes twinkled with humor. "You were staring at my shorts. Intensely."

"I was blinded by their whiteness," Lauren remarked dryly, determined to conquer the rush of adrenaline his nearness brought on.

It was bad enough her unnatural fear of the water was making her act like a spastic fool. She was not about to let herself get pulled in by his effortless charm and good looks and start fawning over him like every other female within a fifty-mile radius. *She* at least had some pride.

"The photographer has arrived," Jonathan announced.

Lauren noticed a skinny young man hurrying down the wooden planks of the private dock. He was balancing a cumbersome black case, a folded tripod and a notebook in his arms. An expensive-looking camera with an obscenely large lens dangled from a strap around his neck.

Jonathan jumped lithely onto the dock, then turned expectantly to Lauren.

She smiled weakly. "I'll just wait here."

His mouth quirked, but he mercifully accepted her decision without comment. Or ridicule. After a brief conference with the photographer, Jonathan returned to the boat with a grim expression on his face.

"What's wrong?"

"Nothing." Jonathan leaped onto the boat, steadying himself on a long rope as he swung over the chrome rail. "This guy is kind of peculiar. He has a list a mile long of different shots and poses to take of us. And he wants you to change into long white pants, a white starched high-necked jacket and one of those tall pleated hats that chefs wear. He even brought the outfit with him. He told me it was in his car."

Lauren blanched. "Are you kidding? We had to dress in those getups in cooking school, especially when we were preparing a special menu. They are the most unflattering outfits imaginable. When I put one on my resemblance to the Pillsbury doughboy is frankly both uncanny and a bit frightening. I'm not wearing that stuff."

"Don't worry. I already told him we wouldn't do it."

"We?"

Jonathan blushed. "The photographer brought white dress slacks, a navy blazer and a nautical cap for me. The Pillsbury doughboy sounds like a step up compared to me looking like Thurston Howell the Third in my outfit."

"I always liked *Gilligan's Island,*" Lauren remarked with a teasing grin.

"Watch it, doughboy."

Lauren laughed.

The photographer approached the sailboat, and Lauren quickly stifled her laughter. He briskly introduced himself and immediately began fussing over them. He heaved a few long sighs and complained several times about the low angle of the sun. Neither Lauren nor Jonathan said a word.

Finally he positioned them at the boat's helm alongside the highly polished wooden wheel. After checking the light with his meter, he began snapping away. Lauren didn't bother to hide her smile when Jonathan politely but firmly refused the photographer's second request for a wardrobe change.

The photographer shouted instructions and they dutifully posed. It was boring, and it was starting to get hot when they paused for a break. Lauren quickly downed half a bottle of water, then, deciding she needed to refresh her makeup, bravely ventured to the fore of the boat. As she tried to comb and repin her windblown hair, she was startled to feel an ominous motion beneath her feet.

"Jonathan, the boat is moving!"

There was no verbal response as the boat continued to drift away from the dock. Fearful that her terrified yell had been swallowed up in the wind, Lauren gripped the rail and hand over hand started working her way cautiously toward the stern of the boat. She kept her eyes locked on her fingers and tried to ignore the panicked voice inside her that screamed, *Oh my God, what am I going to do now?*

Eventually she reached her goal, sagging with relief when she saw Jonathan. For one crazy minute she had feared she was alone on the runaway boat.

He took one look at her and smiled. "Relax," he said calmly, his arm resting casually on the spokes of the wooden wheel. "The photographer wants to take a few shots of us with open water in front of the boat. It's more dramatic."

"Uh-huh." Lauren bit her lip.

"We don't have to go out very far," Jonathan insisted. "Actually I'm not even going to clear the cove."

"Terrific." Since her only other option was jumping over the side and trying to swim to the dock, Lauren plopped down opposite Jonathan. At least she was close enough that if she fell over he could rescue her. That is, if he decided she was worth getting wet over.

The breeze caught her hair, blowing it free of the pins she had carefully secured it with moments ago. She put up her hand to catch the wild curls and rescue the hair clips, hastily stuffing them in the pocket of her shorts.

"It's a fairly windy day," Lauren remarked. She took a few short, choppy breaths and watched the shoreline slowly recede. "I thought the boat would move faster."

"I haven't let out the sails," Jonathan explained. "We're currently moving under engine power."

"Isn't that cheating?"

"Not if it gets you where you want to go."

The boat glided effortlessly through the water. She watched intently as Jonathan expertly guided it through a narrow channel that led to the cove he'd mentioned. Lauren lifted her hand to her forehead to block the sun from her eyes.

Even though it was late afternoon, the glare off the bay was nearly blinding. She thought longingly of the sunglasses nestled inside her purse on the opposite side of the boat, but prudently decided it would be wise to wait until they stopped moving before attempting to retrieve them.

"Watch out for the boom!"

"What?"

Jonathan's reflexes were so fast Lauren barely had

time to be frightened. He reached up and caught the long wooden pole that swung ominously toward her before it had a chance to bang into her shoulder. But while saving her from being attacked by that lethal weapon, he inadvertently threw her off balance.

"Ahhhh . . ." With a startled cry she toppled and rolled completely over, landing squarely on her rear. All the blood rushed from her head, and for the first time in her life Lauren thought she might faint.

"Are you okay?"

Lauren blinked several times and everything slowly came into focus. The blue sky, the white clouds, the blue-green sea. And Jonathan's handsome face filled with concern.

"What happened?"

"It was all my fault. I didn't notice the boom swing around until it was almost too late."

"The boom?"

Jonathan pounded the top of the wooden pole. "The boom. It's attached to the mast and the bottom of the mainsail. It swings back and forth when the boat turns. And if it hits you, you go boom."

Lauren shook her head to clear the cobwebs, then gazed blindly out to sea. "All these quaint nautical terms are starting to give me a headache."

"Sailing sometimes has that effect on people."

"I believe it," Lauren remarked grimly. She rubbed her temples furiously, although they were hardly the part of her anatomy that was aching the most.

"Are you sure you're not hurt?" Jonathan crouched on one knee beside her and ran his hands experimentally across her shoulders. She suppressed the wild impulse to cuddle next to his solid, safe, male warmth.

"I'm fine," Lauren insisted. He was so close she could see the flecks of gold highlighting the green of his eyes. He smelled of sun and citrus cologne and salty sea air.

If she tilted her head just a fraction, she could press her lips against his throat and taste this exotic aroma.

Lauren closed her eyes and turned away. Hoping to regain her equilibrium, she concentrated wholly on the sounds around her: the hard slapping of the waves against the hull, the shrill cries of the sea gulls echoing over the water, the crisp flapping of the flag that was raised above the mast.

"Lauren?"

She reopened her eyes. The warm hand on her shoulder began moving, and she felt a thumb lightly caress her bare neck. A tremor went through her. Lauren fought to calm herself, hoping desperately that Jonathan hadn't noticed her physical reaction. She nonchalantly hugged her fluttering stomach. The slight rocking motion of the boat intensified her queasiness. Or perhaps it was her proximity to so much gorgeous masculine charm.

"I'm not hurt," Lauren insisted in a strained voice. "Just humiliated."

Jonathan was mere inches from contact with her breasts. If she turned at all, they would collide. The thought brought on another bout of lighthearted giddiness. With effort, Lauren held herself rigid.

"You look awfully pale. Are you sure you didn't bruise or sprain anything?"

Lauren winced. "Trust me, I have plenty of padding where I fell the hardest."

Jonathan grinned. "I think we've gone out far enough. I'll drop anchor so we can finish taking these silly pictures." He swiped at some imaginary dirt on his shorts as he rose.

Lauren heard the anchor hit the water with a big splash. Jonathan moved confidently around the large deck of the boat, adjusting, pulling, untying and tying ropes. Lauren slowly stood, then took a step backward to stay out of his way and admire the view. Of him.

Finally he unfurled two huge sails, and the gusting wind puffed them into majestic white clouds.

"I hope we don't have to stay out on the water very long." Lauren cast Jonathan a sly glance. She was starting to recover from her less than graceful fall and decided a bit of retribution was in order. "With all this dipping and bobbing my stomach might turn queasy. I'd be so embarrassed if I got sick all over your nice white shorts. Then you'd have to change into that darling outfit the photographer brought with him."

"Hey, I'm the captain of this ship. If you upchuck on me, I'll make you walk the plank." Mischief sparkled in his eyes. "Naked."

She yelped loudly as he pulled her toward the center of the boat. At his touch her skin became hot and clammy at the same time. A lazy smile hovered at the edges of his mouth.

Lauren's cheeks flamed, and the tension in her chest changed to excited anticipation. Wild erotic fantasies suddenly filled her head. Hot, sweaty, nude bodies; tense, hard, straining muscles; uncontrolled, wild, fiery passion; golden, forbidden, rugged pirates. *Pirates?* Good Lord the sun must be starting to fry her brain.

"Where should we stand?" Lauren asked breathlessly, deciding the sooner she planted her feet on solid, firm ground the safer she would be.

"Let's pose here." Jonathan hauled her to his side and draped a possessive arm around her waist. "Don't forget to smile."

Lauren turned toward the photographer positioned on the dock and smiled stiffly, certain she must look like an idiot. Jonathan mugged unselfconsciously for the camera, and she couldn't help but notice how his dazzling white smile was nearly as bright as the sun.

Fortunately he seemed unaware of the covert looks she kept sneaking his way.

Finally it was over. At a dismissive wave from the photographer Jonathan released his hold on Lauren.

"Let's go for a sail," Jonathan suggested with an all-encompassing glance that turned Lauren's cheeks red.

"I'd prefer going back to the dock," Lauren insisted. "I've done all the prep work and partial cooking of tonight's dinner, but I need to unpack the food coolers and familiarize myself with the kitchen. You do have a kitchen on this thing, right?"

"It's called a galley."

"A galley," Lauren dutifully repeated. *Great. More nautical terms.* "Where is it?"

"Can't you stop thinking about work for one minute?" Jonathan asked in an exasperated voice.

"I'd prefer not to make an idiot of myself later tonight," Lauren retorted. "In case you haven't noticed I'm having a bit of trouble standing upright on this floating booby trap."

He grinned and an irresistible dimple appeared in his cheek. "We won't sail too far. It'll give you a chance to find your sea legs."

With a smile that was full of charm and promise Jonathan set the boat in motion. She watched him as he masterfully took control of the large craft, guiding it carefully past the few smaller boats that were anchored in the cove.

She shaded her eyes with her arm and gazed along the hilly shore, catching an occasional glimpse of a rooftop through the dense trees. Except for an impressive-looking yacht moored at a private dock and bobbing merrily, there wasn't much to look at except water. Lots and lots of water.

All too quickly they cleared the tranquil cove and headed for open water. Lauren twisted her hands together. She really should insist they return to the dock immediately, but the longer she waited to voice her objection the more reluctant she felt to do so.

Jonathan was right. She did work too hard. And it would be smart to learn how to balance herself on this floating monstrosity before she had to serve an elegant dinner. Who knows how much damage she could cause trying to serve hot food?

No sooner had the thought entered Lauren's head than the boat dipped through a wave and her footing slipped. She grasped a nearby rope and managed to sit instead of fall down on a low bench built against the side of the boat. Jonathan appeared to be too busy navigating their course to notice her mishap.

She moved experimentally on the cushion beneath her and realized it was, as the airline flight attendants always said, a flotation devise. She pulled a second cushion from the end of the bench and positioned it behind her shoulders. Leaning gingerly against the sturdy rail of the boat, Lauren discovered it was strong enough to support her weight.

After deciding she was in no immediate danger of drowning, she shrugged philosophically, settled herself more comfortably against the cushions and stared down at the water. She held on tightly to the rail, just in case, but quickly became fascinated by the sight and sound of the whitecapped waves crashing against the boat as they glided through the bay.

Gradually she began to relax. The synchronized slapping of the waves and rhythmic rocking of the boat created an almost hypnotic trance. Her head swayed in cadence with the waves, and she started drifting away into daydreams.

She smiled and lifted her face toward the sun, realizing that sailing could actually be an enjoyable way to spend an afternoon. The speed of the boat, the wind in her hair, the salty sea mist in her face gave her a feeling of reckless abandon.

All too soon Jonathan maneuvered the boat into a secluded inlet. He adjusted the sails and dropped anchor.

"Why did we stop?" Lauren turned lazily in his direction. She felt bonelessly relaxed. "Did you run out of gas?"

"No engines this time, just the power of nature." Jonathan's mouth twisted into a wry smile. "Wind."

"Right, skipper." Lauren gave him a jaunty salute and wiggled back against the cushions of her makeshift lounge chair. She stretched out her legs, crossing them at the ankles. The glowing rays of the sinking sun felt delightful on her bare calves. With a sigh of pleasure, she took a deep breath of moist sea air.

It really was beautiful out on the water. The sky was a brilliant blue, the sea a calm sheet of deep green glass. She could faintly make out the shoreline in the distance, a solid brown etched on the horizon. For the first time in her life Lauren felt a true connection with nature. It was so serene, so utterly peaceful.

"Do you like it out here?" Jonathan's deep voice broke in, but didn't disturb the quiet.

"It's magnificent," Lauren replied enthusiastically. "It certainly gives us a humbling perspective of our importance in the world."

She gazed over at him. He was standing at the helm, one arm casually resting over the top of the ship's wheel and one muscular leg propped against the sparkling chrome rail. And he was staring. Directly at her.

The atmosphere on the boat began to subtly change, and an undercurrent of tension started slowly building.

Lauren's breathing increased as the languid haze engulfing her brain began clearing and a few salient facts registered in her mind. She was alone at sea with two hundred pounds of irresistible male and a strange fluttering deep in her stomach that she knew was not caused by seasickness. It was desire. And it was a definite threat to her sanity.

Flustered, Lauren struggled awkwardly to her feet. Anxious to break the mood, she racked her brain for a neutral topic of conversation. Humor. A good laugh usually diffuses tension. Yet for some bizarre reason all that came to mind were some not so amusing dirty jokes!

"I'm really glad you like sailing on my boat," Jonathan said quietly.

Lauren smiled vaguely, suspecting her voice would sound ridiculously fluttery if she attempted to speak. What was wrong with her? More importantly, where was that barrier of outrage and anger that always kept Jonathan at a distance in spite of the tremendous physical attraction she felt?

That apparently, Lauren admitted to herself, had been left back on dry land. Here in the gently swaying surf, her confused feelings were brought on by doubt. Had she been wrong about Jonathan's character? In her heart she had difficulty reconciling this sexy, charming man with the dishonest looter who had unscrupulously stolen her hard work.

One thing she did clearly understand was that when confined in this small space, Jonathan's powerful male presence was impossible to ignore. He shifted the position of his leg, and her breath caught. He must have heard the sound because he next gave her a look of such naked longing that Lauren knew the tightly coiled watchfulness inside him had finally snapped.

Jonathan stood gracefully and moved toward her with a deep sense of purpose glittering in his eyes. Lauren could hear a roaring in her ears. It sounded like the ocean, pounding surf against the sand, but that wasn't possible. She was standing on a boat in the middle of a very calm bay.

The noise got louder as he approached. She gasped when he reached her and opened her mouth to protest, but it was too late. He bent his head, laced his fingers into her hair and kissed her.

The touch of his warm lips robbed her of speech. *My God that felt good. Better than good. Perfect.* Soft and warm and delicate. Her senses whirled. She wanted more. Lauren leaned into him, adjusting her lips across his and deepening the kiss. She moved her body against him, rubbing her breasts against his chest, her pelvis against his hard thighs.

Her heart was tripping wildly. She had spent so many hours denying her attraction and too many nights dreaming of him to actually believe this was finally happening.

He held her close against his chest, and she felt her feet being swept out from under her. Jonathan went down with her, breaking the fall with his hard body.

"Gotcha," he whispered wickedly in her ear.

He moved again so that his body was pressed tightly against hers. She could feel the hard deck beneath her back and shoulders. He dipped his head and sealed her lips with another hot kiss.

An insistent raw primitive emotion spurred Lauren on. She could taste his desire on his lips, and an uncontrollable need rushed through her. She ran her hands along the shifting muscles of his arms and chest, massaging him with long slow strokes. She could feel his heat and the hardness of his arousal against her belly.

Lauren absorbed that heat. It released the last of her defenses and fed her passion. Freed now, she wanted nothing more than to feel and explore that passion.

She squirmed, pressing her thigh between his legs, slid down, then up, provocatively stroking his turgid flesh.

She heard him groan, hoarse and urgent. His hand closed over her blouse. He unbuttoned some of it, then impatiently ripped away the rest, exposing her heated flesh to his hungry mouth. She shivered as his fingers slid to her neck, gliding sensually down her throat and chest and coming to rest on the lacy top of her bra.

Trembling, she helped him find the bra clasp, sighed with delight when he freed her breasts. He groaned as they spilled into his hands. Greedily he drew the soft flesh into his mouth, flicking his tongue repeatedly over the nipples, until they grew hard.

She tensed when his hand slipped to the zipper of her shorts, but his touch was gentle and smooth despite his urgent need. Lauren whispered his name and shifted slightly, subtly encouraging him. She moaned softly when he pulled off her shorts completely, dragging her underwear with them. Deep inside she knew it was wrong, knew she should stop, but she selfishly lacked the control to put an end to such bliss.

The intensifying ache spread through her as his fingers stroked the springy curls that covered her sex. Wanting to feel more of him, Lauren clutched a fistful of Jonathan's shirt in her hand and yanked it over his head. Thrilled to finally make contact with his naked flesh, she swept her hand appreciatively over his bare, muscular chest. He felt hard and satiny smooth. She nipped playfully at one brown nipple with her teeth and felt the tremor go through him.

"A condom," Jonathan said in a husky voice. He dropped his head and fastened his lips over her naked breast.

His words barely registered in her mind. Light swirled behind her tightly shut eyes, and she arched herself closer. Lauren shifted restlessly and felt the sensual wave of desire building between them.

Jonathan pulled back suddenly, releasing her swollen nipple. She cried out softly in frustration. *Not now. I was so close.* Sighing, Lauren sagged against him, resting her face in the side of his neck. Her breathing was harsh and shallow. Apparently the lack of oxygen was also affecting her brain. Had Jonathan just said condom? How romantic.

Lauren lifted her head.

"I don't have a condom." Jonathan laughed, but he didn't seem very amused. His breathing was as swift and erratic as hers, and his voice sounded strained and tight. "Do you?"

"Of course not," Lauren croaked. She struggled to sit up as reality started seeping into her passion-fogged consciousness. She was sprawled half-naked on the deck of a sailboat out in the middle of the Chesapeake Bay.

"I don't suppose you have any other form of birth control handy?" Jonathan asked.

Lauren stared at him.

"Didn't think so." He had the gall to grin at her. "Guess we'll have to be a little creative."

Lauren decided she didn't like his tone. But there was hardly time to dwell on it. She felt the coarseness of his clean-shaven jaw against her cheek; then his mouth brushed lightly against her temple.

His touch was gentle and strong. He placed a nibbling kiss behind her ear, then another on her throat. He pressed his mouth to first one and then the other corner of hers. His tongue softly outlined her lips, and she parted them. She felt his tongue lightly stroke the edge of her teeth. Lauren shivered. All thoughts of protest vanished.

She slowly reclined onto the deck of the boat. Her hands slid over his shoulders and back. She inhaled the scent of Jonathan's expensive aftershave, and a tide of wanton longing washed over her. Her body was sensitized and aware of his every touch.

This could go nowhere. For several reasons, but most importantly because they did not have the necessary protection to proceed.

"We should stop," Lauren whispered weakly.

"Mmmm." Jonathan bent his head and kissed her navel.

"No, really, we should stop."

He swirled his tongue on her ribs, then moved lower. His mouth was hot against her belly. "Oh, Jonathan I really don't think we should—"

Her hands pushed ineffectively on his shoulders. He kissed her inner thigh, then reached up and curled his fingers over hers.

"Hush," he commanded softly. "We can't make love properly without protection, but there's no need for both of us to be frustrated."

He returned to his task, nuzzling his soft lips against her belly. Lauren heard a low moan and realized it came from her. He continued to press long, hot kisses to her sensitive flesh, and her senses became fully alive, registering each loving caress with anticipatory excitement.

She turned off the puritanical, inhibited part of her brain and allowed herself to become swept up in the sheer passion, the totally natural beauty of the act. Her body quivered with each brush of his lips, each gentle probe of his tongue, until the sensation became almost painful. She twisted as her pulse thundered in her ears, the constant pressure of his lips and tongue driving her to near madness.

She was hot, slick and vulnerable, trusting him totally to bring her release. And he did not disappoint. Just when it became nearly unbearable, a burst of heat exploded inside her.

Lauren couldn't control the strangled cry that rose to her lips as wave after wave of pleasure jolted through her. She shuddered and gasped. Jonathan held onto her as the tension slowly drained out of her, and she closed her heavy-lidded eyes.

Lauren's breathing eventually steadied. As she drifted slowly back to earth she gradually became aware of her surroundings. Cradled in Jonathan's arms, she could feel the tension in his muscular thighs, the tightness of his erection straining against his shorts. She glanced up at his face. His eyes were shut, his expression rigid.

"Perhaps I should . . ." She began lightly stroking his hardness.

Jonathan's eyes shot open. He reached down and closed his hand over hers.

"Don't worry about me," he said tightly, pulling her hand away. "I get my pleasure from pleasing you."

Lauren's eyes widened. In her experience men were seldom that generous. Especially when it came to sex.

Jonathan and Lauren considered each other.

"It must be getting late." Lauren broke the awkward silence and licked her lips nervously. They felt a bit raw. "We had better return to the dock. I'm sure the Spencers will expect us to be waiting for them."

"There's no rush." Jonathan gently rubbed her bare shoulder. "The Spencers called me just before you arrived. They had to cancel the dinner cruise. That's why they sent the photographer. They wanted pictures of the boat to show their grandchildren."

"What!" Lauren pulled angrily out of his embrace. "Why didn't you tell me this before?"

Jonathan shrugged. "I wanted you to come sailing with me, and I figured the moment you knew the Spencers weren't going to be here, you'd bolt."

"So you thought you'd trick me into taking a ride with you? How nice."

Lauren felt like sobbing. She pulled her gaping blouse together. Her fingers were trembling. Not only from anger, but from a deep sense of betrayal. *What had she done?*

"I'm sorry," he said with quiet puzzlement. "I never imagined you would get this upset."

"I'm not upset. I'm angry." Lauren's throat tightened. "I hate it when people lie to me, Jonathan."

"Of course. So do I."

She felt his lips brush gently as a feather against her temple. Her eyes filled with guilty tears. Perhaps if she had been standing on solid ground instead of swaying sensually on this sinful boat, she might have been able to resist the romantic magic of the moment. But now it was too late.

"I want to go home." Lauren sniffed.

"Can't we at least have dinner first?"

"No." She hastily pulled on the rest of her clothing. This was embarrassing enough without being half-naked before him. "I couldn't possibly eat a thing."

"Can we discuss this? Calmly?"

"No." It was impossible. She was far too confused and emotional to discuss anything right now. Besides, what was there to say? He liked to lie, and she wouldn't tolerate it. End of discussion. "I want to go home."

Lauren flinched when she saw the trace of unhappiness in Jonathan's eyes. Despite everything, it hurt to know she was responsible for it.

He sighed heavily. "Whatever you want."

Lauren was shaken by the gruffness of his voice. She wanted to reach out and comfort him, but she knew that was insane. She was mad at him. And rightfully so.

She remained perfectly still while he hauled up the anchor and set the boat in motion. Darkness had completely fallen, but the bright light of the moon and several strong running lights on the boat guided their journey.

They motored back to the shore in utter silence, the mood on the boat heavy and somber.

Jonathan cut the engine as they made the approach to the dock. It too was lit with twinkling white lights. Lauren might have appreciated the fairy-tale beauty if she weren't so miserable.

All was silent and still except for the gentle lapping of the waves against the solid hull of the boat. Jonathan politely held Lauren's hand as she jumped off the boat. Her eyes welled with unexpected tears.

"I brought the food in disposable styrofoam coolers that I don't need. They're stored at the front of the boat. You can eat the food if you want. Or throw it out. It doesn't matter."

"Okay."

She fought to keep her nerves steady as they walked to her car. The air seemed oppressive, and all she could think about was escape. Lauren fumbled with her car keys, but once she unlocked the door, Jonathan swung her around to face him. He took her firmly by the upper arms, lifted her off her feet and gave her a hard, passionate kiss. It left her breathless.

"See you later, Lauren."

Then he turned and walked away before she had a chance to even consider a reply.

ELEVEN

"It was the sexual attraction. That's what really screwed up my head."

Jonathan flopped down on the couch in his den next to Chesapeake and poured out his troubles to his uninterested dog.

"I should have walked away from Lauren the first time I met her at the pastry shop. She made it perfectly clear she had no interest in me. But uncontrollable carnal thoughts, visions of creamy, smooth flesh and mind-blowing kisses overwhelmed my judgment."

Jonathan rubbed Chesapeake's furry head absently. "It got worse each time I saw her. I don't understand why. She isn't close to being the type of woman with whom I always imagined I would invest my time and emotions. She's certainly attractive enough and intelligent and has an offbeat sense of humor that I enjoy.

"But she also hides behind large plants at parties, walks into waiters and makes Mother's hair practically stand on end every time they meet." Jonathan laughed. "Truthfully I get a charge out of watching Mother's reaction to Lauren, but that is not the point."

Jonathan pulled on the dog's ears, and Chesapeake tipped her head lazily in his direction.

"I have a date tonight. Spending time with other

women will cure me of this odd obsession I've developed for Lauren."

Chesapeake yawned and stretched out her hind legs.

"I can see you have some doubts," Jonathan said. "Well, so do I, but I have to try something. I acted like some crazed, oversexed teenager on the sailboat yesterday. It was disgusting. Lauren was really upset.

"And don't get me started on the cooking show. It was that fiasco that made me realize I'm capable of causing her real hurt. She wants a professional relationship, and that is what we are going to have. It is the only civilized solution."

But how could he so easily dismiss the depth of physical pleasure he felt when he touched Lauren? Kissed Lauren? And how could he simply ignore the emotional connection they shared, even though it appeared they both wanted desperately to ignore it?

It was the ignoring part that probably irritated Jonathan the most. Just when things started getting interesting with Lauren, she deliberately distanced herself from him. It was damned annoying, mostly because he didn't have a clue why she did it.

She was a very busy, very ambitious woman. Maybe she felt it wasn't the right time to start a relationship. Or maybe she just didn't like him. Well, whatever the reason Jonathan had philosophically decided it was Lauren's problem and only she could overcome it.

He nudged Chesapeake aside and pulled out one of several cookbooks the dog was lying on. "I raided the cooking section at the library today and checked out all the books featuring seafood dishes. Lauren made it very clear that I'm on my own, and I have enough misplaced male pride to steer clear of her. I won't pathetically beg for help no matter how much I need it. There has to be something here that I can cook for the show."

Jonathan flipped through the book and made notations on a legal-sized yellow pad.

"There are certainly tons of oyster recipes. Which one should I make? How about Sotterley oyster pie? The recipe makes ten first-course or six main-course servings."

Jonathan read through the entire recipe and shook his head. "No way. Too complicated. I'd have to make a pie pastry and something called a béchamel sauce. Maybe I can make oyster soup with watercress. It looks easy. But what's with these weird ingredients? Where do I buy julienne carrots? They probably only sell them in specialty stores. And what is crème fraîche? Better skip that one. Geez, doesn't this book have a beginners' section? Or a section for the culinary impaired? Let's try another book."

After hemming and hawing for another thirty minutes, Jonathan finally selected a recipe. Chesapeake followed eagerly in his wake as he entered the kitchen and began organizing the necessary ingredients.

"This variation on the usual recipes for oysters Rockefeller is perfect. I can chop everything in the food processor," Jonathan explained as Chesapeake stood beside him, watching the cooking preparations with a hopeful expression. "Now I won't have to figure out the correct knife to use."

The Cuisinart hummed while Jonathan dumped the ingredients inside. Fortunately he'd had the limited number of simple ingredients needed to make the dish in his refrigerator. Mel down at the oyster plant had given Jonathan a few dozen unshucked oysters, so he was even able to cook the oysters in their half shells exactly as required. The only parts of the dish missing were lemon wedges and parsley sprigs, and Jonathan figured he could skip them because they were to be used for garnish.

Jonathan baked, then broiled the oysters according to the directions and removed them from the oven. "They smell awful, but they look just like the picture in the cookbook."

He stood back and compared his creation to the photograph in the cookbook, tipping his head to view the dish from every angle. Then he scooped the oysters from their shells and placed them in Chesapeake's dog-food dish. When they were cool, he set the bowl on the floor. With a few sniffs, slurps and snorts Chesapeake devoured the contents, then gazed longingly at Jonathan.

"Did you like it, Chesapeake? Was it good? Of course you don't have the world's most discriminating palate. I've seen you grab a drink from the toilet when you thought I wasn't watching." Jonathan glanced down at his dog's sparkling clean dish. "Looks like we have a winner. I'll make this recipe for the first show. Too bad I can't taste the stuff myself, but I'd gag if an oyster touched my lips."

Jonathan rinsed off his cooking utensils and the empty oyster shells, then removed a timer from the cupboard. "You are in luck, Chesapeake. I have enough ingredients to make one more batch, and Lauren told me to time my preparation. I have to fill a six-minute television segment with my culinary demonstration."

Chesapeake's ears perked up the moment Jonathan switched on the food processor. He smiled fondly at his dog and sighed, "If only my feelings for Lauren were this easy to understand."

Lauren had never considered herself much of a risk-taker. She had been an inquisitive but not overly adventurous child. Her teenage years included a healthy dose of rebellion against parental authority, but more often than not Lauren had defied her parents in order to conform to her peers.

Even pursuing her dreams of being a pastry chef and writing a cookbook were being enacted in a relatively safe environment. Lauren had deliberately returned to her home town because it was safe and familiar, a place where she felt accepted and comfortable.

Experimenting with dessert ideas, creating and refining recipes, were activities Lauren did in solitude, where there was no one to witness her failures. Only successful desserts were served to family, friends and customers. The less than stellar creations ended up exactly where Lauren thought they deserved to be—the garbage.

Today, however, Lauren was about to become a risk-taker. As she stood behind the large TV camera and watched the crew make all the necessary technical adjustments to the kitchen set, she knew she was about to enter a situation that had the potential for unlimited disasters. Aside from her own nerves and inexperience working in front of a camera, she had a co-host who couldn't cook and a director who couldn't function unless he consumed copious amounts of caffeine.

At least the set looks good, Lauren thought as one of the young assistants strategically placed two large ferns on the back countertops. The plants added a hint of the exotic to the stylish yet homey kitchen configuration. The wispy leaves of light green perfectly complemented the rich jade counter and brought out the golden hues in the sleek oak cabinets.

Lauren spotted Jonathan entering the studio and she automatically tensed. Her mind reeled with the image of her wanton behavior on the sailboat last week, lying practically naked on the deck of Jonathan's boat, panting and writhing in sexual abandonment, her body flushed with excitement, his eyes glittering wildly as he ignited her blood with his sinful kisses and sensual caresses.

She remembered the strength of him, the power and force of their mutual passion overwhelming every rational thought. It was a mystical and mortifying memory that she could not ignore.

Lauren took several measured breaths, trying to calm the panic that seemed instantaneous whenever she was near Jonathan. The worst part was that this was not the first time she had seen him since the sailboat incident. They had spent a great deal of time together, both in person and on the phone, preparing for today's show.

And instead of becoming easier, these meetings were getting Lauren more and more flustered. Especially because during each encounter he had been polite, kind and professional, yet uncharacteristically distant and reserved. This subtle change in Jonathan's attitude puzzled Lauren and instead of being relieved by his impersonal manner, she felt strangely sad.

Jonathan stopped to talk and joke with the crew, and the sounds of companionable male laughter echoed through the set. Dressed in a navy blue polo shirt, pleated khaki slacks and tasseled loafers, he looked like a preppy ad for men's cologne.

Lauren could see that the crew clearly accepted Jonathan as part of the crowd, yet he somehow stood out from the other men. There was an intangible air about him that marked him as being someone special. He was distinct, noticeable and unforgettable. No question about it, Jonathan had panache.

Lauren lowered her gaze and started arranging her notes. The last thing she needed was to have Jonathan catch her staring at him like a wide-eyed adolescent.

"Time to get started people," George called out. "I need Lauren and Jonathan on the set so we can block the show. Everybody else stand by for cues."

Lauren spent another much needed minute on the mundane task of organizing her notes to give herself time to calm her nerves. Then firmly burying her feelings of trepidation, she lunged forward.

Jonathan greeted her with a polite smile. She knew he had to be nervous, but nothing in his voice or mannerisms suggested a trace of doubt. Jonathan seemed perfectly at ease, standing with his hips resting against the sink and his ankles casually crossed, listening earnestly while George gave them instructions.

They first rehearsed the brief introduction to the show that George had written. Lauren's throat felt tight and her stomach quivered as she read her lines, but to her relief she managed to utter them without making any mistakes. Jonathan also delivered his lines error-free, and Lauren envied his natural delivery. She was sure she seemed stiff and wooden in comparison.

"That was fine," George said. "We'll start rolling tape now. Have the completed dishes been placed on the set?"

"One of the crew took the platter of oysters Rockefeller I brought and put it in the oven," Jonathan answered.

"My dessert pizza is in the refrigerator," Lauren replied.

"Great. Let's get started." George backed off the set and slipped on a pair of headsets.

"Lauren, watch out for that cable!"

Jonathan's scream sent Lauren's pulse rate galloping. She turned a frightened eye in his direction, but the bright studio lights obscured her vision. She felt his fingers dig into her upper arms; then he roughly shoved her to the floor.

"Why did you do that?" Lauren asked, blinking her eyes in astonishment.

"I'm so sorry," Jonathan said. He reached up and

caught the thick, black cable that swung past them before it knocked into his shoulder. Holding the heavy wire with one hand he smoothed the other over her head, neck and shoulders. "Are you okay?"

Lauren blinked again and stared up at him. "I'm fine," she insisted, pushing herself into a sitting position. It did strange things to Lauren's heart when she realized the frantic, worried look in his eyes was for her. "What happened?"

"It's all my fault. I pulled on the cable to move it out of the way, but I was so busy leering at your legs I wasn't paying attention. I must have yanked on it too hard and it swung free."

"Lauren are you hurt?" George rushed over and knelt beside her.

"No." Lauren brushed the wrinkles from her skirt and stood. Her chest tightened with delight. *So he likes my legs, huh?* "I guess my co-host decided he wanted to do a solo show."

Jonathan raised one eyebrow. "What else would you expect from an innately competitive male?"

Lauren made a comical face at him. It felt wonderful to catch a glimpse of Jonathan's lighter, teasing side again. He grinned at her in amusement, but she saw there was more in his smile. Admiration. Maybe even a hint of approval. Her heart started pounding erratically.

"Let's try it again. Everyone keep an eye out for stray cables," George shouted as he adjusted his headset. "Lauren, Jonathan, try to relax and have fun. You want your viewers to enjoy cooking as much as you do. Remember everything you're doing is on tape. We can edit out mistakes and reshoot anything that doesn't go smoothly. Jonathan you're up first."

Now that the excitement of her near accident had passed, Lauren's nerves were starting up again. She took her wobbly knees to the stool near the refrigerator and gratefully sat down while Jonathan began his demonstration.

"Oysters Rockefeller is an elegant and simple dish even the novice cook can enjoy preparing and eating. Personally I think the most challenging aspect of the recipe is opening the oysters."

A few crew members chuckled, and Jonathan grinned boyishly.

"There are several tricks and a measure of luck involved in shucking oysters, but trust me, if I can do it, anyone can learn. You'll need a kitchen towel and an oyster knife with a two-and-a-half to four-inch blade. It has recently come to my attention how important it is to use the correct knife when cooking, so make sure you have a proper oyster knife before you try opening one."

Lauren glared hard at Jonathan, but his wily green eyes stared directly into the camera.

"Before you begin, scrub the shells clean with a stiff brush under cold running water so no debris will fall into the oyster. There is a flat side and a rounder side to an oyster. Fold the towel so it covers your left hand, place the rounder side down in the towel and grip it tightly. Gently force the oyster knife into the side opposite the hinge. Then with a twist of the knife blade, slowly force the oyster shell open."

Lauren leaned forward for a better view. Jonathan twisted the knife slowly and the shell opened easily, revealing a plump, gray oyster.

"Remember not to exert too much force when twisting the knife or you will break the shell, cut the oyster or maybe even skewer your hand. After opening, cut the muscle that holds the shells together; then cut the muscle that holds the oyster to the shell. Discard the flat, top shell, leaving the oyster in the rounder bottom shell. Don't forget to pick out any bits of shell that cling to the oyster. One of your guests might be a lawyer, and if he cracks a tooth it could mean litigation."

More laughter greeted that comment, and even Lauren found herself smiling.

"Now place the oyster half shells on a layer of rock salt in the bottom of a large broiling pan. Rock salt is used to hold the shells upright and to keep the oysters hot."

There was a smattering of applause as Jonathan nestled the oyster among the salt. "Now we're ready to make the 'Rockefeller' part of the dish."

Lauren noticed George holding up three fingers, indicating Jonathan had three minutes left to complete his presentation. Jonathan turned up his smile, rapidly dumped spinach leaves, an onion, garlic cloves and Worcestershire sauce into a food processor, then pulsed the ingredients together. He moved so quickly and spoke so rapidly Lauren could barely keep track of the ingredients and amounts.

"Top the oysters evenly with the spinach mixture," Jonathan said while he slathered the oysters with the green sauce. "Then sprinkle with parmesan cheese and top with a combination of bread crumbs, sherry and melted butter. Bake at four hundred degrees for fifteen minutes; then place under the broiler for two minutes until browned. Garnish with lemon wedges and parsley sprigs."

Jonathan removed the completed version of the dish from the oven, placed it on the counter, then tipped it forward for a better camera angle. Lauren saw several crew members lick their lips appreciatively.

Lauren had to concede the oysters looked appetizing and inviting. Even the presentation was excellent. They were geometrically arranged on a beautiful blue and white ceramic dish, accented with green parsley sprigs and yellow lemon wedges.

"These oysters make a terrific appetizer or can be served as a main course," Jonathan said. "But if you want an outstanding dessert, listen closely while Lauren Stuart teaches us how to make a very different kind of pizza."

With a stiff smile Lauren exchanged places with him. "Thanks, Jonathan. I know how difficult it is trying to come up with new and different foods that your family and friends will enjoy. So for a complete change of pace, I recommend pizza for dessert."

Lauren tried to relax and speak enthusiastically, but she felt as though her tongue was stuck to the roof of her mouth. She stuttered a line, tried to repeat it, then became totally lost.

George smiled encouragingly at her, and at his cue, Lauren tried again. She forged determinedly ahead, but her presentation did not go nearly as smoothly as Jonathan's. The hot camera lights melted the cookie-dough crust of the dessert pizza to an unworkable consistency. Taping had to be stopped briefly while the dough chilled in the freezer.

Lauren had planned to arrange an intricate design of strawberries and kiwis on top of the pizza, but was unable to complete the task because a hungry crew member apparently had eaten a large portion of the sliced fruit. Taping was stopped while the extra fruit Lauren had brought, just in case, was cleaned and sliced.

After what she calculated to be the longest twenty minutes of her life, she finally displayed the finished dessert. Relieved to be done, Lauren tipped the pizza up to the camera. It slid off the platter and would have crashed to the floor if not for the quick reflexes of a nearby assistant.

"Cut tape," George shouted. "Lauren, Jonathan, terrific job." George shook their hands enthusiastically.

"I'm sure I have more than enough footage for a twenty-six-minute program. I'll edit the piece later this afternoon with one of the station's interns. We'll even make a copy for each of you so you can watch the show on your VCR before it airs."

"How nice." Lauren managed a tight grin.

"Thanks, George," Jonathan said. "It will be great to have an opportunity to critique our performances before the next episode."

"Your performances were fine," George insisted in a jovial tone. "In fact, things went so well today I want to tape three episodes next time. It will be far more efficient. There is no sense lighting the set and gathering the crew for only one show."

Lauren smiled weakly at George, and struggling to look unaffected by the request. *Three episodes!* She had barely managed to survive one. She closed her eyes and pinched the bridge of her nose with her thumb and index finger, hoping to ease the headache that was starting to throb behind her eye sockets.

"Hey everybody, we certainly can't let all this beautiful food go to waste," Jonathan called out. "Help yourselves."

It was all the invitation the crew needed. They rushed forward like a swarm of angry bees. Lauren was jostled, nudged, then bumped from behind. Trying to keep her balance, she turned quickly and nearly collided with Jonathan. He flashed her that sexy grin that always made her forget her name and held out a platter of oysters Rockefeller.

"You're going to hurt my feelings if you don't try one."

Lauren stared at the dish for a full minute. She selected an oyster, lifted it to her mouth and took a small nibble. The strong, pungent taste of garlic ambushed her tongue, obliterating all other sensations. "Wow!"

The burly lighting technician standing next to her was not nearly as circumspect in his opinion. "Damn! What is this crap!"

"Garlic," Lauren explained, wiping a tear from the corner of her eye. "Lots and lots of garlic."

She noticed most of the other crew members were having similar negative reactions to the oysters. Some were gulping water, while others spit their uneaten food into paper napkins. One enterprising young woman was furiously sucking a lemon wedge.

Pieces of Lauren's fruit pizza were suddenly in high demand as everyone scrambled to replace the lingering garlic taste invading their mouths. Except George. Lauren gasped in astonishment when she saw the station manager reach for a second oyster. Lauren laughed. Apparently he had finally discovered something that gave him as much of a jolt as caffeine.

"I don't believe this," Jonathan exclaimed. He dumped the remaining oysters into the garbage pail and snapped the lid shut. "The garlic must have been spoiled. How can a reputable grocery-store chain get away with selling customers rotten garlic? I will definitely be lodging a complaint with the produce manager."

Swallowing the bubble of laughter that was rising inside her, Lauren hustled Jonathan into George's office for a private chat. The moment they were alone, she shut the door.

"I know you tested this recipe because you prepared it flawlessly on camera," Lauren said. "Yet somehow you got your amounts mixed up. Everyone was eating the oysters you brought from home. Were you distracted when you were cooking the dish?"

"No." Jonathan crossed his arms defensively. "I even kicked Chesapeake out of the house so she wouldn't get in my way. She was starting to get ridiculously excited every time I switched on the food processor and refused to leave my side."

Lauren opted to let that comment pass, since she had no idea what he was talking about. "The recipe you sent me for the program guide calls for two cloves of garlic. Did you decide to get creative and add a few more for good measure?"

Jonathan frowned. "I did not change the recipe. I will admit the first time I made the dish, I didn't know you were supposed to peel the garlic, but my housekeeper showed me how to do that. It took me awhile, but when I cooked the oysters for today's show I made sure every single piece of garlic was properly peeled."

Lauren's eyebrows rose. "Every piece? There should have been only two."

"Two cloves," Jonathan insisted. "When you break the cloves apart, you get lots of small pieces."

"Jonathan, the small pieces *are* the cloves. The big piece is called a head of garlic."

"Oh." Jonathan furrowed his brow. "Then I guess I did use a little too much garlic."

"Yeah, about thirty cloves worth." Lauren started laughing. He flashed her a look of annoyance, and she laughed even harder. "Two full heads of garlic! You sure shook up the crew. The last time I saw that many people spitting was when my Dad and I went to an Orioles' baseball game last summer."

"God, I hope nobody gets sick." Jonathan raked his fingers through his hair. "I knew I should have had someone besides Chesapeake taste the food. She isn't exactly a finicky eater."

"I can't believe you fed those oysters to your poor dog." Lauren clucked her tongue disapprovingly. "I should report you to the ASPCA."

"I really messed up. My housekeeper is allergic to oysters so she wasn't able to taste the food. I probably

should at least have tried to choke one down myself."
Jonathan lifted his eyes to the ceiling, as if searching
for divine guidance. "Can eating too much garlic be
poisonous?"

"Oh, Jonathan."

Lauren stopped smiling. She reached out and captured his hand. It really was a harmless and funny mistake. She was trying to be casual about the situation,
but she could see he was genuinely worried. Lacing her
fingers through his, she squeezed gently, offering comfort and support.

"Seriously, Lauren, could someone get ill from eating
those oysters?"

"No one actually swallowed the oysters," Lauren said
softly. "Except George. I think the only side effect he'll
have is garlic breath that could stop a train."

Jonathan didn't even crack a smile. "I'm sorry I ruined the show," he murmured in disgust. "I wanted
everything to be perfect for you."

He sounded tired and baffled. Nothing like the confident, in-control man she knew. She heard the edge of
desperation in his voice, and for some odd reason it
made her heart ache.

"The show was fine." Lauren stared down at their
linked fingers, then softly rubbed her thumb across the
back of Jonathan's hand. "You were great on camera.
Relaxed, funny, competent. I was the one who looked
like a fool. Flubbing my lines, squashing my pizza
dough, nearly dropping the entire dessert at the end.
Thank goodness we do this on tape. Can you imagine
me in front of a live audience?" Lauren shuddered. "I
doubt I'd have the courage to try another show if you
weren't with me."

"Oh, sure." Ironic disbelief flashed in his eyes.

"I'm being truthful," Lauren insisted. The guilt crept
slowly into her conscience, and she lowered her chin a

fraction. "Besides, I am partially to blame for any problems you had today. I knew you couldn't cook, and I refused to give you help when you asked for it."

Lauren lifted her head, leaned closer and studied Jonathan's face. "I promise to help you prepare for the next three shows. We'll plan the menus together and coordinate our presentations. I'll even come to your house tomorrow evening and start teaching you basic cooking techniques. From now on, we work together as a team."

"Thanks. I appreciate the pep talk." Jonathan turned his head and gave her a long, considering look. "You are one classy lady, Lauren."

He smiled at her, and an intense feeling of joy pierced Lauren's heart. Followed immediately by a jolt of panic as the truth hit her. She was in love with him!

Lauren froze. *Oh my God.* She had fought so hard to keep her life sane and her heart untouched, yet he had still captured her affections. She had difficulty understanding her insatiable response to him, could not fathom why most of the time he left her feeling like she was going in circles. Until now.

She loved him. That was why she'd felt so sad when Jonathan had acted distant. It was why she'd felt hurt because he was unhappy. It explained the strong need she'd had to offer him comfort when he was distressed, and it was part of the reason her heart beat faster when she was near him.

She loved him. Lauren gulped noisily and lowered her head, trying not to focus on the emotions that were overwhelming her. Her first reaction was denial, but she couldn't generate enough dishonesty to make it stick.

"Are you coming back to the studio?"

Lauren's head shot up in panic. The emotions inside her head and heart were screaming so loudly she was certain Jonathan could hear them. She felt trapped by her feelings and tried desperately to hide the apprehension she felt.

"I'll be there in a minute. You go ahead without me."

Lauren fought to keep her nerves steady as Jonathan walked out of George's office. She literally sat on her hands to keep from fidgeting and rubbing them together. When she was finally alone, she collapsed against the desk. Lauren briskly massaged her temples and commanded herself to think logically. She could handle this, learn to cope with it. Somehow.

She was in love with a handsome, charming, intelligent man who could turn her knees to water and make her breath catch in her throat with one sexy smile. The only problem was she didn't trust him.

Good Lord. What was she supposed to do now?

TWELVE

The next evening Jonathan learned how to clean, peel, slice, dice, chop, cube, mince and julienne all manner of vegetables. He learned the difference between frying and sautéing, boiling and simmering, blanching and poaching. He learned how important it was to use one cutting board exclusively for meats and another board exclusively for vegetables to avoid bacteria cross-contamination. He learned the clever trick of lighting a small candle near the cutting board to avoid eye tearing when slicing onions.

And as he spent the evening storing up all this essential information, Jonathan also learned a lesson in sexual frustration that he swore brought him to the very brink of insanity.

Lauren, seemingly unaware of his regard, moved confidently around his kitchen as she patiently instructed him. Her occasional innocent shoulder squeeze of encouragement drove him nuts. As it became increasingly difficult for Jonathan to keep his hands off Lauren, he found himself starting to deliberately bump into her, just so he would have an excuse to touch her.

I really have lost it, Jonathan decided. He watched as Lauren's elegant hands with the long, tapering fingers and pale oval nails expertly wielded a lethal-looking knife, and a sharp sting of desire flooded his body. *I absolutely cannot sink any lower. I'm getting aroused watching a woman slice squash.*

Jonathan sighed in frustration, a helpless victim of his baser urges and uncontrollable emotions. He raked his sleeve across the beads of sweat forming on his forehead and realized he couldn't remember ever feeling this kind of fervor for a woman. He had sworn to keep their relationship on a strictly professional level, but it was becoming nearly impossible, especially since every time Lauren stepped closer his mind was flooded with memories of their steamy afternoon on his sailboat.

He had honestly made an effort to find a new female companion. He had gone on dates with two different women over the weekend. They had been pleasant outings enhanced by intelligent conversation, a relaxed atmosphere, even a slight sexual attraction. Of course comparing them to how he felt about Lauren was like saying Niagara was just a waterfall or Michael Jordan was just a guy who happens to play a little basketball.

Lauren flashed Jonathan a comfortable smile and rolled a thick zucchini onto the cutting board. He felt the urgency within him rise to a higher level. He wanted to kiss her. Hard. He wanted to slip his hands beneath her shirt and caress her full, round breasts. He wanted to smooth his fingers over her hips and stomach, and bring out the heavy warm passion within her sensitive body.

Jonathan noticed Lauren catch her bottom lip between her teeth, and he realized his intentions must have shown on his face. Her hands shook slightly as she lifted the cutting board and pushed the sliced vegetables into a copper bowl. Moving closer, Jonathan grazed his knuckles gently across her cheek and stared down at her with a sexy, intimate look.

Lauren cleared her throat. "Now I'll show you how to stir-fry all these vegetables."

"Mmmm, sounds fascinating." The fingers caressing her cheek slid down to the nape of her neck. "But first I'd like to show you something."

Without giving her any more warning, Jonathan pulled her close. He extended his head and met her lips. He kissed her slowly and gently, deepening the kiss only after he felt Lauren's acceptance. His tongue slipped past her soft lips, and he tasted a hint of the raw carrot she had been munching.

It felt so good to hold her in his arms. There was something so endearing about Lauren despite her occasionally prickly moods and that sweet stubborn streak that drove him crazy. He stroked her cheek with his thumb and slanting his mouth over hers pressed another passionate kiss on her soft lips.

Lauren gave a small sigh and melted into him. Jonathan was startled by her encouraging response, but he quickly seized the chance to allow his repressed passion free rein. Nearly shaking with need, his hands began a sensual assault, wandering over her soft, curved form with playful abandon. Jonathan ran his hands over the gentle swells of her breast, the round curves of her hips, the lean muscles of her thighs. His fingers moved around her waist, and he turned her so that her back was pressed against the counter.

He buried his face in her neck and brushed it with butterfly kisses. Lauren whimpered, wrapped her arms around the back of Jonathan's head and pulled his lips over on hers. Waves of heat rolled through him as her darting tongue tickled the crevices of his mouth. His muscles grew taut and a tight, twisting tension gripped him. Mindlessly he rotated his hips against hers, driving his male hardness against her female softness.

Anticipation and desire coursed through his veins like a raging fire. Jonathan lifted his mouth from Lauren's and blazed a sensual trail of moist kisses along the edge of her throat, alternating his lips and teeth, his teeth and tongue.

"We really shouldn't." Lauren's words had a breathless, choked sound.

Jonathan reluctantly drew back his head. The air felt trapped in his lungs, and he had to concentrate hard to steady his breathing.

"It was just a little kiss," he said huskily, nuzzling the side of her neck with his jaw. He refused to remove his hands from her waist. She was soft and round and felt too good, too sweet to let go.

"If that was a little kiss, then a big one will surely kill me," Lauren said, laying her head on his shoulder.

Jonathan pulled her slumped body closer and ran his fingers up and down her spine. "I can't imagine a better way to die."

Lauren gave an exaggerated groan, and Jonathan felt a tiny shock of unleashed passion shiver down her back. Her passion pleased, no, thrilled him. The feelings he had for her were a jumbled mix of desire and admiration and respect, and he hungered for a chance to explore them.

Stroking her hair tenderly, Jonathan planted a soft kiss on Lauren's swollen lips. His fingers moved to the buttons of her cotton blouse; then his hand slipped inside to cup her breast. She trembled as he sensuously massaged her round flesh. He circled her nipple with his thumb, enjoying the silky smooth sensation of the lacy fabric contrasting with the hardening flesh inside.

"Mmmm."

Her languid moan encouraged him. Searching along her back, he found and released the hooks of her bra and pushed aside the wispy lace that covered her. Lauren moaned again, loudly this time and arched her back.

"Jonathan—"

"You're so beautiful, Lauren," he muttered thickly.

"So passionate, so alluring. I need a taste. Just one small taste."

He bent his head lower and captured her aching nipple in his mouth. Lauren threw her head back and screamed. He drew the nipple further into his mouth and tasted her sweetness. She surged urgently toward him, cradling his head against her breast, her fingers twisting convulsively in his hair as he suckled.

"Oh, Jonathan," she whimpered, pressing his head closer.

Her skin felt hot. She tasted like passion and sin, and he couldn't get enough of her. He grabbed her hand and brought it down, pressing it against the front of his jeans, over his straining erection. Her fingers encircled him and he groaned low in his throat. She whispered his name. He pressed feverishly against her hand, rocking his hips back and forth. She stroked him rhythmically, and he felt himself growing larger. It was an unbearable mix of pleasure and pain.

He licked her nipples with urgent thoroughness until they were rock hard, then pressed his lips hotly to the curving flesh of her breasts. Jonathan was going out of his mind. He grasped Lauren's hips firmly, preparing to lift her onto the countertop. He was going to slowly peel those sexy jeans off her legs, kiss every square inch of her creamy skin, spread her legs wide and bury his face between her naked thighs.

And when her breathing grew frantic and quivering, when she was nearly begging for release, he was going to fill her with his hardness. He was going to satisfy this ache, this hunger they both felt, give in to the desire and blinding passion they needed to physically express.

As Jonathan started lifting Lauren, a sudden high-pitched canine whine reverberated through the room.

"What?" Lauren cried out in alarm and stiffened in his arms. She twisted, and he slowly placed her feet back on the tile floor, afraid she might fall. But when she tried to pull away, Jonathan held her tightly against his chest. "What was that?"

"Nothing." His arms tightened around her hips as he buried his face in her hair, nuzzling aside the silky tresses so he could nibble on the delicate lobe of her ear.

The whining increased. A cold wet nose touched Jonathan's hand. Chesapeake tried nudging herself between them, butting her head insistently against their thighs.

"It's only Chesapeake," Jonathan whispered. He blew out a harsh breath. His hands stroked Lauren's hips and bottom lovingly. "If we ignore her, maybe she'll go away."

Lauren laughed breathlessly. "I think the chances of that actually happening are slim to none."

Chesapeake continued whining, then switched to short, loud barks. Completely frustrated Jonathan turned to his pet and shouted, "Shut up, Chesapeake!"

The silence lasted three seconds. The retriever jumped up on her hind legs, placed her front paws on the counter next to Lauren and barked even louder. Jonathan groaned.

"Down girl!" Lauren commanded. The dog stopped barking and started to whine. "Chesapeake, get down!"

Chesapeake hesitated only a second, then jumped down, sat on her hind legs and gazed up at Lauren with liquid brown eyes.

"Good dog." Lauren pulled away from Jonathan and stroked Chesapeake's golden ears. The dog's tail instantly started sweeping the floor. "She really is a smart puppy. With just a bit of training, she could be very obedient."

Jonathan blinked with astonishment, his gaze bouncing back and forth between his dog and Lauren. He couldn't believe it. Chesapeake had actually listened to

Lauren. That dumb dog had managed to quickly and correctly obey a command.

The flippant remark he so often made to his mother unwittingly popped into Jonathan's head: *When I find a woman that can make Chesapeake obey a simple command, I'll marry her on the spot.*

He'd been kidding. It had been a joke. A dumb joke. Chesapeake never listened to anyone. Jonathan rubbed his temples and tried to force his brain to think. Lauren was speaking. He struggled to listen.

"It's getting late, I have to leave."

"Leave?" He looked about the kitchen in a confused stupor. The cutting board was shoved to one side, most of the knifes were dirty and there was an enormous bowl of chopped vegetables near the sink. Chesapeake, that amazing dog, was still sitting at attention, patiently waiting for acknowledgment.

"I'll walk you down," Jonathan heard himself offer.

"Thanks." Lauren reached shyly for his hand, and they left the kitchen with Chesapeake trailing respectfully behind them.

Jonathan walked Lauren to her car in a daze, his subconscious mind running at full speed. He wanted to say something to her, something deeply profound and meaningful. But all he could think of was, *You made my dog obey, therefore I should marry you.* And that idea was nearly as preposterous as it sounded.

Or was it? Had he been on guard against his mother's matchmaking efforts for so long that he had closed his mind against marriage with anyone but an imaginary perfect female who existed nowhere except in his subconscious?

On some level he knew it was crazy, knew he had momentarily lost touch with reality. You did not fall in love with a woman and marry her because she was able to control your dog. But Jonathan had learned that sometimes in life you needed to look at a situation from a different angle in order to see the truth.

It appeared that Chesapeake had just provided him with that different angle.

They arrived at Lauren's car and Jonathan automatically took her hand to assist her inside. When his fingers touched her palm, a pleasant tingling sensation traveled up his arm and a soothing, intimate feeling invaded his chest.

"I'll talk to you later," Lauren said. She squeezed his hand tightly before pulling her fingers away. Once the car door snapped shut, she peeled out of the driveway.

Still in mild shock, Jonathan watched her drive away. Lauren wasn't sophisticated or subtle or glamorous. His mother disapproved of her, his dog adored her and he'd probably fallen in love with her the afternoon he'd met her at the library when he'd practically had to wrestle a book from her hands in order to assist her.

He hadn't considered it before, but they shared many things in common. Lauren was independent, motivated to succeed in her career and devoted to her family. And she was the first woman he had ever known who made him feel comfortable about who he really was. She carried no expectations or images of the man he should be.

He wondered if she could learn to enjoy sailing. Well, maybe if they bought Dramamine by the case. He really hoped she didn't like opera. Of course he could always invest in an excellent pair of earplugs if she did. Jonathan glanced down at his beloved dog, the prophet of his destiny.

"Don't look so smug, Chesapeake. There is intense chemistry between Lauren and me, but she fights it all the time. If we want her in our lives, we need to find a way to win her heart."

* * *

From Jonathan's, Lauren drove directly to her sister's house. With each passing mile she felt her control slipping, yet not until she had dragged herself out of the car and arrived at Eileen's front door did she realize she was crying. Knocking urgently, Lauren waited impatiently for a response.

"Hi, Eileen. Can I come in?" Lauren's breath caught in a series of hiccups. "I've had kind of a rough evening."

"Good heavens, Lauren, are you all right? What happened?"

"Oh, this and that." Lauren waved her fingers dismissively through the air as she stepped inside. Eileen placed a sisterly arm of consolation around her shoulders, and tears welled in Lauren's eyes. "I was over at Jonathan's house. I've been teaching him how to cook."

"Gracious, Lauren, he can't be that bad a chef."

"No jokes please, Eileen. This is serious." Lauren threw herself onto the living-room sofa. "There was a lot more going on at Jonathan's tonight than cooking lessons. And I'm not sure I can handle it."

"What kinds of things?" Eileen tilted her head and stared at Lauren. "Did you sleep with him?"

"Almost." Lauren started squirming on the cushion. "If his dog hadn't interrupted us, I would probably be rolling around on his bed this very minute. Or maybe even the kitchen floor. He makes it awfully easy to get carried away." The images made her blood race. She sighed, then slid Eileen a swift, sideways glance. "I've fallen in love with Jonathan." It felt like admitting a crime.

"I know."

"How can you?" Lauren cried indignantly. "I only realized it myself yesterday afternoon."

Eileen sank down next to Lauren. "You've been fighting your attraction for him so intensely, I knew he had to be someone special."

Lauren pressed a tissue to her nose and blew loudly. "I feel like a fool."

"Warren!"

Michael burst into the room, a bundle of three-year-old energy. He launched himself at Lauren, and she caught him instinctively. She sniffled when he wrapped his arms around her neck and hugged her noisily. He smelled of baby shampoo and crayons.

"How's my best boy tonight?"

"I'm good. It's my birthday!"

"Ummm, not for a few months. You were born in September."

"It's my birthday!" Michael insisted. He wriggled off Lauren's lap and ran from the room.

As Michael rushed away, Lauren noticed his right foot was encased in a red slipper with a dalmatian head on top while the left sported a gold slipper with a lion's head.

"Cool slippers." Lauren glanced up at her sister. "Why is he wearing two different kinds?"

"Don't ask," Eileen replied with a grim smile.

Michael soon returned, his small arms laden. He dumped everything on the sofa next to Lauren. Proudly sorting through the piles, Michael displayed the items to his aunt. She dutifully admired the brightly colored party hats, plates, napkins, cups, balloons, horns, blowers and streamers. The design on each item was either a dalmatian or a lion.

"I think I'm starting to recognize the theme," Lauren said. She tooted one of the lion horns at Michael, and he laughed. "These are fun."

"I guess some genius who's never had children decided three-year-olds need help making noise," Eileen commented dryly. Michael snatched up one of the horns and tore out of the room. "I'm hoping if I hide them in a closet after he goes to sleep, he'll forget about them."

Lauren smiled briefly, then flopped back against the sofa cushions and sighed. "Oh, Eileen, what am I going to do about Jonathan? The cooking contest will be held in two days, and he is still going to bake *my* cheesecake.

"For weeks I've relished the idea of exposing him as a fraud and embarrassing him in front of half the town. It seemed appropriate for his stealing my recipe. But how can I hurt so cruelly the man I love? If I reveal the truth, will I forever lose my chance at a relationship with him?"

Eileen grimaced. "Does everyone have to know the truth?"

"I feel I'm betraying myself if I don't hold Jonathan accountable."

"Well, we all know how impossible it is for you to keep quiet about anything." Eileen folded her hands in her lap. "But love involves sacrifice and compromise, Lauren. You have always understood that fact."

"I'm willing to make sacrifices and compromises, but this is definitely not a compromise situation." Lauren flung her head back and closed her eyes, silently assessing the situation. "Sitting through a plotless action-adventure movie where something gets blown up every five minutes because your husband or boyfriend really wants to see that film is a compromise. Or letting your son wear two different slippers to avoid a major battle is a compromise. Or buying plain old vanilla ice cream instead of chocolate fudge chip—because that's his favorite.

"I know in the grand scheme of life my cheesecake recipe stacks up at the bottom of importance. I accept that. Heavens, I agree with that assessment. But my culinary talent has inspired and challenged me in a way nothing else ever has, and it has given me a sense of purpose in life. In a very real way, my cooking has helped me find a sense of self.

"I can't allow Jonathan to take that away from me, regardless of how I feel about him. Love complements, enhances, even completes your life. It shouldn't force you to sacrifice your integrity."

"Oh, Lauren, this is a tough call." Eileen reached over and stroked her arm gently. "Although the ice-cream analogy really is a no-brainer. Vanilla or chocolate fudge chip? Heck, just buy both kinds."

"Ahhh!" Lauren opened one eye, then sat up, throwing the pillow she was mashing at her sister. "I'm spilling my guts over here, and you're making fun of my analogies."

"I'm just diffusing the tension with humor," Eileen insisted, hurling the pillow right back. She ducked as another pillow sailed her way.

"I'm serious, Eileen."

Eileen stopped in midthrow. "Of course you are. Sorry." She let the pillow drop into her lap. "I'm not going to start quoting all those horrific statistics like Mother does, about how a single woman your age has a better chance of being struck by lightning than she does of finding a suitable mate. I have faith in both your judgment and your integrity. I know you will ultimately make the choice that is right for you."

Eileen hesitated, then smiled. "I like Jonathan, even though I barely know him. He has a reputation in this town for being a man of accountability and honesty, not an easy feat for a business owner. Actually I think this is one of those rare moments when it is important to recall one of the quaint sayings Dad has spouted at us for years, 'To err is human, to forgive divine.' "

Lauren stifled a groan. She might have found her sister's advice a bit patronizing if she hadn't known how sincerely it was given. The human heart was more than capable of forgiveness, which was an essential element in the survival of any relationship. After all, everyone makes mistakes on occasion. But could she forgive and forget Jonathan's mistake?

"Oh, great. Now Dad's advice is actually making sense to us," Lauren sighed. "This hysteria must be contagious. Clearly we're both cracking up."

"Talk to Jonathan," Eileen urged.

"I want to," Lauren replied softly. "I just can't figure out what to say. My emotions are so jumbled and confused. I have to sort it out myself first. Somehow."

Lauren had never believed it was necessary to have a man in her life in order to achieve happiness, yet the thought of losing Jonathan brought a hollow, empty feeling to the pit of her stomach, and it would not ease, no matter how many sighs and deep breaths she took.

Lauren dug deep within herself, searching for the determined, driven aspect of her personality that would help her find an answer to her dilemma. It eluded her. She pressed her lips together and tried to concentrate. Eileen was right. This was a rare moment when one of her Dad's many clichéd expressions was appropriate. Unfortunately the saying that nagged at Lauren was, "A no-win situation."

Jonathan punched the security code into the cleverly concealed electric box and waited while the large, wrought-iron gates slowly opened. Once cleared of them, he drove along the gravel drive slowly, car tires crunching loudly in the quiet of the morning. After he rounded the final bend, the house came into view.

The formal gray stone mansion, built in the style of an eighteenth-century English manor house was the home of his mother's childhood, an estate that had been in the family for over four generations. It had aged gracefully over the years, an impressive structure that bespoke of money, power and elegance.

It had been built as a showpiece, a testament to one man's financial success, but over time had gradually become a comfortable home. There was still much that was formal about the place, but Jonathan thought this more a reflection of its current occupant, his mother, rather than the personality of the house.

The quiet remained as Jonathan exited his car and jogged toward the back of the house. He was pleased to note the absence of his mother's car. The cooking competition was starting in less than an hour, and the last thing he needed was to face an inquisition.

He passed through the sunken west garden, only one of many landscaping masterpieces on the property. It was a formal sea of color with vivid orange azaleas, blue delphiniums and yellow lupins all in flower.

The scent was sweet and fresh, contrasting sharply with the pungent spices of the walled kitchen garden, which Jonathan entered next, in search of the family cook, Regina. She had been helping him learn the intricacies of using the dreaded pastry bag, and he needed just one more favor.

"Hi, Regina. I have a problem I'm hoping you'll be able to solve." Jonathan stepped into his mother's kitchen, and over the clatter of pots and pans spoke to the family cook. "I need a fresh pastry bag for today's cooking contest. I forgot to buy some last night.

"I'm supposed to be at the restaurant at eight, and the baking supply store doesn't open until ten-thirty. Do you have a clean pastry bag I can use? One that will fit the decorating tip you taught me yesterday?"

"I might." Regina wiped her hands on the dish towel hanging off the waist of her apron and walked to the far side of the spacious kitchen. Jonathan followed closely at her heels. She was a large woman with a quick temper and a ready smile. He had always admired her honesty and the way she stood up for herself against tyrannical employers. Like his mother.

"There should be some new bags in the tin on the top shelf." Regina pointed at one of the many pantries in the enormous kitchen.

"I'll get it," Jonathan said, moving forward before Regina had a chance to start climbing on the step stool. He pulled out the shiny tin box the cook indicated, then descended to floor level. Prying the tight lid off the canister, he looked hopefully inside.

"Here's one." Regina reached over and removed a white bag. "It's been an awfully long time since I made any fancy company's-coming cakes, but these bags don't go bad. I think this will work fine."

"Looks good," Jonathan agreed. "Thanks, Regina. I can't begin to tell you how much I appreciate all your help. I didn't have a clue how to use one of these gizmos until you showed me yesterday. Thanks to your patience and excellent instruction I believe I have a decent chance of winning today's contest."

"I hope you do win, Jonathan." Regina smiled fondly at him. "I daresay you've worked harder than anyone else in the competition."

Jonathan smiled modestly. Regina's praise was given sparingly, making it all the more prized. Jonathan closed the lid, then climbed back up on the step stool to return the tin to its original position. While he was rushing to complete the task, his hand accidentally knocked against a sturdy cardboard box.

"Watch out!" Jonathan yelled in alarm.

Regina screeched and moved out of the way, no easy accomplishment for such a large woman. There was a loud thud as the box hit the floor, then a swishing noise as the top split open and the contents spilled out. Jonathan swore under his breath. Magazines were strewn haphazardly across the tiles. "Are you hurt, Regina?"

"I'm fine," Regina answered. "No harm done. You just dropped one of my boxes of old cooking magazines." The older woman went down on her knees and started gathering the journals into a pile.

"Leave them," Jonathan insisted. "It's my mess, I'll clean it up." He noted with a wry grin that Regina didn't have to be told twice. The cook grunted and moaned as she clutched the small of her back with her fist and slowly rose to her feet. Huffing from her exertions, she gave Jonathan a wry smile, picked up her vegetable-harvesting basket, garden shears and gloves, and left the kitchen.

Moving quickly, since he didn't want to be late for the contest, Jonathan started scooping up the magazines and stacking them inside the box. Many of the covers sported mouthwatering photographs in vibrant, bold colors. Lively-looking fresh vegetables cut and molded to look like exotic flowers, stark fresh berries artfully arranged on a pure white plate, elaborately formed pastries baked to a delicate golden brown.

Everything looked amazing, appetizing and appealing. But it was a headline on one cover that captured Jonathan's complete attention.

Original Recipes from the Most Promising Graduates of the CIA.

The words made him think of Lauren, made him remember how much he missed her. Jonathan hadn't seen or spoken to her since the night she'd come to his house. The night he'd learned to slice and dice and chop. The night he had kissed and caressed her. The night he'd realized how hard he had fallen for her.

Work and preparing for the cooking competition had kept him busy for the past two days. He had tried to contact Lauren several times, but had been unable to reach her. She apparently was just as busy as he was, so they had played phone tag, leaving messages on each other's answering machines.

Maybe it was better that way. They needed uncomplicated time together so they could talk, discuss the future. He wanted her undivided attention when he made his pitch. He acknowledged convincing Lauren to take a chance on their relationship was probably going to be the toughest sale he'd ever made.

Jonathan hunched his shoulders and started flipping through the pages of the magazine. He wondered if Lauren had seen this article. Maybe he would ask Regina if he could borrow the journal so he could show it to Lauren. He found the section featuring the CIA chefs and quickly scanned the text. Then he turned the page.

Jonathan's eyes widened. He drew in a deep breath and stared at the page for several minutes, uncomprehending. There was a picture of Lauren. She was dressed in a starched white chef's uniform with a tightly buttoned collar and a ridiculously tall, pleated white hat. Her hair was longer, her eyes looked darker and her smile was wide, happy and genuine.

Printed on the opposite page was a cheesecake recipe that Jonathan could easily recite in his sleep. The article claimed this exciting original creation was proof of her budding talent.

"Damn."

All this time and she had never said a word. Why? Why had she kept it a secret? Too stunned to take it all in, Jonathan read the section on Lauren again. He felt a sharp pain in his chest. Betrayal? But Lauren wasn't like that. She was open and honest and up-front. He looked again at her picture, and his mind raced with unanswered questions. *What the hell was going on?*

THIRTEEN

Lauren pulled into the already crowded parking lot of La Maison restaurant, ten minutes late for the start of the cooking competition. *Whose brilliant idea was it to start this darn thing at eight in the morning? Certainly not hers.* Well if anyone said anything to her about being late, she decided that was going to be her first line of defense.

Her heels clicked in a staccato rhythm as she raced along the brick sidewalk, clutching her skirt so the wind couldn't make a total mockery of its modest length. She arrived out of breath, but fortunately it wasn't necessary to use her prepared excuse for lateness.

Lauren slipped casually into the restaurant without anyone noticing her tardiness, smoothing her wild, wind-ruffled hair as she sidled casually over to the judge's table. She located the large manila envelope with her name on it and hastily stuffed it into her already overflowing purse, silently blessing Eileen's superior organizational skills.

Armed with her recipe information and judging forms, Lauren sauntered over to the huge coffee urn set up on a side table and poured herself a full cup.

She greeted a few of her fellow judges and smiled at the nervous contestants milling about on the fringes of the room. Lauren sipped her coffee as she quickly read through the cooking schedule. Jonathan was not scheduled until ten. Good. That would give her time to settle into the judging routine before she had to face him.

She had spent the past two days in a fog of distraction, with fragments of emotions, advice and desire floating around in a confusing mass inside her head. One minute she was determined to follow through with her original plan and confront Jonathan loudly and publicly. The next, she was ready to quietly dismiss his crime and eagerly embrace the feelings of love she carried for him.

The indecision haunted her, yet she knew there was no one to blame but herself. She had reached for the phone a dozen times over the past two days, wanting to have it out with Jonathan. Confront him directly with his duplicity and wait, if her temper would allow it, for his explanation. Yet she never made the call.

But it would all end tonight. Or perhaps begin. Lauren honestly had no idea which mad, reckless side of her feelings would carry the day. Would she expose him or forgive him? Who knew? Her biggest hope was that she could end the evening with at least a shred of her dignity intact.

"We're ready to start the competition, Lauren." Chef Henri approached her in his customary theatrical manner. They exchanged air kisses.

"Eileen will be so pleased we are keeping on schedule," Lauren replied, after glancing at her watch.

"Your sister is magnificent," Henri insisted. "So organized, so professional. The hospital is lucky that she is willing to do all this work for them. At no charge! I hope they appreciate what a gem, what a jewel they have in their chairwoman."

"I'm sure they do," Lauren replied automatically as she followed Henri and the other baking judges to their section of the kitchen. She waited tensely for the usual

burst of resentment over the endless praise of her perfect sister to bubble up, but it barely simmered inside
her. Lauren relaxed. Perhaps she was finally learning
to overcome her obsession with Eileen's accomplishments.

Henri made a brief opening announcement, and the
contest began. Lauren smiled encouragingly as Mrs.
Hathaway started preparing her marzipan cake, but it
had little effect on the poor woman's nerves. Within
ten minutes of starting her presentation, Mrs. Hathaway
had dropped a mixing bowl filled with dry ingredients,
incorrectly measured the sugar and forgotten to separate the eggs she was beating. Near tears she asked for
a second chance, and Lauren gently persuaded the
other judges it would be acceptable.

Lauren was relieved Mrs. Hathaway was eventually
able to overcome her nerves and concentrate on her
cooking. Her next attempt at the dessert proved far
more successful, and the kitchen was soon filled with
the sweet citrus scent of the marzipan cake. By the time
Mrs. Hathaway whipped the meringue topping, she was
humming softly and appeared to be enjoying herself.

The morning passed quickly. After a spectacular Bos-
ton cream pie and a delicate apple strudel were prepared by two more contestants, Jonathan entered the
kitchen. He was dressed in khaki pants and a crisply
pressed light blue oxford button-down shirt. Lauren's
heart started its customary dance against her ribs. He
looked sexy, virile and impossibly handsome. When he
glanced at her solemnly, her lungs struggled for air.

Lauren dropped her gaze, hastily scribbling several
lines on the margin of her judging form. She could
hear the muted conversation from other sections of the
kitchen, the sounds of merry laughter, the distinctive
clanking of pots and pans. Yet above it all she distractedly heard the loud thumping of her own heart.

She made a few more scribbles on the paper, stalling for time. Finally doubting that her little ruse was fooling anyone, Lauren lifted her head and risked another peek at Jonathan.

His eyes were already on her. They had probably never left. He seemed a bit edgy, a bit nervous. Before she could stop herself Lauren smiled at him, but he didn't respond. Instead he gave her a curt nod of acknowledgment then organized his cooking materials with military precision in a rigid line.

Without once cracking a smile, he proceeded to make the Amaretto cheesecake with such swift, sure movements that Lauren knew he had been practicing. A lot.

The muscles on the back of his neck corded with tension when he removed the cake from the oven. Jonathan set it gently in the center of the cooling rack, threw the oven mitts almost defiantly onto the counter and lifted his head. His gaze locked with Lauren's.

Something hot and smoky flared in his eyes. Passion? Triumph? Anger? Lauren couldn't be sure, but the coffee she had consumed earlier that morning bubbled in a jittery mass in her stomach.

She cleared her throat loudly and stood up. Her knees felt wobbly, but she managed not to falter. "The cheesecake looks fine, Mr. Windsor," she said in her best judge's voice. "We'll call you back when the cake has sufficiently cooled so you can decorate it."

"I'll be waiting," Jonathan replied.

The next contestant entered the kitchen. With a final, mysterious glance Jonathan left. Lauren tried to focus her attention on the cream puffs Mr. Johnson was making, but her mind kept wandering back to the memory of a pair of green eyes, taut rippling muscles and chocolate Amaretto cheesecake.

* * *

"Mr. Windsor, the judges are ready to observe your final cake preparations now."

Lauren made her announcement in the crowded restaurant dining room and looked about anxiously for a response. She didn't immediately see Jonathan, but she knew he was there with the other contestants, waiting to finish his competition entry. She heard a burst of female laughter and craned her neck forward, strongly suspecting he would be surrounded by a group of giggling, fawning women.

Sure enough, after one more fit of merriment, Jonathan slowly raised his head and glanced in her direction. The dimples gracing his handsome face disappeared the moment their eyes met. He didn't look very happy to see her.

Lauren nodded in his direction and tried to look casual, but her fingers tightened around the clipboard as he approached. He had rolled up the sleeves of his shirt, revealing muscular forearms that were tanned and dusted with golden hair. In a room filled mostly with women he was an imposing foreign presence. Lauren's throat constricted.

Jonathan kept walking toward her with his long, steady stride and didn't stop until she had neatly backed herself against a wall. He pressed the advantage of his height and glared down at her. He was so totally in control, so unabashedly male that Lauren realized she had never really felt the full impact of his superior size and strength until this moment.

"We need to talk," he stated firmly. "Privately." The set of his mouth was cold and grim.

Lauren's stomach curled with nervousness. There was a gruffness in his voice that made her skin prickle. With guilt. He sounded very serious. And angry. He had seemed uncharacteristically glum when preparing his entry earlier that morning. Had he finally discovered

that she was the one who'd signed him up for this contest?

"I'm rather busy at the moment," Lauren retorted.
She glanced over his shoulder and saw a room full of
curious onlookers pretending not to stare. She lowered
her voice. "Can't it wait until after the competition?"

"I know you're busy, but this is important."

"Oh?" Lauren tilted her face and bumped the top
of her head smartly against the wall. It stung, but she
refused to give Jonathan the satisfaction of seeing her
wounded.

"Isn't there something you'd like to tell me about
the cooking competition?" Jonathan asked, with a
pointed, expectant stare.

"Isn't there something *you* want to tell *me?*" Lauren
countered with an equally expectant frown on her face.

He was standing so close that he was practically on
her toes. The deep green of his eyes reminded her of
a spring thunderstorm. A bit wild and a bit unpredict-
able.

Yet instead of feeling intimidated, Lauren felt empowered by his obvious emotion. She could feel the warmth
of his powerful body, but she refused to back away from
him, even though she couldn't actually go anywhere
with a solid brick wall pressing against her shoulders.

His expression remained stony. She wondered idly if
he had a strong temper. She'd seen him annoyed with
his mother and angry with his dog, even frustrated over
his own inadequacies, but she had never seen him completely lose control. Maybe it was time.

"I'm waiting," Jonathan declared pointedly.

"Really? So am I."

She started tapping her foot annoyingly and tried to
look bored. The buzzing hum of conversation from the
dining room increased in volume. They must be attract-
ing quite a bit of attention, Lauren decided.

The hostile silence was just starting to rattle her nerves when Lauren suddenly realized how juvenile their behavior was. She had been waiting for three weeks to have this conversation with Jonathan, and the best she could manage was a tit-for-tat sparring match and a staring contest?

"Jonathan," Lauren began, reaching out and putting her hand lightly on his arm. "We do have a lot of things to say to each other, but this is neither the time nor place."

His muscles tensed under her fingers. "I'm not anticipating a long, drawn-out discussion. I just need to solve a mystery."

He glared at her and she glared back. Lauren was suddenly furious. What did she have to feel guilty about? She might have crossed the line a bit when she'd registered Jonathan for this contest, but he was the one who dishonestly took the accolades for something that wasn't his.

"Lauren?" Henri sounded anxious. The chef came rushing over, apparently unaware of the tension surrounding them. "The other judges are waiting. Is Mr. Windsor ready?"

Lauren's chin shot up. "I don't know. Are you ready, Mr. Windsor?"

"I'm ready." Jonathan's face contorted as he gave Lauren a meaningful stare. "But I'm not finished."

Lauren smiled hesitantly at the uniformed valet attendant as he assisted her out of the car. She handed him the ignition key, but waited until he had driven away before crossing the street. Even though she was her customary hour late, Lauren didn't rush, knowing that she felt emotionally unprepared to enter the country club and witness the presentation of the cooking-competition awards.

Much to her regret, there had been no opportunity for a private word with Jonathan after the contest had ended. When she was finally finished with her judging commitments, she had marched into the restaurant, prepared for the argument of her life, but he was nowhere to be found.

It was rather a serious letdown, Lauren decided. Getting all worked up into a fine temper and then not having anyone to vent her frustrations on. Of course, she might very well get that opportunity tonight.

She thought she had a fairly strong grip on her nerves, yet her pulse was racing madly by the time she reached the entrance to the club. After another wan smile for the young man who politely held the door for her, Lauren entered the building.

It felt cool in the open foyer. The structure had been built over a hundred years ago by a prosperous sea captain who had grand illusions, great wealth and a wife determined to display them both. Unfortunately the couple had lived only a few years in the rambling mansion before succumbing to an influenza epidemic. They'd left no heirs, and the house had fallen into neglect in the ensuing years.

The matrons of several established, well-to-do local families eventually rescued the place and spent the past fifty years happily raising funds and restoring the mansion to historic-preservation status. The interior boasted soaring ceilings with ornate plaster moldings and medallions, intricate wood paneling, crystal chandeliers and long multipaned windows accented with burgundy moiré draperies.

All of the country club's public functions were held at the mansion, and club members fought tooth and nail for the opportunity to host their parties in these elegant surroundings. The club had already been booked for another event, but in typical Eileen fashion, Lauren's sister had persuaded the other group to defer to the hospital auxiliary so the big formal gala and awards presentation could be held here.

Lauren could tell by the noise and movement of the crowd that tonight's event was taking place in the second-floor ballroom. She passed several people on the stairs as she made her way up and felt relieved that she didn't recognize anyone. She was hardly in the mood for social chitchat.

When she reached the top of the grand staircase and caught a glimpse of the crowd, Lauren could feel her palms start to sweat. The ballroom was filled with glittering, expensively dressed people who carried themselves with the poise and self-assurance of the privileged. Muted classical music mingled with discreet conversation as the throng moved about in an orderly, random fashion.

Lauren's eyes darted anxiously about the room, and her heart started beating faster when she spotted her prey.

"Have they presented any of the awards yet?" Lauren asked breathlessly as her rapid shuffle through the crowd brought her beside her sister and brother-in-law.

"Finally!" Eileen threw her arms around Lauren and gave her a tight hug. "I've been stalling everyone for over an hour. Where have you been?"

"I fell asleep," Lauren admitted, feeling guilty over Eileen's slightly worried, slightly annoyed tone. "The judging ended later than we planned, and I stayed to organize the transfer of all the food from the restaurant to the club. I was so tired when I got home I figured I'd rest for an hour before getting dressed.

"I haven't been sleeping well these past few nights, so I must have really zonked out. The next thing I knew it was dark outside, my head felt like lead and I was already late."

"The wait was certainly worth it," Rob interjected. "You look fabulous, Lauren."

"Thanks, Rob. I really needed to hear that." Lauren smiled gratefully at her brother-in-law, then wriggled her shoulder self-consciously, hoping her daring dress was staying in place.

Suspecting she was going to need every bit of false courage she could muster, Lauren had splurged on an outrageously expensive evening gown for tonight's formal awards presentation. It was strapless, cut from luxurious red crepe material and clung indecently to her every curve. She felt wicked and strong wearing it. When it stayed in place.

Lauren adjusted the position of her tight bodice again and with a forced casual air inquired, "Am I the last one to make an appearance? Has everyone else arrived?"

"Jonathan is here." Eileen jumped in with a response before her husband had a chance.

Lauren's heart thumped. She'd thought she had a fairly strong grip on her nerves, but hearing Eileen's simple statement started her stomach churning.

"Did you talk to him?"

"Briefly." Eileen drew back, glancing sideways through the crowd. "I also spoke with Jonathan's mother. She's a real frosty one."

Lauren gave a nervous giggle. "Quite the little charmer, isn't she? Actually I think she's really more of a dragon than an ice queen. I always feel a tad singed each time I'm near her."

"Dragon fits," Eileen agreed. "Well, now that you are here, I had better get this show on the road. The bar has been open for over an hour, and they ran out of canapés twenty minutes ago. I'm going to have a room full of rowdy drunks if I don't get some food in these people soon."

Rob gave Eileen's shoulder a comforting squeeze. "I'll introduce you," he offered with a kind smile.

As Eileen started to leave, Lauren grabbed desperately for her sister's wrist. "I have to know, Eileen. Who won the prize in the dessert category?"

Eileen raised her hands helplessly. "I have no idea. Henri tallied all the judge's scores, then sealed the results inside special envelopes that he's been carrying around inside his jacket pocket. He won't reveal anything. If you ask me, Henri is definitely one of the people here tonight who needs to eat more and drink less.

"He's acting like he's a partner in the prestigious accounting firm of Price Waterhouse and these are the Oscars. He won't drop subtle hints about any of the winners, even to me. And I'm the chairwoman of this event!"

"I'll have a stroke if I have to wait much longer to find out the results," Lauren wailed. "I gave Jonathan good marks, but ranked him fourth in the overall standings. The other judges' scores could move him higher, maybe even place him as the winner."

Lauren captured Eileen's hands between her palms. "Please, please, present the dessert awards first."

Eileen gave her a look of such intense uncertainty Lauren almost felt guilty.

"What are you planning to do?" Eileen asked cautiously.

Lauren slowly released her sister's hands. "I'm not sure," she admitted with a weak smile. Then she stiffened her back. "Stop looking so panic stricken. I promise I will not ruin this lovely fund-raiser you have worked so hard on with an embarrassing, hysterical outburst."

Eileen seemed unconvinced. She narrowed her eyes,

but Lauren returned her gaze steadily. Finally Eileen shrugged.

"Just try to keep the melodrama down to a theatrical level." Eileen gave her a sisterly kiss on the cheek. "No matter what happens tonight, Rob and I will support you."

"Thanks." Blinking back sudden tears, Lauren watched Eileen and Rob make their way toward the awards podium. Lauren sniffled, wishing she had a hankie or a tissue but her tiny purse was mostly ornamental, not functional.

She wrinkled her nose, then took a deep breath and forced herself to scan the crowded room. She caught a glimpse of Jonathan's granite profile, and her blood froze.

He was standing among a select group of people gathered near the orchestra. Dressed in an elegant designer dinner jacket and black trousers, he was the perfect picture of masculine beauty. The starched white shirt beneath his jacket emphasized the healthy glow of his tanned features, and the expertly tailored fit of his coat showcased his broad, muscular shoulders.

Jonathan's mother was positioned next to him, guarding her son and heir with a strong grip and a possessive attitude. She was wearing a flowing emerald green gown that Lauren begrudgingly admitted looked very flattering on her. Flanking Jonathan's other side was a girl of average height and average features in a dreadful-looking gown of vivid purple.

The girl was staring up at him with rapacious eyes. Someone must have made an amusing remark because they all laughed suddenly. Jonathan's smile was charismatic, his white teeth sparkled sexily. The insipid girl by his side was clearly transfixed by it.

Lauren stifled her anxiety. Had he brought a date? The thought disturbed her. Immensely. But Lauren didn't have time to dwell on her jealous feelings because Eileen, bless her heart, was presenting the first cooking award of the evening. In the dessert category.

"Good evening, ladies and gentlemen, and welcome," Eileen began. "I'd like to thank you all for your enthusiastic support of our fund-raising efforts and say that I hope to see you all in next year's competition."

That comment brought the expected laughter and good-natured mumbling from the crowd. Eileen continued.

"The old saying goes, 'You should save the best for last,' but tonight I thought it would be appropriate if we indulged our childhood fantasies a bit and began the evening by awarding the prizes in the dessert category first. Henri?"

After a bit of tussling through the crowd, the flamboyant chef joined Eileen on stage. The slightly inebriated Henri looked as though he wanted to say something, but Eileen wisely held the microphone out of his reach. Somewhat reluctantly, the chef handed Eileen three envelopes. She wasted no time.

"In the dessert division, the third-place award goes to Norman Johnson for his delectable cream puffs."

There was a smattering of applause as Mr. Johnson accepted his prize. His head bobbed enthusiastically as he nodded his thanks to the crowd; then he raised the small trophy Eileen handed him high above his head.

"Congratulations, Mr. Johnson. I sneaked a bite of one of your cream puffs earlier, and they truly are wonderful. In second place, Becky Hathaway's marvelous marzipan cake."

The volume of applause increased. Mrs. Hathaway smiled as she received her award, yet her eyes shone suspiciously with unshed tears when she dipped a quick curtsy to the crowd.

"Excellent job, Mrs. Hathaway," Eileen proclaimed.

"I haven't tasted your cake yet, quite frankly it looked much too beautiful to cut, but I'm saving room for a slice later tonight."

Lauren took a deep breath, closed her eyes and focused totally on the sound of Eileen's voice.

"And now, ladies and gentleman, the winner. It gives me great pleasure to announce this year's first-place dessert winner of the hospital's auxiliary cooking competition. Jonathan Windsor. Chocolate Amaretto cheesecake!"

Time stopped. Lauren lifted her head and opened her eyes. She saw Jonathan embrace his mother while several of the men near him patted him heartily on the back. He shook hands with two of them, then turned and walked up to the stage.

Lauren took several steps forward, but halted. A strange feeling of inevitability came over her. For almost forty-eight hours she had agonized over what she would say to him, and everyone else, and how she would say it if Jonathan won this contest. She had planned her revenge in anguish and bitterness and ambivalence.

The moment was at hand; the struggle had finally ended. It was time to have her say. But Lauren remained silent. In this final moment of truth, her indignation and self-righteousness collided directly with her heart.

Despite everything, she loved this man. She respected this man. She could never willingly cause him pain or embarrassment. It just wasn't part of her nature.

Her mom had once told her there were no rules in love. Unbelievably, Lauren realized that her mother had been right. Everything else faded to insignificance. With a deep sigh, she took a step backward.

Oh, she wasn't about to let Jonathan get away without any retribution. She would never be anyone's doormat, especially someone she loved. But there was a big difference between being a pushover and being prudent.

One of her dad's favorite Shakespearean quotes was "The better part of valor is discretion." Lauren decided this was a most appropriate time to act with both valor and discretion.

Jonathan reached the stage and turned to address the applauding crowd. An unfamiliar heat invaded her chest as he searched among the faces in the crowd. *Please let him be looking for me!*

Finally Jonathan's intense gaze settled on her. She stiffened her spine and tilted her chin. Their eyes met and held. He gave nothing away, and Lauren would have sold her soul to know what he was thinking, what he was feeling at that exact moment.

"Thank you all very much for this wonderful recognition. I'm rather surprised and certainly honored to be receiving this award," Jonathan said with a trace of irony in his voice. "But I can hardly take all the credit for the extraordinary cheesecake I baked today. Some of you may have read an article about me that appeared in *Washington Today* magazine a few months ago. In that journal it was incorrectly reported that I developed the original recipe for this cheesecake.

"The real genius and talent behind this fabulous dessert is a special woman I care about very, very much. I feel it's only fair and proper that she share this award with me. Lauren, sweetheart, will you come up here?"

Lauren's eyes remained pinned on Jonathan. She distantly heard a curious buzz rippling through the room. She forced her shoulders back and lifted her chin higher. Running solely on emotion and adrenaline, she took that long walk through the crowd and stepped up onto the stage beside him.

He welcomed her with a loving smile, his sexy green eyes filled with warmth and temptation. He put his arms around her shoulders, and she turned her face into the warmth of his chest.

The emptiness she had felt inside, the doubts and anguish all vanished. She had fought her destiny long enough. It was time to enjoy the spoils. Her throat grew so tight she could barely swallow. She knew she had to hurry. It was now or never.

"I love you, Jonathan," she whispered boldly in his ear. "I love you very much."

FOURTEEN

Jonathan felt as though someone had just punched him in the gut. His senses whirled, his heart raced, yet he somehow managed to retain a calm veneer. He pulled back and focused his complete attention on the woman he held in his arms. Lauren returned his stare with a hungry, yearning expression on her sweet face and an unmistakable gleam of love in her warm brown eyes.

Jonathan waved disinterestedly at the crowd of applauding people. Eileen thrust a trophy in his hand, and his fingers automatically closed around the cold, metal base. His eyes stayed on Lauren. He felt something hot and primitive pass between them.

"Let's get out of here." Jonathan clasped Lauren's hand and pushed through the crowd, tugging her along behind him.

He heard Eileen's voice announce the next group of contest winners. He caught a brief glimpse of his mother as he shoved past a knot of people blocking the exit. She was horrified. The expression on her face was so sour, she looked as though she had just swallowed a lemon. Tough. If she disapproved of Lauren that was her problem, not his. He fully intended to make Lauren a part of his life, and his mother was going to have to accept it.

"Wait a second, Jonathan. There is something else I have to tell you."

He whirled around and faced her. She was panting and slightly disheveled from their escape. Her hair was wispy and wild around her face and her cheeks were flushed, and he knew he had never in his life seen a more beautiful woman.

"If you're going to tell me that you registered me for the cooking contest, don't bother. I figured that out on my own."

"I suspected that was what you wanted to discuss with me this afternoon." She gave him a guilty stare. "How did you find out? Or more importantly *when* did you find out?"

"I accidentally stumbled across an old cooking journal this morning. Inside was a fascinating article featuring promising new chefs of the CIA. Imagine my surprise when I started reading the text and discovered a picture of you along with a cheesecake recipe I could easily recite in my sleep."

"Oh, no. You saw that horrible picture?"

Jonathan slanted her a teasing look. "I really liked the hat you were wearing."

Lauren groaned. "Please don't remind me. I look like a moron in that photograph."

"I thought you looked beautiful. But I suppose I'm biased. 'Cause I'm in love with you." Jonathan heard Lauren catch her breath, and he smiled. Now wasn't the best moment to explore these incredible feelings, however. He first needed to put to rest all the tension that had plagued them the last few days.

"I always thought my mother was responsible for entering me in the cooking competition," Jonathan explained, "but when I discovered it was your cheesecake recipe I had been baking I knew it had to be you."

"I've been very upset about this." Lauren shifted nervously, and the slit in her red gown opened, revealing a tantalizing glimpse of shapely leg. "Why did you steal my recipe? It was really nasty and dishonest."

"I agree it was wrong, but I can only plead guilty by reason of ignorance. The first time I saw your recipe was when I read the magazine article about me in *Washington Today*. Most of the stuff in that piece was a gross exaggeration of the facts, but that was completely my fault. I barely spoke with the reporter who wrote the article." Jonathan ran a hand impatiently through his hair. "I was so busy thinking about all the other inaccuracies, I never gave the recipe much thought. My mother supplied the journal with all their information. The best I can deduce is that she got the recipe from our family cook."

"Your mother!" Lauren squeaked, swaying momentarily with shock. "I don't believe it! She must be kicking herself in frustration. She can't stand me. And we might never have met if she hadn't chosen my recipe to be published in that magazine article."

"Poetic justice, huh?"

Lauren tossed her head back and laughed. Jonathan found himself grinning at her. He had to admire her style. He bent his head and kissed her smiling lips. It was a long, gentle kiss that gradually evolved into something hot and charged with desire.

He could feel the current of love flowing easily between them, and Jonathan embraced the emotion. A strange sense of calm and completion entered his soul. They belonged together. Lauren had just openly acknowledged her feelings for him. He could hardly wait to get her alone so he could properly express his own feelings of love.

"Did you drive your car here tonight, Lauren?"

"Uh-huh."

"Perfect. We came in my mother's sedan because she

doesn't like to ride in the Jaguar. She says I drive too fast." He flashed Lauren an overtly sensual look. "Give me your parking ticket."

Lauren silently fished the slip of paper out of her purse and passed it to him. Jonathan blindly held the stub out in the general direction of the parking attendant, feeling unable to tear his gaze from hers, even for a second. She looked soft and vulnerable and primed for loving. He was fairly mesmerized by the vision of love and desire he saw reflected in Lauren's eyes.

"The valet is here with my car," she said softly. Lauren moved closer and broke the enchanting spell by kissing Jonathan's throat. "It's time to go home."

Jonathan's emotions were riding high when they entered the car. The moment he closed the door, the car's interior seemed to shrink. The darkness, the anticipation, and the silence, broken only by the sound of their labored breathing, were all magnified to an almost fevered level.

Jonathan knew he had to get a handle on his charged emotions or else he wouldn't be able to drive. He took a deep breath, then flung the cooking trophy over his shoulder. It landed on the back seat and bounced onto the floor with a dull thud.

Lauren giggled. Jonathan deliberately avoided making eye contact with her. The sound of her laughter made his body tense with excitement. He could practically feel the blood pounding through his veins.

A deep yearning coupled with acute frustration grew steadily inside him. His body felt tight, in a state of excited sexual anticipation that reminded him too much of being a hormone-crazed teenager on his first date. Jonathan searched for the reins of his calm rational self-control as he buckled his seat belt.

He turned the key in the ignition, revved the engine

and tore away from the curb with tires screeching, admitting he had only found a small part of it. Hopefully it would be enough to get them to his house in one piece. He shook his head and stomped down on the accelerator. The speedometer needle jumped. The car shot onto the highway, and the tense silence inside the vehicle escalated with each rapidly accumulated mile.

Jonathan snuck a quick glance at Lauren. She was staring at him intently. Through the flickering highway lights, he could see her biting her bottom lip between her teeth. Her brown eyes blazed with passion.

"Hurry," she whispered softly.

Jonathan did a double take. Lauren blew him a kiss, and the heat of her gaze shot directly to his crotch. Her scent tortured his brain, a tantalizing combination of feminine softness, sexy perfume and hot desire. He gunned the engine and neatly executed a tight lane change. With the skill and determination that would have made an Indy 500 driver proud, Jonathan weaved in and out of the traffic, easily overtaking the slower cars and trucks as he sped down the highway.

Lauren reached over and ran her hand from his shoulder, down his forearms, to his fingers, then back up again. Her touch felt feather light, but it flooded Jonathan's body with the most unbearable sensations. His knuckles turned white as he gripped the wheel tighter.

He exited the interstate and made a hairpin turn. The tires squealed in protest. Jonathan swung onto the long driveway that led to his house. When they reached the end, he slammed on the brakes and the car screeched to a shuddering halt, barely missing the merrily tinkling water fountain in the center of the drive.

There was a moment of complete silence and total inertia. Then Jonathan sprang into action. He unbuckled his seat belt, threw it off his shoulder and turned to Lauren. She was sucking in short, gasping breaths of air. Jonathan swiftly unsnapped her belt and pulled her against his chest. Then he kissed her. Hard.

"Tell me," he whispered, running his moist tongue over her sweet lips. "I need to hear you say it."

"I love you."

"Ahhh, Lauren . . ."

Jonathan felt Lauren sag into her seat and shiver with pleasure as he pushed himself against her and claimed her lips in another wild, passionate kiss. The smell of her skin and taste of her mouth was intoxicating.

"We should get out of the car," Lauren gasped when the kiss finally ended. "We're starting to fog up the windows."

Jonathan groaned. It was far too easy to lose his head when he started kissing Lauren. He reached across her lap and pulled on the door handle. The car door swung open and she nearly tumbled out. His strong hand on her shoulder steadied her. Cursing softly, Jonathan jerked open his door and jumped from the car.

She was searching for her purse when he yanked Lauren's car door all the way open, clasped her waist and practically lifted her out of the car.

"Oh, my." Lauren sank her fingers into the taut muscles of his forearms as she found her footing and snuggled between his splayed thighs. He leaned back against the car and held her close, breathing in the spicy fragrance of her silky hair.

He momentarily lost himself in the warmth of the embrace. Lauren fit well in his arms. She leaned in closer, burying her nose in the crisp folds of his elegant dress shirt. He smiled. No one made him feel the way Lauren did.

He rested his chin on top of her head and started caressing her bare shoulders. She looked fabulous in her red evening gown, sultry and tempting. Jonathan's stroking fingers moved from Lauren's shoulders to her neck, then down to her breasts.

He could feel her chest rise and fall in rapid breaths when his questing fingers found a tight, puckered nipple. He rubbed his fingers repeatedly over the swollen bud and she shuddered violently. He kissed her lips with lingering tenderness and she moaned with pleasure.

"Easy, Lauren. Let's take it nice and easy."

Jonathan's voice was tight and labored. His advice to Lauren seemed ridiculous, given his aching need. It took every bit of self-discipline he possessed to keep from tossing her onto the hood of the car, pressing her thighs wide and filling her softness with one powerful thrust. Right here. Right now. Under the stars.

"You're right, we should stop," Lauren muttered. She took a shuddering breath and swayed toward him. "If you don't stop kissing and caressing me, I'm going to collapse. Then you'll have to carry me all the way up that long, long hill, then up each step of that long winding staircase to get to your bedroom."

"Sounds like an excellent plan," Jonathan replied.

"It's a flawed plan. All that climbing and carrying will be exhausting for you." A provocative smile played around the corners of Lauren's mouth. "You're going to need every ounce of strength tonight. I have my own ideas on how to make you very, very tired. And I intend to execute every one of them."

"Is that a challenge, Ms. Stuart?"

"It sure is." She nipped at his chin.

"A Windsor never backs down from a challenge," Jonathan declared loudly. He bent down, hoisted a shrieking Lauren over his shoulder and climbed up the grassy hill. A few minutes later he deposited her in the middle of his bed.

"I'm impressed." Lauren sat up and brushed the hair out of her eyes. "You're not even breathing hard."

"The minute I start kissing you I will be," Jonathan said, an unmistakable look of lust in his bold green eyes.

"Oh, goody."

Lauren folded her legs beneath her and sat up straighter. A surge of euphoria struck her, and she started grinning like a fool. She felt wonderful. On top of the world. She was head over heels in love with Jonathan and they were about to consummate that love.

"Practical matters?" Lauren asked.

"Never fret, my dear, this time I'm prepared." He yanked open the top drawer of his dresser and removed a box of condoms.

She gave him a shy smile. "Excellent. The large economy size. I like a man with ambition. Now where is your lovable mutt?"

"Locked in the basement with a fat, juicy doggy bone." Jonathan leaned forward and skimmed his lips slowly over Lauren's. She tingled with pleasure. "Chesapeake sleeps all over the furniture. Some of my uncle's antiques are starting to look a bit shabby, so when I leave the house I've been confining my dog to the room where she can do the least damage. The basement."

"Brilliant." Lauren rose to her knees. Her hand settled on his chest for support as she leaned forward. Her warm breath fanned his cheek. "You are a truly brilliant man." She kissed his lips lightly, then snuggled back in the bedding.

From her perch on the wide king-sized bed Lauren studied Jonathan's every move with avid interest. He removed his jacket and black silk bow tie, then tossed his gold cuff links casually on the mahogany dresser. He pulled the onyx studs from his shirt, and they hit the dresser with a loud *clunk*.

Next he unbuckled his black leather belt and drew it

slowly off his waist. He unbuttoned his fly, and Lauren gulped. His movements were casual, yet deliberate. Unconsciously she inched forward on the bed for a more revealing view.

Lauren licked her lower lip as she caught a naughty glimpse of curly blond hair through the opening of his shirt. Jonathan was certainly a fine-looking man, with or without his clothes. Of course, right now she definitely preferred him without the clothes.

He gracefully slid the white formal shirt off his shoulders and leisurely pulled the T-shirt underneath over his head. They hit the heavily padded carpet without making a sound. Lauren couldn't take her eyes off his now beautifully naked chest, broad muscular shoulders and flat belly. His little striptease was the most erotic thing she had ever witnessed. The desire inside her, so briefly explored when they stood together in the moonlight, now raged through her.

"That's a very wicked-looking grin, Ms. Stuart. What can you possibly be thinking?"

Lauren blushed and lowered her head demurely.

Jonathan kicked off his shoes, peeled down his socks and shucked his trousers. Clad only in a pair of very sexy blue silk boxers he came toward her. In his glittering eyes Lauren saw fierce determination and pure male aggression.

Jonathan lifted his knee onto the bed. The mattress sagged beneath his weight, and Lauren pitched forward. He caught her easily.

He peeled off her dress before she even had a chance to catch her breath. His hands cupped her breasts, and Lauren's whole body responded to his touch. She wrapped her arms around his neck and pulled him close.

They kissed endlessly, again and again until she was clinging to him, squirming and moaning with mindless excitement. She reached longingly for him, stroking his hair and neck and broad shoulders. Her hand dropped to the deep valley of his spine and curved over his firm buttocks. She squeezed experimentally, then gave a breathless laugh as he jerked back his hips.

"Tell me what you want," he said huskily.

"You," she panted. "I want you."

Jonathan bent his head and pressed a warm, wet kiss to one breast, slid lower and kissed her navel. She released a tortured sigh and arched her back. He ran his fingers lightly through the soft hair between her legs and gently parted her with his thumbs. Lauren caught her breath. Then she felt a soft tickle on her inner thigh and the moist hot tracing of his tongue.

"Oh, my love," she sobbed. The sensations he invoked were wickedly delicious.

The barely controlled passion that had been hovering just below the surface in Lauren burst forth in a firestorm. She twisted and turned on the bed as waves of desire rolled through her, swollen and heavy with a desperate need that Jonathan created and only he could assuage.

Everything happened very fast. Jonathan's hands were everywhere, stroking, caressing, exciting her flesh almost beyond endurance. He whispered sweet words of love in her ear and harsh, earthy phrases of desire. Lauren's body and mind and heart responded joyously.

She ran her palm up the inside of his thigh. The darker hair at his groin felt springy and soft, the muscles of his flat abdomen hard. She cupped his straining erection, curling her fingers lovingly around the smoothly rounded tip.

"You feel so good," she whispered. "Hard and rigid, hot and silky."

Jonathan sucked in his breath sharply. "I can't wait any longer," he declared with urgent passion. He flipped Lauren on her back. Bracing himself on his elbows, he rose above her.

"Are you ready, sweetheart?" he asked gruffly.

She answered by rising to meet him, her knees bent, her feet flat on the mattress. He spread her legs even wider with his strong thighs, grasped her hips between his hands and drove himself deep inside her.

Lauren welcomed him with a soft cry of pleasure. She curled her legs around his hips, hugging his body tightly against hers. Her fingers clung to Jonathan's arms as he thrust inside her warm moist flesh with slow and deep strokes. The sensations were unbelievable. Rough, driving tension mixed with a turbulent rhythm of love and trust.

"You are so perfect," he whispered as he surged inside her, his hips thrusting forward again and again. She whimpered softly and clutched at him, her hands pressing into his back, his shoulders, his hips. Her legs wrapped around his as she strained closer to him, needing his heat and strength to be even deeper inside her.

Reality slipped away as the tension mounted to an unbearable pitch. Lauren's body literally tingled as it shuddered its convulsive release. She called out his name, and he groaned. The physical and emotional connection between them was so gripping that Lauren's climax triggered Jonathan's.

Tears welled unexpectedly in her eyes as she felt him go still and rigid, then felt the wild pulsing as hard flesh deep within her body exploded. Lauren savored each sensation, lifting her hips in response to his movements, stroking his back and shoulders tenderly, planting tiny, moist kisses on his throat.

Finally Jonathan stopped shaking and collapsed on top of her. Lauren didn't mind his crushing weight. It seemed warm and secure. She rubbed her cheek back and forth against his shoulder, just like a kitten. The room filled with a beautiful, serene silence.

"You are an amazing woman, Lauren." Jonathan let out a long sigh of pure male satisfaction. "I sure do love you."

Lauren sniffled her response. The moment was simply too emotional for her to express in mere words. Fortunately he didn't seem to mind.

"I'll be right back, sweetie."

He slipped out of bed and headed toward the bathroom. Lauren blushed when she realized he needed to dispose of the condom he had somehow managed to don despite their mindless passion. When he returned to the bed she gave him a long, lingering kiss of thanks.

Jonathan flopped onto his back, and Lauren immediately sprawled on top of him. She rested her face against his, chin to chin, nose to nose. There was so much to say, yet she found herself too languid and content to speak. She pressed her lips softly to Jonathan's and stroked his hair with her fingers.

A look of utter contentment flitted over his face. He took a deep breath, and Lauren moved up and down on his chest. She searched his eyes and noticed the sudden gleam of purpose in their green depths. Sensing he was about to begin a serious discussion concerning their future, Lauren took a cleansing breath and waited.

"Man, am I starved." Jonathan brushed a light kiss on Lauren's forehead and gently rolled her off his chest. "All I had to eat at the reception were a few measly crackers and a wedge of cheese. There were some interesting-looking hors d'oeuvres, but they ran out of all the good stuff really fast. Let's go down to the kitchen and raid the refrigerator."

Lauren snorted. Oh, yeah, she was certainly in tune with Jonathan's thoughts and feelings. She yanked the edge of the bedspread up around her chest, figuring it would be far more effective if her breasts were covered when she gave him a glowering scowl. How could he be thinking of food at a time like this?

She practiced scowling while Jonathan jumped out of bed and pulled on a pair of shorts. She waited for him to face her, but when he turned toward the bed, he quickly dropped to his knees and disappeared. Lauren scrambled to the side, tugging the spread with her. She leaned over and watched his every move with growing fascination. Jonathan's head and shoulders glided under the bed frame. When he reappeared a minute later he was clutching her evening gown in his fist.

"It will take you an hour to get into this thing. Why don't you wear my shirt instead?" He tossed the gown on a nearby chair, then held up the tuxedo dress shirt he had worn earlier for her inspection. "You'll look just like one of those sexy women in a James Bond movie."

"That shirt closes with studs, not buttons," Lauren observed, forgetting to scowl. "It will hang wide open."

"Precisely."

Lauren cocked an eyebrow. "Pass me that comfortable-looking faded gray sweatshirt, and I'll agree to wear it braless."

Jonathan's eyes lit up with delight. He threw the sweatshirt at Lauren, then frowned. "Hey, wait a minute. You didn't have a bra on tonight."

"That's right. My gown is strapless, and I didn't have time to buy a bustier."

"A bustier?"

"Yeah, you know those tortuous garments that rock stars wear? It sort of squashes everything from your waist to your chin and pushes it up. And out."

"Hmmm, that bustier sounds very interesting. I'd love to see you model one." Pulling a clean shirt from his dresser, Jonathan asked hopefully, "Maybe you'd like to exchange that big sweatshirt for this skimpy half T-shirt?"

"No way. But I'll wear the sweatshirt with only my underwear if you keep your chest bare," Lauren volunteered.

"Deal." Jonathan slanted Lauren a lecherous look. "Who said compromise between men and women was difficult? We reached a mutually satisfactory agreement in less than a minute."

"On an eminently important topic." Lauren pushed the dangling sweatshirt sleeves up past her elbows. "It's a well-known fact that underwear can be a highly volatile subject."

"Smart aleck."

Lauren yelped as Jonathan cupped her buttocks and squeezed lightly. She ran ahead, and he quickly followed. Their playful shouts echoed through the vast rooms of the large house. On the way to the kitchen, Jonathan opened the basement door. An exuberant Chesapeake bounced out and greeted them enthusiastically.

Lauren helped Jonathan set out a feast of leftovers. Despite her earlier disdain at the idea of food after experiencing the most emotional and profound lovemaking in her life, Lauren found herself eating nearly as much as her lover.

"Chesapeake's going to get fat real fast with you around," Jonathan remarked conversationally.

Lauren guiltily returned the small piece of ham to her dish. "Sorry," she whispered to the panting dog. "We'll have to wait until he turns his back."

"Guess this means I'm going to have to watch you both like a hawk after you move in," Jonathan declared good-naturedly. He put another large slice of ham on his plate.

"Move in? Here?"

"Sure. It's a great house, you said so yourself. Eventually we can move somewhere else or even build a home if you want. Maybe something on the water so we can dock the sailboat on our property. But it makes sense to start out here after we get married."

"Married?"

Jonathan crossed his arms over his bare chest. "Why do you keep repeating everything I say?"

"Nerves. I'm definitely nervous."

"I love you, Lauren."

"I know." She closed her eyes briefly. "Loving you and being loved by you makes me very, very happy, Jonathan. But marriage is a huge step. A forever step. We haven't known each other long. I don't know how you feel about having children or if you realize how important my career is to me or if you ask for paper or plastic bags when you buy your groceries."

Jonathan reached across the table and stroked her cheek with the backs of his knuckles. "I'd like us to have a family, one, two, ten kids, it honestly doesn't matter. Ultimately it has to be your choice since you are the one who's going to go through the pregnancies.

"I think you are a world-class culinary talent, and after trying to cook myself, I appreciate your skills even more. I'm proud of your success and hope to accompany you on all your book tours. As for my groceries, Mrs. Ryan does all my shopping so I have no idea what type of bag I use. But I'd be happy to ask her."

Lauren's expression turned misty. "Would you really come with me if I ever go on a book tour?"

"Absolutely."

"You say the sweetest things." A sense of deep happiness and contentment unfurled inside Lauren. She leaned toward Jonathan. He immediately copied her movement. They met and shared an affectionate kiss over the center of the table.

"You're probably right about waiting to get married," Jonathan said, shifting back against his chair. "There's no need to rush. We should wait until we both agree it's the right time. Then we can take a quick trip out to Las Vegas and elope. I always thought it would be a blast to get married in one of those tacky, neon wedding chapels."

Lauren was grateful the fork full of potato salad she had just placed in her mouth helped hide her panic. Las Vegas. Gracious. He probably thought it would be fun to be married by an Elvis impersonator, too. Oh, Lordy.

Who would ever have suspected her sophisticated, preppy boyfriend was a closet good old boy? Needing a moment to gather her thoughts, Lauren took a long swig of beer and washed down the salad.

"I only plan on getting married once in my life," she said lightly. She slowly wiped the corners of her mouth with a paper napkin. "I'm not the most conventional woman in the world, but when it comes to weddings I've always envisioned something a bit more traditional."

"Sure, honey. Whatever you want." Jonathan patted her arm. "As long as it's legal, I don't care. In the meantime I think you should move in with me. I want to start waking up next to you every morning of the week. Besides, living together will help prepare us for marriage."

Lauren was horrified. "Are you nuts? What would my parents think? And your mother?" She shuddered and gulped some more of her beer.

Jonathan looked worried. "You're not going to carry this premarital thing too far, are you? I'm warning you right now if you say we can't sleep together again until we're married, I'm booking the next flight to Vegas. We can have a quick wedding and be back by Monday."

"Stop jumping to ridiculous conclusions. I never said

anything about abandoning our physical relationship. I just don't feel comfortable living together before we're married." Lauren took a careful breath. "I really don't want to get married in Las Vegas. I want a traditional church wedding, with our family and friends in attendance and tons of fresh flowers.

"I want a reception with an open bar, progressive nouvelle cuisine and a five-tier golden genoise cake layered with white chocolate mousse and fresh raspberries, iced with classic French white butter cream."

"Anything else?" Jonathan asked in an amused tone.

"Yes. I want an orchestra, at least five pieces, so our guests can spend the night dancing."

"Dancing? You are really pushing it, lady."

Lauren closed her eyes and pictured it all in her mind. The small church decorated with flowers, the sound of organ music, a frothy wedding gown, Jonathan looking impossibly handsome in a morning coat and cravat, the chatter and laughter of the guests.

She opened her eyes, and conflicting emotions pierced her. "On the other hand eloping does have its advantages. Weddings can be very stressful. Especially for the bride. My mother will probably badger me until the last moment to call it off. After all, she didn't hand-pick you as my husband. She'll be whispering in my ear as I prepare to walk down the aisle that you're the wrong man for me, warning me ominously that you'll be ogling other women constantly during our honeymoon.

"And your mother! Heavens, she'll probably show up at the church dressed in black from head to toe and sob pitifully through the entire ceremony."

"You're scaring me."

"I'm scaring myself." Lauren rubbed the knot of tension that was forming at the base of her neck. "Promise me we won't even consider getting married until next year. Late next year. That will give us plenty of time to decide exactly what we want and will allow our families time to vent most of their disapproval. Our wedding doesn't have to be grand or expensive, Jonathan. I just want it to be special."

"We could get married on my sailboat," Jonathan suggested with a grin. "If any of our family members start acting up, we'll toss them overboard."

"Now that would certainly be special."

Jonathan shoved his chair back and moved around to Lauren's side of the table. She wrapped her arms tightly around his waist and squeezed. He folded her close to his bare chest, and her earlier panic melted away.

"I promise we won't get married until we both agree it's the right time." Jonathan rubbed his cheek against the top of Lauren's head. "I promise my mother will not wear black to our wedding. I promise not to have an affair with another woman while we are on our honeymoon. And I promise I will always love you."

"Thank you. It's very comforting knowing I'll have your support. And your love." Lauren angled her chin so she could stare into Jonathan's eyes. "I promise you will always be first in my heart. I will love, honor and cherish—"

A subtle canine whine interrupted Lauren's speech. "And I promise not only to tolerate, but to love your undisciplined dog. How does that sound?"

Jonathan's rich laughter triggered the joy in Lauren's heart. "Sounds like a recipe for happiness to me!"

EPILOGUE

Eleanor Windsor stood alone in the small entrance foyer of the quaint inn, waiting impatiently for the hostess to lead her to a table. She brushed her fingers over the sides of her neatly coiffed hair and sighed with annoyance. Jonathan's actions at the cooking competition last evening had left her feeling unsettled and emotional, and to make matters even more unbearable she found herself uncharacteristically late for a luncheon appointment.

Deciding it was far too inconvenient to continue waiting for a member of the staff to assist her, Eleanor stepped into the dining room and quickly scanned the occupied tables. As she had expected, the restaurant was uncrowded. She caught a glimpse of her lunch companion, and the tension that had been eating at her all morning slowly rose to an almost unbearable level.

Plastering a cool smile on her lips, Eleanor forced herself to tread slowly across the room. She was pleased that she encountered no other friends or acquaintances to impede her progress. She also managed to reach the table without being seen by her lunch date.

"I'm sorry I'm late," Eleanor said. "I had to run an important errand this morning, and it took longer than I had planned."

"I was beginning to wonder if we had gotten our wires

crossed and I had mistakenly come to the wrong restaurant," the woman seated at the table responded.

Eleanor heard the note of uncertainty in the other woman's voice and understood her anxiety. So much was riding on the outcome of this seemingly innocuous lunch.

Eleanor slid into an empty chair. A young waiter approached them, but Eleanor shooed him away. He persisted, and after a brief debate she reluctantly allowed him to leave a menu, but she placed it off to the side, unopened. Eleanor believed a conversation of this magnitude required the complete attention of both parties. She considered food and drink unnecessary distractions.

At last the overly attentive waiter left. Eleanor repositioned her water goblet, stalling for additional time. She waited several tense moments until she felt certain she had the undivided attention of her lunch partner. Finally she spoke.

"Lauren was seen leaving Jonathan's house at seven o'clock this morning." The words were issued in a challenging tone. Passion stirred in Eleanor's eyes as she added, "Naturally I'm very interested in hearing your opinion of *your* daughter's rather rash behavior."

Julia Stuart swallowed a small, choked sob. "Are you sure?" She sounded dazed. "Absolutely certain?"

"Yes. Jonathan's housekeeper, Mrs. Ryan, called me this morning. She takes her daughter to swimming practice every day, and her route brings her past Jonathan's house. She saw Lauren pull out of the driveway." Eleanor lowered her voice to a whisper. "According to Mrs. Ryan, Lauren was wearing a red evening gown, the same gown she wore at the awards banquet last night."

"Oh, dear." Julia blushed, then took a hasty sip of ice water. "Jonathan certainly knows how to sweep a girl off her feet. Spending the night with a man is hardly typical behavior for my Lauren."

"I think he's fallen in love with her." Eleanor blew out her breath dramatically. "In fact, I believe he might actually marry her."

Julia's bottom jaw dropped open. "Marriage? Already? They've only known each other a few weeks." Julia frowned at Eleanor. "What should we do?"

The women stared at each other with equally solemn expressions. There was a long moment of pin-dropping silence.

"I think we should celebrate." Eleanor lifted her arm and beckoned the waiter. "A bottle of your finest champagne, young man."

"What a relief! Oh, Eleanor, it feels like we've been waiting an eternity for this to happen." Julia laughed merrily. She fanned her napkin in front of her face. "I knew the moment I saw Jonathan he was the perfect mate for my Lauren. I exchanged only a few words with him at that luncheon you gave, but I had such a strong feeling about him I could barely contain my exhilaration."

"Thank heaven for your marvelous, rare gift of intuition, Julia. I get so angry when I think of all those countless years I wasted searching for a suitable girl for my son to marry. It's rather ironic that all I really needed to do was ask my friend and golf partner if her charming older daughter was still single."

Julia laughed again. "It's odd how we never thought to match the children up before. After meeting Jonathan, I knew he and Lauren were fated to be a couple, but fate always needs a bit of help." Julia reached over and squeezed Eleanor's hand affectionately. "Yet I believe the ultimate success of the plan was due to our excellent strategy, of which you were a major contributor, Eleanor."

"I did strive to be imaginative and avoid the obvious."

"Don't be so modest. You were brilliant," Julia insisted. "We agreed from the beginning we couldn't let the children suspect we were trying to bring them together. They never would have cooperated, but you came up with the inspiring idea of printing one of Lauren's recipes in that magazine profile of Jonathan. It proved to be the perfect catalyst for their subsequent romance."

"It was one of my better notions," Eleanor said with a pleasant grin. "But you selected the chocolate Amaretto cheesecake, Julia. I doubt another recipe would have affected Lauren so deeply."

"The cheesecake was her first big success. When I left the magazine at Eileen's house that morning for Lauren to 'stumble upon' I knew she would be compelled to confront the man who claimed he created her masterpiece. She couldn't possibly allow someone to steal her work and let it go unchallenged."

Eleanor nodded her head vigorously. "Of course not. Lauren is a woman of character and conviction. I cannot begin to tell you how thrilled I am knowing she will soon become a member of my family. I will be so proud to have her for a daughter-in-law." Eleanor smoothed the linen table napkin across her lap. "I only hope Lauren will be able to overlook my previous behavior. I really have acted quite wretchedly toward the poor girl."

"That was just another important aspect of our plan," Julia said. "Our stubborn children deliberately rejected all the prospective mates we tossed in their paths. The only possible counterattack was to raise objections. I deliberately expressed doubts about Jonathan to Lauren, although it was difficult to hide my true feelings. As my dear husband would say, 'Forbidden fruit is always sweeter.'"

The waiter arrived with a wine stand of crushed ice and a bottle of champagne. "The wine needs to chill for at least another ten minutes," he said. "May I bring you an appetizer while you wait? Or would you care to order lunch?"

"We'll both have a spinach salad with house dressing on the side. You can bring them out as soon as they are ready," Eleanor answered. She waited for Julia to indicate her agreement with the order, then waved the waiter away from the table so they could continue their celebration in private.

Grinning broadly, Julia leaned forward and remarked, "Spinach salad is an excellent choice for lunch. We both need to keep our figures for the wedding. How soon do you think we can organize a proper celebration?"

"With both of us working on the arrangements, it shouldn't take more than a few months." Eleanor reached into her black leather purse and removed a small jewelry box. "I went to the bank this morning to get my great-grandmother's diamond ring from the vault. Do you think Lauren will like it?"

Eleanor flipped open the lid and Julia gave a strangled gasp. The diamond nestled in the center of the ring was pear-shaped and easily weighed ten carats. Its many faceted edges sent rainbow shafts of glittering light bouncing around the room.

"The ring is absolutely stunning. Lauren will be thrilled."

"Excellent." Eleanor snapped the box shut and returned the ring to her purse. "All Jonathan has to do is have the ring sized. As soon as he presents it to Lauren, we can announce their engagement. I want to give a lavish party for all our friends and relatives. Naturally I'll need your help in preparing for the event."

"I can hardly wait." Julia's fair eyes glowed with excitement, but a sudden thought brought a worried crinkle to her brow. "I am concerned that Lauren might be a bit skittish over rushing into marriage. I might need your help in devising a plan to circumvent her objections."

"I'm confident we can have them properly married before the year is out," Eleanor stated forcefully. "Look how far we've brought them already and in such a short time! Think how delightful it will be spending the holidays together."

"You're right, Eleanor. I'm being silly." Julia nibbled the corner of her lip. "Is the champagne ready?"

"It hasn't been chilling the additional ten minutes the waiter recommended, but who cares. Let's open it anyway. I'm too happy to mind a little warm champagne."

Eleanor removed the already loosened cork from the champagne bottle and filled their glasses.

"A toast," Julia offered, raising her glass high. "To true love, stubborn children, crafty mothers and elegant weddings."

The women clinked glasses and drank deeply. Eleanor lifted the champagne bottle, refilled both glasses, then smiled slyly. "A toast. To grandmotherhood."

About the Author

Adrienne Basso lives with her family in New Jersey and is currently working on her newest Zebra historical romance set in the Regency period: *His Noble Promise* (to be published in February, 2000). Adrienne loves to hear from readers and you may write to her c/o Zebra Books. Please include a self-addressed envelope if you wish a response.

COMING IN DECEMBER FROM
ZEBRA BOUQUET ROMANCES

#25 SEDUCING TONY by Jona Jeffrey
__(0-8217-6439-X, $3.99) Caught in the juiciest scandal to hit New York City in years, maverick newspaperman Tony Ross finds his life in ruins—until he meets Eden, a beautiful, mysterious woman who offers solace and nights of sensuous abandon.

#26 MOUNTAIN MOONLIGHT by Jane Anderson
__(0-8217-6440-3, $3.99) Vala Channing can't decide which is more dangerous—the fact that she's about to take her troubled young son trekking in Arizona's Superstition Mountains or that the guide who will lead them is the one man from her past she's never managed to forget.

#27 EVERY BREATH YOU TAKE by Suzanne McMinn
__(0-8217-6441-1, $3.99) When harassing phone calls turn more menacing, Natalie Buchanan makes a desperate call to the police, never expecting Officer Miller Brannigan to show up at her door. Years ago, she'd broken their engagement. But Natalie underestimated the depth of Miller's love . . . and the persistence of her own feeling for him.

#28 FIREWORKS by Cindy Hillyer
__(0-8217-6442-X, $3.99) Assuming responsibility for a five-year-old niece has softened New Orleans divorce attorney Bullock Stockwell in ways he could've never imagined. For when beautiful pediatrician M.K. Channing arrives in his office to give a deposition in his latest case, he finds himself considering a partnership . . . of the romantic kind.

Call toll free **1-888-345-BOOK** to order by phone or use this coupon to order by mail.
Name_____
Address_____
City_____ State _____Zip _____
Please send me the books I have checked above.
I am enclosing $_____
Plus postage and handling* $_____
Sales tax (in NY and TN) $_____
Total amount enclosed $_____
*Add $2.50 for the first book and $.50 for each additional book.
Send check or money order (no cash or CODs) to:
Kensington Publishing Corp., 850 Third Avenue, New York, NY 10022
Prices and numbers subject to change without notice. Valid only in the U.S.
All books will be available 10/1/99. All orders subject to availability.
Visit our web site at **www.kensingtonbooks.com**